Finally the Car Squealed to a Stop . . .

The door opened and Mallory got out. He didn't bother closing the door behind him.

In the trunk, Bryan wondered what was happening. His fears for Julia and Adrienne mingled with relief that the wild ride was finally at an end.

Following the kidnappers' instructions, Mallory had driven to the site of an abandoned strip mine. In the middle of a totally denuded area, fifty feet in front of him on a mound of yellow clay, he could see Adrienne's car. At first this spurred him to walk faster, hoping his daughter was inside instead of the Valenti girl. But then some deep, inner, gut-wrenching fear took hold of him; he slowed down and almost timidly pulled open the door of the red Fiat.

When he saw what was inside, he emitted a loud, ugly moan full of animal despair and collapsed against the side of the car, his eyes bulged wide in horror and disbelief.

Adrienne was lying tied up, and unconscious, on the front seat. Her left leg had been amputated at the thigh.

Books by John Russo

Limb to Limb
Majorettes
Midnight

Published by POCKET BOOKS

LIMB TO LIMB

A NOVEL OF TERROR

BY JOHN RUSSO

PUBLISHED BY POCKET BOOKS NEW YORK

This novel is a work of fiction. Names, characters, places and incidents are either the product of the author's imagination or are used fictitiously, and any resemblance to actual persons, living or dead, events or locales is entirely coincidental.

Another *Original* publication of POCKET BOOKS

POCKET BOOKS, a Simon & Schuster division of
GULF & WESTERN CORPORATION
1230 Avenue of the Americas, New York, N.Y. 10020

ISBN: 0-671-41690-1

First Pocket Books printing June, 1981

10 9 8 7 6 5 4 3 2 1

POCKET and colophon are trademarks of Simon & Schuster.

Printed in the U.S.A.

Special thanks to Pat Riblett, Floyd Coles, Mary Ellen Tunney, and Mike Gorney for technical advice important in the telling of this story

Science does not have a moral dimension. It is like a knife. If you give it to a surgeon or a murderer, each will use it differently.

—Wernher von Braun

LIMB TO LIMB

PROLOGUE

DR. BERNARD AUGENSTEIN STOOD OVER THE DISSECTING table, looking down at the corpse of a premature baby. In his hand, on a sheet of memo paper, were typed instructions from his brother Louis. "Examine this cadaver from a clinical point of view. Take exact measurements. Maintain comprehensive pathological records including all interesting details."

The dead infant, whose birth in the seventh month of pregnancy had been induced by drugs, appeared outwardly normal. On noting this, Bernard Augenstein was surprised and puzzled; he checked the name tag tied to the baby's toe to make sure he had the right baby. Two days ago he had heard his brother coercing the mother into docile submission to the induced delivery by assuring her that the child she was carrying, if it lived, would be "a brain-damaged monster." By this Louis meant that the fetus was hydrocephalic, Mongoloid, its enormous enlarged head having been revealed by X rays.

But the tiny pathetic-looking corpse curled up on its side on the dissecting table had a normal-sized head, not the grossly enlarged cranium caused by hydrocephalus—water on the brain. There was no overt evidence of Mongolism.

Bernard wondered if Louis had made a terrible mistake. Could he have gotten the X rays mixed up with those of another fetus? Or had he simply wanted this baby to experiment upon, even if he had to lie to its mother? Maybe he had told the mother what she wanted to hear, after sensing that she really wanted an abortion.

What, Bernard wondered, was he expected to do? Falsify his autopsy report? If so, he oughtn't to be shocked. Louis was getting crazier and crazier in the chances he was taking.

Bernard went to his desk and leafed through the baby's file. There were charts and descriptions, results of blood tests and spinal taps, evaluations of the secretions and functionings of vital glands and organs. Every medical examination that could be performed had been done. So the baby must have been born alive. The pathological report would complete the brief but thorough history of her life and death. Well, almost thorough. The file contained no prenatal X rays at all—nothing to confirm or deny Mongolism.

Returning to the dissecting table, Dr. Augenstein began his autopsy by removing the infant's brain pan. He almost hoped he'd discover hydrocephalus in its beginning stages, thus confirming his brother's diagnosis. But the cerebrum and cerebellum were normal.

Louis' diagnosis was irrefutably in error. Or he had lied. This baby should not have been aborted.

Shaken, but spurred on by curiosity, Bernard Augenstein continued working. He opened the baby's thorax and removed the sternum. Then he disconnected the tongue by making an incision beneath the chin. He examined the tongue, the respiratory tract, and the lungs, first washing the organs so they could be inspected thoroughly. He found no abnormalities. The bones were flexible and easy to work with; the insides of the lungs were pink and clean. The newness and delicacy of the body parts were a constant reminder of life that had come to a young, unfortunate end.

The doctor made a transverse incision across the pericardium and drained out the fluid. Then he removed the heart and washed it, turning it over and over carefully in his hands. He noticed something and stopped, peering at the organ closely. To his surprise, the exterior of the left ventricle showed a pale red spot, which scarcely differed from the color of the tissue around it. A less-skilled pathologist might not have seen anything unusual. But Bernard had no doubt—an injection had been made with a very small needle. But for what purpose?

Bernard almost did not dare to find out. He hoped that the injection had been a life-saving measure, perhaps an infusion of adrenaline in an attempt to keep the tiny heart beating in an emergency. Well, he would know soon enough, whether he wanted to or not.

With trepidation, he opened the baby's left ventricle. Normally, he would have drained the blood out and weighed it, but in this instance he could not do so, because the blood was coagulated into a compact mass. He extracted some of the coagulant with his forceps and brought it to his nostrils. He smelled chloroform. His eyes widened, and he froze with the forceps in

3

midair, stunned by his discovery. He began to perspire. It slowly dawned on him, against his will, what his brother had done. Louis had administered a hypodermic injection of chloroform so that the blood of the ventricle, in coagulating, would deposit on the valves and cause instantaneous death by heart failure.

This baby had been delivered unnecessarily before the mother's pregnancy had come to full term, on the pretext that it would be born a Mongoloid. Brought forth from the womb alive instead of dead, it had then been subjected to every sort of medical test imaginable. And finally it had been murdered.

This was the furthest Louis had ever gone in his obsession with his experiments. He had done some abortions under conditions that were not quite legal, but these were always done with the parents' approval, fetuses that could not legally have been aborted because the gestation cycle had progressed into the third trimester. In such cases, Louis would circumvent the law by certifying that the pregnancy was a danger to the mother's health.

But now Louis had committed murder. And Bernard had no choice. He had to protect his brother. Perhaps Louis had expected him not to notice the needle mark in the baby's left ventricle, or if he did notice it, to keep it out of his autopsy report. Bernard sighed. He knew what he had to do. He had to keep his mouth shut, not even mention the incident to Louis, and record merely that the baby had died of heart failure.

1 ⋘

THE MOTION PICTURE THAT BRYAN SINCLAIR WAS MAKING about Tiffany Blake was called *Portrait of a Ballerina*. Her doting father had thought up the title. Three weeks ago Tiffany had been scouted by Arthur Silvera, world-famous director of the New York National Ballet Company, and he had made her an offer. Right now she was dancing for the Artov Ballet Company in its production of *The Nutcracker* at Heinz Hall for the Performing Arts in Pittsburgh. But she would probably be leaving soon for the Big Apple.

Euphoric over Silvera's offer, Andrew Blake had decided that it would be wonderful to make Tiffany the subject of a documentary. He could well afford to squander money on whim, and Bryan wasn't about to discourage him. The struggling twenty-eight-year-old filmmaker needed the cash because he was planning to marry Julia Valenti, Tiffany's understudy.

For over a week, ever since New Year's Day, he hadn't even seen Julia, and he missed her. She had been busy rehearsing and performing, and he had been working long hours at the editing table, putting the finishing touches on a sales film for a paint company. A few hours ago he had shipped the film's components by Greyhound to the laboratory in Cleveland, he hoped in time to meet the tight deadline. Then he and his partner, Paul Smith, had driven across town to film the second act of *The Nutcracker*. At least he would get to see Julia on stage tonight, in the background.

Crouched behind an Arriflex camera on the balcony, Bryan squinted through the eyepiece, zoomed in tight, and used the folds of the curtain to get a sharp focus on center stage. When the dancers came out, he would be ready. But he wished he could be a spectator this evening instead of a filmmaker. He would rather sit back and enjoy the ballet without worrying about lighting, composition, and camera angles. Grimacing, he told himself he probably wouldn't feel so glum once the curtain opened. The trouble was, he had his doubts because the project wasn't going well.

It wasn't so much that Andrew Blake was a hard man to work for. Bryan had gotten used to that six months ago when he and Paul had produced a series of TV commercials for Hot Dog Heaven, Blake's chain of fast-food franchises. In addition to franchising, Blake was into meat-packing, restaurant equipment wholesaling, and numerous real estate ventures. He might be arbitrary and demanding, but he represented plenty of potential future business that Bryan wanted to cultivate.

The problem was Tiffany. Over the past few weeks of working with her, interviewing and filming her at her home and at ballet rehearsals, Bryan had decided he liked her and felt sorry for her, too. Some inner struggle seemed to be going on. She was only nineteen and seemed even younger, unable to cope. When she was offstage her personality shriveled—that was the only way the change could be defined. It was hard to believe that she was the very same young woman who appeared mature, sensuous, captivating—when she was dancing.

She acted resentful of Bryan sometimes. Other times she kidded him and almost relaxed. His toughest task was to get her to be less withdrawn when she wasn't onstage. So far, her interviews were as terrible as her dancing was superb. Her only form of self-expression seemed to be the ballet. She had no boyfriends; she didn't even date anyone, so far as Bryan could discover. He prided himself in his skill as an interviewer, but he couldn't get anything out of her that he could use. She would have to open up, give something of herself, or his subjective approach to the documentary would be a flop.

Anxious for the second act, the capacity audience filled the theater well before intermission ended. Part of their excitement was the knowledge that Tiffany would soon be a star in New York. The orchestra played its opening bars and Bryan had the film rolling from the first wave of the baton. An indicator at the rear of the camera told him he had established synch with Paul Smith's Nagra tape recorder downstairs in the orchestra pit. Bryan tilted his lens at the ceiling. Then he began a very slow tilt-down and zoom, capturing the ambiance of Heinz Hall, a splendid gilt palace of white marble, plush red velvet, and sparkling gold filigree, a fitting milieu for the wistful, nostalgic, almost intangible delights of *The Nutcracker*.

Tchaikovsky's music was lyrical and thrilling, a

perfect vehicle for the extravagant costumes, scenery, and dancing. In the original version of the choreography, first performed in 1892, a young girl, Clara, dreamed that her Christmas nutcracker was transformed into a prince. But in the Rudolf Nureyev version, being performed tonight, Clara dreamed that her aged and stern godfather, Drosselemeyer, became a brave and handsome prince and took her on wonderful romantic adventures in the Kingdom of the Sweets. At the end of the ballet the prince would be once more transformed into Drosselemeyer and the dream would end.

When Bryan's slow zoom brought her to focus at center stage, Tiffany as Clara was in her dream world of a bygone century. Panning with her across stage, Bryan, like everybody else, was entranced by the magic she was weaving. She seemed vibrant, mysterious, alluring—truly the prisoner of a bittersweet dream. A flow of excitement and adrenaline had her dancing to the peak of her ability. The audience was enthralled; she was feeding off their energy and enthusiasm and giving it back manyfold. If only, thought Bryan, if only she would come off in person with any semblance of the way she danced!

The ballet swept to its resolution and concluded to thunderous applause. As the curtain closed, Bryan quickly removed the camera from its tripod, slung the battery pack over his shoulder, and rushed downstairs to get audience-reaction shots and up-angle close-ups of the dancers taking their reverences. The applause went on for a long while, giving him the time he needed to run down the aisle and join Paul Smith.

The supporting cast had already come out from behind the curtain. Bryan seized the opportunity to get some good close-ups of his fiancée—pretty dark-haired Julia—who was out of breath, smiling, radiantly happy.

She had been part of the corps de ballet in the Kingdom of the Sweets. So had Adrienne Mallory, Paul's girl friend. Bryan shot some footage of her, too.

Markian Teslovic, who had played the prince, escorted Tiffany back out onstage and the applause increased in fervor. The curtain parted for Nicolai Artov, lean and handsome, beaming and confident, as if he stood no chance of losing his prima ballerina. He pranced across the footlights and presented Tiffany with a lavish bouquet of flowers. She gave her curtsies of appreciation while the audience went wild, clapping and yelling "Bravo!"

Bryan turned the camera on the audience, centering Tiffany's father in a medium shot. Seeing the lens pointed in his direction, Andrew Blake pretended to be unaware of it. Bryan had him in three-quarter profile—a handsome, craggy-faced aristocrat with alert blue eyes, ruddy complexion, and thick, wavy white hair. Suddenly he arose, continuing to applaud, unabashedly inaugurating a standing ovation for his own daughter. Two men on either side of him got up; then gradually the entire audience followed suit. Blake stood proud and erect in the center of Bryan's lens, everybody in the packed theater standing up applauding right with him. Zooming back to a wider shot, wishing he had the tripod for steadiness, Bryan allowed the camera to record the tribute to young Tiffany Blake, knowing that when it was edited into the finished movie it would appear spontaneous.

2 ❧

A BALD MAN WITH DEEPSET BLACK EYES MUNCHED TUNA salad in a coffee shop across from Heinz Hall. His lips were thin and tight, his complexion pallid. After each bite he sipped coffee, then meticulously used his napkin. He had an air of being insulated from the outside world. Yet, his eyes seemed keenly alert.

Sitting at the counter, he peered through lettered plate-glass at the tall poster across the street advertising the Artov Ballet Company presentation of *The Nutcracker* starring Markian Teslovic and Tiffany Blake. Swallowing the dregs of his coffee, he considered buying a ticket. The Blake girl was supposed to be a phenomenon, a rising star.

But Dr. Louis Augenstein knew he wouldn't go to the ballet. It was out of the question. He was soured on ballet, on symphony, on all the aesthetic pursuits that in days gone by had meant fully as much to him as his profession. Imprisonment had made him bitter, and the bitterness had grown around him like a cocoon, shutting the world out.

Leaving the coffee shop, he walked resolutely in the cold of January, head bent to the icy wind. Large wet snowflakes blew, plastering themselves against him. He pulled his collar up and gripped the brim of his hat. When the wind gusted, the tails of his topcoat slapped against his legs. At four o'clock it was already getting dark. The city streets, still decorated for Christmas, contained sparse traffic and few pedestrians because of the cold.

Dr. Augenstein took his time walking to the morgue. He would be as late as he dared. Having to care about being late goaded him. He was a clock-puncher now, a nobody. Once he had been an eminent surgeon. Now he cut up the dead. They didn't trust him with anyone live. His true skills were being wasted. He felt humiliated, belittled, demeaned. It was the way they wanted him to feel. He fought against it, reminding himself that he knew more than all of them put together.

He certainly knew more than Dr. Walter Kerrigan, his so-called "superior" on the four-to-twelve shift. Kerrigan had to pretend he liked being a pathologist, when the truth was he didn't have the nerve to operate on anything except cadavers. Pathology was a safe outlet for his mediocre expertise; if the scalpel slipped, the patient wouldn't complain. Louis Augenstein hated being an underling to Kerrigan. He despised the stupid redundant formality of listening to Kerrigan's preliminary observations concerning each corpse he was assigned, and then doing the autopsies himself and turning over the findings so Kerrigan could write up and file the required reports. As if Louis couldn't write up the reports on his own and put his name to them, after doing all the work. But it was part of the price they were making him pay for losing his license.

When he arrived at the morgue, a female corpse was waiting for him, naked and already bathed. It was a form of chastisement from Kerrigan, who had prepared the corpse while Louis was taking his time. As soon as Louis got his coat off, his boss pointed out some things concerning the cadaver that were perfectly obvious and gave Louis some instructions that were unnecessary. Louis gritted his teeth till Kerrigan went away.

He already knew something about the girl from reading the newspapers. Her name was Helen Ann and she was seventeen, an honors student, and a cheerleader. For three days she had been the object of a city-wide police search. Her body had been found under some brush on the outskirts of the park where she had gone jogging.

The table on which she now lay was made of metal grating over a long shallow basin. Constantly running water would flush away blood and other body fluids exuded during the autopsy procedure.

Helen Ann was in a good state of preservation— thanks to the cold weather. She had obviously been quite attractive. Some pervert had found her irresistible. Augenstein could see that she had almost assuredly been raped; there was a bruise on her left inner thigh above the knee and a tear in her vagina probably made by a fingernail. The apparent cause of death was a blow to the head, judging by the soft skull and caked blood, but the autopsy would ascertain this.

Louis began by making a neat incision across the top of her head; then with a quick expert movement he turned half the skin down over her face and the other half over the back of her neck, like peeling back a grapefruit. Next he used a circular saw to cut through bone and remove the top of her skull. Before scooping the brain out and weighing it, he noted that the blow to the head by an obviously blunt instrument had indeed produced a fracture and resultant concussion sufficient to have caused death.

He made a Y-shaped incision in the girl's torso, opening her in such a way that her chest could be flapped back to cover her face and her abdomen could be peeled to either side to make her internal organs accessible. To facilitate this, he used the saw to cut her sternum. He observed no wounds or other damage to her internal organs. A healthy and beautiful girl, who could have made some lucky man very happy.

Well, she must have brought a little happiness to somebody, Dr. Augenstein thought, when after opening her pelvic area he saw that her uterus was markedly enlarged. The outline of a fetus could be discerned in its amniotic sac. The doctor estimated that Helen Ann had been about two months pregnant. The cold weather would have preserved the fetus perfectly, as it had her internal organs. What would the parents say if told their sweet little honors student had been screwing somebody—probably a big dumb football player? It wouldn't shock them in this day and age. Nothing unusual for little girls to be going at it by age twelve. Pretty soon the age of consent and the first day of kindergarten would coincide.

Should he report the pregnancy to Kerrigan, or should he remove the fetus and keep it for his own private experiments? It would be wonderful to have one so perfectly preserved. There were experimental findings he needed to verify, and this specimen would be ideal. In hot weather it would have been macerated, ruined.

Momentarily, the thought of getting caught stealing it gave Louis pause. He didn't want to lose his job or, worse, be sent back to prison. But he swallowed his fears. Furtively, he noticed that Kerrigan was busy with another autopsy down at the far end of the lab. The correct procedure would be to remove the fetus and place it on the dissecting table to be weighed and measured. But a chance like this might not happen again soon. He might as well go ahead and remove the fetus. Nothing wrong in that. It had to be done, anyway. Then, if Kerrigan wasn't looking . . .

Louis deftly extracted the fetus and placenta and preserved them in a bottle of formaldehyde. Kerrigan was still busy and as his saw began whining, cutting through bone, Louis knew he was safe. He wrapped the specimen bottle in a clean handkerchief and secreted it in the pocket of his coat.

Kerrigan's saw stopped at that moment, and Louis tensed. Kerrigan would notice the pregnancy if he came over right now. He would see the swollen uterus and ask where the fetus was, why it hadn't been weighed and measured. Louis quickly stitched the girl back together, sewing expertly in large, neat stitches. He felt guilty about what he had done, not because he had stolen the specimens, but because he had potentially interfered with a criminal investigation. The fact that Helen Ann had been pregnant could have a bearing on helping the police find out who had killed her. But Louis tried to convince himself that this was unlikely. The parents had enough grief already; now, thanks to him, they could at least bury their daughter believing she had been pure. Besides, if her murderer went free, Louis believed it would be justified by his higher purpose in taking the fetus.

He needed it for his experiments, which had to go on as long as he wasn't caught. He had been imprisoned only for the abortions. He had kept the experiments secret. The world didn't know what he had accomplished. If they did, they would realize he was a genius.

In his apartment Louis kept a file of newspaper and magazine clippings about people he could have helped if he had wanted to, if the results of his experiments could be made public. Some were rich and talented. Others were poor, like the little boy who had lost a hand in the blades of his father's power mower. The latest was the famous cellist with the Boston Symphony whose arm had been amputated above the elbow because of bone cancer.

Louis knew he could become an international celebrity just by helping the cellist. But he couldn't announce his discoveries, not yet, not in America, a democracy, where current ideology refused to accept that the ends could sometimes justify the means. He would be denounced because of the way he got his results; they would put him in prison again. Some Russian scientists were more advanced in their thinking; they were already proposing that human vegetables with total and incurable brain damage should be used as living organ banks for transplants. This sort of thing was related to Louis' own ideas. But his discovery was more astounding.

Leaving the morgue at midnight, he kept his gloved hand around the specimen bottle in his coat pocket as he walked past Heinz Hall on his way to a bus stop. The theater crowd suddenly gushed out into the street, milling around despite the cold, smiling and swapping comments about an obviously enjoyable performance. Louis shunted off to one side to avoid being jostled. It annoyed him that *The Nutcracker* was the only ballet that could have drawn such a mob on such a bitterly freezing evening. It was a beautiful enough ballet, but a Christmas fad. Even some of the top companies footed their year-round operating costs mostly by putting on *The Nutcracker*. Of course, Louis had to admit, ballet in general was now undergoing a sudden, rather startling upswing in popularity. What could be the reason? Mass taste couldn't have improved very much. Perhaps in America, in a culture almost totally undisciplined and purposeless, people were beginning to find an attraction in an art form that required the utmost in self-discipline, practice, and precision.

Louis congratulated himself that he had loved the ballet before it became so popular. Wistfully, he looked up at the poster of Tiffany Blake, the young and pretty ballerina. The newspapers said she wasn't going to stay here in Pittsburgh. Arthur Silvera had made her an offer. If *he* wanted her, she must be pretty good. At this moment her career was in ascendancy.

But it could all come crashing down, Louis thought. It would only take some unforeseen illness or injury. He had once had a career, too.

3 ❦

"I GOT SOME GREAT STUFF," BRYAN SAID. "WAS THE sound okay?"

"Naturally," Paul replied with a grimace, showing his resentment of any implication that his job could be less than perfect.

While the dancers were in their dressing rooms and the theater was emptying, the two filmmakers had begun breaking down lights, cables, and other gear.

Bryan was dismantling the camera when Andrew Blake brought over the two men who had sat beside him during the performance and introduced them to "the talented writer and director of our motion picture production about Tiffany." Embarrassed by the verbose compliment, Bryan obligingly shook hands with Bert Snyder and Morris Hoffberg—fat, doughy-looking executives from the bakery that supplied buns for all the Hot Dog Heaven franchises—then turned around and introduced them to Paul Smith, as it didn't seem Blake was going to bother. In which case Paul would've been offended. Blake and Paul had never quite hit it off, and Bryan had taken charge of producing the ballet film so he could act as a buffer between them.

"I hope you got some damned good camera angles," Blake said, showing off for the gentlemen from the bakery. "I don't want anything less than a topnotch movie."

Paul backstepped and pretended he had to give full attention to putting away a set of headphones.

"I think you'll be pleased when you see the finished product," Bryan said, hoping he wasn't lying. It *could* still turn out all right. It was up to Tiffany.

Blake said, "When we get together to look at what you've filmed, Bryan, I want to talk with you about getting that feature-film project under way."

"All right, Mr. Blake," Bryan replied, not allowing himself to become excited by what Blake was saying. It was more eyewash for Hoffberg and Snyder.

Paul had glanced up from what he was doing, keenly taking in the exchange and mulling it over as he twisted the ends of his bushy, dark blond mustache between thumb and forefinger. He always got excited over the slightest possibility of making "a real movie"—and if he had more self-control, he wouldn't let himself in for so many disappointments.

"Feature film?" Bert Snyder said, grinning drolly and glancing from Blake to Bryan. "Surely you aren't serious. I thought feature movies had to be made in Hollywood."

Paul flashed him a dirty look behind his back.

"Good features can be made anywhere," said Bryan,

18

"with the right talent and the right script." It was an argument he had made many times, with varying degrees of success. He wasn't interested in convincing Snyder. Especially since Blake wasn't listening—he and Hoffberg were talking about something else.

"Somehow I can't picture Robert Redford and Jane Fonda working out of Pittsburgh," Snyder snickered.

Bryan would have been content to let the subject drop.

But Paul gave a loud snort and butted in. "*Night of the Living Dead* was made here. I know some of the people who worked on it."

"A funky little horror flick," Snyder scoffed. "Hardly big-time production." He pivoted, disdainfully walking away from any further discourse, as if the people he was talking to were obviously his intellectual inferiors.

Glowering at the roll of fat on the back of Snyder's neck, Paul muttered an obscenity under his breath and slammed the lid on the Nagra tape recorder—an expensive piece of equipment to ruin by a pointless outburst of temper.

"Take it easy, Paul," Bryan said. "What he thinks doesn't pay our bills."

Like Paul, Bryan wanted to make feature films someday instead of commercials; it was why he had gotten into the motion picture business six years ago, right after college. It had been a tough struggle making a name for himself, and tougher still making a decent living. Often his true goals didn't seem any closer at all. But he had more patience, more tolerance, than Paul. If he had to make commercials for a while, he'd do it the best way he knew how; whereas Paul hated the people who paid him and gave them less than his best effort when he could get away with it. But he did take their money willingly enough.

"Did the Big Wiener mean what he said about backing a feature film?" Paul asked, after Blake and the bakery men had meandered out to the lobby.

"Hard to tell," said Bryan. "I'll follow through on it, but don't get your hopes up, Paul."

"What do you think of showing him my sexploitation script?"

"He's too prudish. He'd want to be involved with something he considers more respectable. I wish we had some kind of story based around ballet—maybe a murder mystery. Exploitable, but stylish, too. Know what I mean? Something that could feature Tiffany in a supporting role. Blake isn't going to put up cash for anything less than a showcase for his daughter."

"Maybe you'd rather sell him on a script you wrote yourself," Paul said sulkily.

"Come off it, Paul!" Bryan snapped. "I don't care who writes the script as long as it's a good one. Write the kind of movie I just described and I'll try to talk Blake into putting up the money."

"I'm sorry," Paul mumbled. "I guess I lost my head."

Bryan silently accepted the apology. He didn't want his partner going off half-cocked. Paul needed time to mature; he was only twenty-two and sometimes he acted like a flower child. Lately this was getting harder and harder for Bryan to take. But maybe the partnership would survive if he stuck it out a while longer.

Nicolai Artov's wife, Natalia, a trimly built brunette in a neat red suit, came down the side aisle with her five-year-old daughter, Stephanie, and chatted with Bryan as he finished packing the camera.

"I'm going to be a ballerina!" Stephanie blurted out and did a cute, almost-not-awkward interpretation of a demi plié.

"Bravo!" said Bryan, laughing.

20

"Oh, Bryan, what's going to happen to us?" Natalia lamented.

"Don't worry," Bryan consoled her. "In the long run, things will turn out fine." He had a great deal of faith in Nicolai Artov's ability to rise above adversity. But obviously Natalia knew better than he that the loss of Tiffany Blake would be a major setback for her husband. If Tiffany stayed, Nicolai would have a star, a sure draw at the box office, plus continued monetary support from her father, who had been a strong patron of the weak but promising Artov Ballet Company.

"It's Nicolai's own fault, you know," said Natalia in a soft, sad voice.

Bryan knew what she meant. By putting Tiffany in the limelight so aggressively, Nicolai had put himself in danger of losing her. Now others with more money and prestige had seen what he had discovered—that this shy, ingenuous blonde, pretty in an unremarkable way offstage, could infuse her dancing with such vitality and precision that on stage she was transformed. Well, Nicolai couldn't keep her under wraps, could he? Such intrigue went against his nature. He was honest and forthright to a fault.

"Nicolai is a true artist," Bryan said. Natalia thanked him for saying so before hurrying to catch up with pretty little Stephanie, who was skipping energetically out toward the lobby.

Secretly, Bryan looked upon the ballet movie as a way of helping the people he liked. Besides telling Tiffany's story, he wanted to get across the poignancy he saw in the Artov Ballet Company, struggling to make a name for itself much in the same way as he himself was struggling. Since Blake's money was footing the bill, he planned to shoot enough extra footage on the side to put together a good film for Nicolai, not featuring Tiffany, since she would probably be heading for New York. The star of this corollary film would be Julia.

Bryan had met Nicolai and Julia two years ago when the three were guests on a local television talk show. Nicolai had been a famous dancer and choreographer in Eastern Europe, had defected from a Communist country, and was fighting an uphill battle for recognition in America. He was living proof that not every defector gets rich and famous automatically. He and Julia performed a *pas de deux* for the studio cameras and talked about ballet, and Bryan showed some TV commercials he had made and answered questions about Pittsburgh film production. He felt totally eclipsed by intense, charismatic Nicolai and modest, sincere Julia, who had expressed herself so eloquently in her dancing. Over dinner and drinks, after the taping of the television program, he felt a compulsion to get across the point that he didn't always intend to be making mere TV spots.

"But you should be proud of what you do," said Julia. "It's a fine beginning. I don't know how you manage to make it all come together—the sound, the color, the music. I thought the films you showed were marvelous."

"Of course, of course," said Nicolai emphatically in his Russian accent, making it clear that there was no need for Bryan to demean himself.

They were impressed with the expertise, the slickness, of his film work, not the content, which was trivial. But knowing that they approved of him, for whatever reason, made Bryan feel good. Nicolai was such a strong personality. And Julia was so pretty and intelligent that he was attracted to her immediately.

If Tiffany went to New York, Julia would be the leading candidate for prima ballerina. Her rival would be Adrienne Mallory, the attractive but pushy redhead who had started going out with Paul Smith. Even though it would be an opportunity for Julia, Bryan would rather that Tiffany stayed, for Nicolai's sake.

By the time all the film equipment was dollied out to the sidewalk and loaded into Bryan's station wagon, Adrienne and Julia were out front in their street clothes, in high spirits about the way the performance had gone. Tonight had been the night everything clicked. Bryan hugged Julia and gave her a congratulatory kiss. She was still keyed up from the dancing; her body against his felt excited, vibrant. "You must be awfully tired," she said, hoping he wasn't, "after being on the go all week long."

"I'm just now getting my second wind," he joked, knowing she wasn't ready for the evening to end. Actually, he wasn't, either. He had to unwind and he wanted to do it with her. It was so nice being with her again.

"The footage we got is going to look and sound great," Paul said enthusiastically.

"I hope you got some of me," Adrienne purred, believing it was charming to let her self-interest openly show.

"We got some beautiful stuff of you, love," Paul said, although he had not looked through the camera.

"Is everybody hungry?" asked Julia.

They all agreed that they were. But they were so wound up that their conversation rambled on in front of Heinz Hall for a while longer before they were able to decide on a cozy, inexpensive Italian restaurant where they could go to celebrate.

"You realize we're the peons, don't you?" Paul said, getting into the car. "Blake is taking the Artovs and his two ass-kissers from the bakery out to some fancy place for dinner. But he didn't invite *us*. We're not part of the aristocracy."

"Probably someplace where you have to wear a suit and tie," Bryan conjectured. "And we're wearing jeans."

"That's not the reason he didn't invite us," Paul sneered. "You think everybody respects you, Bryan. But to people like Andrew Blake, you're nothing but hired help."

4 ❧❧❧

RIDING HOME ON A NEARLY EMPTY BUS, SNOW FLURRYING against the windows, Louis Augenstein felt sorry for himself. If accused of harboring such feelings, he would have denied it. It was a momentary weakness in the hard inner core of pride and determination that had seen him through the hardships of six years in prison. His bitterness against the world was like a suit of armor, protecting against scorn and derision and fortifying his willpower.

He was in good physical shape. He had exercised relentlessly in his cell and in the prison yard and the weight room. Despite everything, he wanted to keep on being a surgeon, and a surgeon needed stamina to endure long hours of delicate and precise operating procedures. Even though he had lost his freedom,

Louis didn't want imprisonment to erode the skills he cherished. Night after night, day after day, alone in his cell he imagined himself doing operations, remembering each detail so minutely that his imaginings, so vivid and so exact, were the next closest thing to reality. He was almost rehearsing instead of merely fantasizing.

Now that he was out of prison, he wanted to find a way to resume his life's work. He didn't want to go on cutting up dead bodies.

It wasn't that he had a compulsion to help people. Although he had never openly admitted it, his self-image wasn't that of a merciful healer. He knew that he was arrogant and proud. The intricacies of surgery gave him pleasure. He loved the godlike feeling of power that came from tinkering with life itself. Making mangled, broken parts of human beings function again was the next best thing to creating a human being from scratch.

The thing that had started Louis feeling sorry for himself while riding home on the bus was the specimen bottle in his overcoat pocket. He shouldn't have to sneak around stealing specimens to do his work. He was a genius! And the world had punished him for it.

At home in his apartment, he had a small laboratory that he had set up by scrimping on the money he made at the morgue. He was able to do dissections and various small-scale experiments, constantly amassing data to corroborate his major discovery. But the facilities were woefully inadequate and he felt frustrated, constrained. The limitations of his present circumstances oppressed him almost as much as a prison cell and increased his bitterness.

Once he had had his own clinic to work in, modern and fully equipped—a marvelous place that he viewed as a shrine to his accomplishments. But he had lost it to bankruptcy, all the money had gone to legal fees, and in the end he had been convicted and sentenced. And for what?

For trading the lives of tiny undeveloped creatures, fetuses, who could have turned out to be anything—heroes, punks, or murderers—for knowledge that could be of real benefit to selected individuals whose true worth and potential had come to fruition. Saving an adult of *proven* intelligence and accomplishment was infinitely preferable to saving a fetus of unknown destiny.

Take Tiffany Blake, for example. Something bad could happen to her, as had happened to the Boston cellist whose arm had been taken by bone cancer. Not that Louis wished it on her, but he enjoyed thinking about the position it would put him in. He would be the only person in the world with the skill and knowledge to help her—if he came forward. One of these days, probably long after he was dead, they would realize that he, even more so than Jonas Salk, Louis Pasteur, and Christiaan Barnard, was one of the great entrepreneurs of modern medical science.

5 ❧❧❧

TIFFANY WAS HAVING A MISERABLE TIME AT HER FATHER'S club. She barely touched the filet mignon her father had insisted she order, instead of the chef's salad she would have ordered on her own. She sipped claret sparingly, since she wasn't much of a drinker. Her father had been badgering her all during the meal.

"You've already *proved* that you stack up with the New York talent," he argued heatedly. "Actually going there would be anticlimactic. Besides, New York is squalid. Tell her, Bert."

"The crime rate is horrendous," said Bert Snyder. "Rape is how they pass their time when they're not mugging old ladies. Everybody has triple locks on their doors. I wouldn't live in New York if you paid me. I'm telling you, you can get raped just going out for the milk."

"I shouldn't think anyone would want to rape *you*, Bert," said Morris Hoffberg, and got some laughter. When the laughs died down, he corroborated: "New York is a disgusting city."

"There, you see?" said Andrew Blake.

Tiffany nodded as if she agreed, hoping the subject would be dropped. She wasn't going to debate the most important step of her life in front of these people. She wasn't good with words, anyway. Why couldn't she just follow her impulses for once? Without interference from her father. He called it "guidance." Lately she was beginning to see that it was the guidance you would get from a leash.

She wished she could just go someplace quiet and curl up, now that the dancing was over. She didn't want to be with anyone, not even to hear herself praised. Why wasn't it possible to enjoy dancing for people without having them try to make you into a celebrity? Maybe the more important they thought *you* were, the more important *they* felt for being with you. Snyder and Hoffberg had already done enough gushing to last her the rest of her life. They had complimented her on being a "movie star"—as if she didn't realize that the movie about her, which she didn't even want, was her father's way of competing with Arthur Silvera, proving she didn't need to run to New York; she could have all the trappings of fame and glory right here in Pittsburgh, thanks to Daddy's money.

She felt sorry for Bryan Sinclair. He was so honest and sincere and he wanted to do a good job. Not giving him what he wanted made Tiffany feel mean and petty. But she couldn't help it. She liked him, but when he tried to pry into her personal feelings, she choked up. It was really none of his business, though, was it? Did being a successful dancer mean that you had to give the public pieces of yourself? What did all this have to do with the beauty, the enjoyment, of ballet?

Sitting across from Nicolai Artov and his wife and child didn't help Tiffany relax. She felt so much pressure and guilt. So far she hadn't had the nerve to talk with Nicolai about her big decision, and he hadn't mentioned it at all, had gone on being his usual self, perfectly courteous and gracious. But the hurt look in Natalia's eyes seemed to say: "Don't you realize you owe my husband your loyalty?"

Of course Tiffany realized it. Nicolai had worked with her patiently and caringly since she was eight years old. It was obvious to her now that he had groomed her to be his prima ballerina. Through her growing-up years she had idolized him; and she still did. She had something close to a crush on him. Now she was in a position to help him, and she wanted to, but at the same time she wanted to get away. She felt like a traitor. At age forty, Nicolai was past his prime as a dancer, but he was striving for recognition as a choreographer and director. His dream, which Tiffany knew full well, was to be considered on a par with Silvera and Balanchine. He had stood by her, awarding her the lead in *The Nutcracker*, when he could have ensured success by bringing in an established star. For this, Tiffany owed him. . . .

What, exactly?

Did he hold a mortgage on her future happiness? Or was her father the sole landlord in that department? All her life she had felt constrained, her drives and true feelings channeled in directions she couldn't control, except in her dancing. She had looked upon the offer from the New York National as an excuse to go off on her own, without hurting her father. And yet, why did she keep on feeling that in harboring these desperate yearnings she was being somehow selfish and ungrateful?

"Nicolai." Andrew Blake's voice rang out loudly. "Tell my daughter how badly you want her to stay."

Tiffany glowered at her father, rebuking him for trying to pressure her ballet instructor.

"Tell her what a terrific ballet company we can build here," Blake prodded, "provided, of course, that she stays. I have the money and you two have the talent. Silvera is a tyrant, a maniac—both critics and dancers say so. We can make him look like a bush leaguer."

"A maniac and a tyrant, he may be. But he is also a genius," said Nicolai. Then he turned toward Tiffany and spoke only to her. "I want you to know that you have my blessing, whatever you decide. Silvera wants you very badly. This is a compliment to me, as well as you. I can't hide the fact that I dislike losing you. But maybe someday you'll favor one of the Artov productions by appearing as an honored guest performer. Promise me *now*, won't you?"

Tiffany spoke softly, almost in a whisper, her mouth dry. "I promise. And I only hope you'll still want me. I don't know how well I'll do without you, Nicolai, if I can remember all you've taught me."

Meeting her father's eyes, she saw that he was seething. He had not expected Nicolai to go against him and his money. Tiffany sipped some more claret. The wine was making her a bit light-headed. The dancing had taken a lot out of her. And she was under such a strain.

Oh-oh—she was going to have to meet someone. A blustery red-nosed man in a yellow leisure suit had come over to the table and was shaking hands with her father. He always introduced her proudly to everyone who came along, even if she didn't care to meet them and would probably never see them again. She excused herself and got up from her chair, figuring to avoid the introduction by scampering to the ladies' room. As she got away she heard her father saying, "Yes, we just came from the ballet, my daughter—"

The door to the ladies' room swung shut and Tiffany, exhausted, leaned on the sink, staring at herself in the mirror. She looked haggard. She wanted to be alone for a while, away from everybody. She considered locking herself in one of the stalls. Just then the door opened and Tiffany was startled, seeing Natalia's reflection behind hers in the mirror.

"Are you going to leave us, then?" Natalia asked, her voice soft and lightly accented; like Nicolai, she, too, had been born behind the Iron Curtain.

"I don't know," replied Tiffany—but in truth the constant pressure from all sides was making her decision for her; she wanted to just run away from it all.

"Do what's best for yourself," said Natalia, surprising Tiffany with her gentleness. "Honestly, I mean it. Nicolai and I have talked it over, and we won't hold it against you. We want you to be happy. Seize opportunity where you can. Nicolai should have done that five years ago, instead of sticking it out here, sacrificing himself to build a company when he could have gone off on his own."

Tiffany was stunned. Everybody was being so nice, so understanding—except for her father. She hardly knew what to say. "Thank you, Natalia," she blurted out. "You don't know how much this means to me. I dreaded hurting you both."

The two women embraced, each unsuccessfully fighting back tears. It had not occurred to Tiffany that Nicolai could fail. But Natalia obviously lived with the possibility every day. It was an act of genuine unselfishness for her to bestow her good wishes in this way.

When they came out of the ladies' room, they heard a loud crash and then commotion. Andrew Blake, his fists clenched, was standing over the man in the yellow leisure suit, whose nose was leaking blood. The man's chair had been knocked down and Nicolai picked it back up. Stephanie, who had been dozing, was now on her feet, hanging onto her father, sleepy-eyed and puzzled. The man with the bleeding nose struggled to stand up, using a handkerchief to stanch the flow of blood that had spattered his yellow suit.

Tiffany stopped in her tracks, eyeing her father coldly.

"Bastard insulted you," he explained lamely, some of his pride in being the male victor suddenly wilting under his daughter's level, chastising gaze.

Tiffany turned her back on him. Her disapproval was the one thing he couldn't stand. Sometimes it even enabled her to get her own way.

He was still crowing, maintaining his ego. "Bastard deserved it, didn't he, Bert? Any father worth his salt had to let him have one right in the kisser."

"Damned right," Bert Snyder promptly agreed.

"You sure popped him a good one," Hoffberg chipped in.

Stephanie had started crying while Nicolai and Natalia were struggling to get her into her coat. The man Blake had punched sat off by himself, leaning his head way back in an effort to stop his nosebleed.

Tiffany was embarrassed for her father. "Let's go home," she said. "The evening is ruined."

Sometimes she felt like his wife. A nagging one at that. In a way, she was glad to be given any excuse, even this rather pathetic one, for going home and locking herself in her bedroom. She needed time to think things out. Maybe she would use this incident to stay mad at her father until he came around to agreeing that she should go to New York.

What would he think if she told him that she had used a trick of her imagination to *become* Clara, to work herself into her role? She had imagined Drosselemeyer and the prince as the two competing sides of her father's nature—the one wanting to free her, and the other wanting to keep her a prisoner forever. He had smothered her with love and protection ever since her mother had died when she was four years old. If she danced well enough and hard enough, she might escape. But she feared that come tomorrow, like Clara, she would see all her finest dreams evaporating. The handsome prince would disappear, the Kingdom of the Sweets would fade to nothing, and she would be back in the arms of stern old Drosselemeyer, her father having found a way to spoil her chance with the New York National.

6 ❧❧❧

ON THE NIGHT OF THE FINAL *NUTCRACKER* PERFORMANCE, on the first Saturday of the New Year, Dr. Louis Augenstein sat alone in his apartment watching the news on television, hoping to hear a follow-up report on the police investigation into the rape and murder of Helen Ann Marx. Louis was worried. Yesterday the cop in charge of the case, Lieutenant Manderson, had phoned him at the morgue.

"Any chance the Marx girl could've been pregnant?" the detective had asked, barking the question at Louis and catching him off guard.

It was all Louis could do to keep cool. "Pardon me?" he said, to buy himself time. To make matters worse, Walter Kerrigan was nearby, making an undisguised attempt to overhear what was going on.

"I already talked to Walt Kerrigan," came Manderson's rhythmic staccato voice over the line. "He said you performed the actual autopsy; he only filed the report. He relied on the information you gave him. Any chance you could've screwed up?"

Louis had to brazen it out. He didn't want to act panicky with Kerrigan watching, obviously wise to the fact that it was Manderson on the phone. "If she had been pregnant I certainly would have discovered it," Louis said with just the right touch of sarcasm, as if offended by the affront to his expertise. He shrugged at Kerrigan, whose white morgue coat was spattered with blood. Why didn't the man get back to his cadaver, where he belonged?

"She had been dead three days," said Manderson.

"And?"

"Maybe you couldn't tell so easily."

"If she was pregnant? Nonsense. I'd have spotted it immediately. The cold weather had all her organs perfectly preserved. I was even able to detect the presence of acid phosphatase in her vagina, to confirm for you that she had been raped." Louis fell back on jargon and an attitude of haughty professionalism to put Manderson off. How ridiculous all this is, was the tone he put into his voice. He must have been successful, for Kerrigan's attention seemed to have waned; his eyes flickered toward the cadaver on the autopsy table in the middle of the lab, a woman in whom the Y-shaped incision had already been made, her greenish color and sickening smell evidence of the fact that she had been dead for some time in a relatively warm place.

"Of course you've had plenty of experience diagnosing pregnancies," Lieutenant Manderson said, trying to rattle Louis by this reference to his conviction.

Louis decided not to dignify this with a reply.

"I'll be talking to you again," said Manderson ominously, then hung up. He didn't even say good-bye.

Louis uneasily went about his business the rest of the day at the morgue, but he couldn't wait to get his hands on a newspaper that evening. Fortunately, the reason for Manderson's stubborn probing became clear in an article on page three.

Helen Ann had had a boyfriend, an older man—in fact, twenty years older than her seventeen years. This man, a copywriter for an advertising agency, had become a suspect in her murder. He hadn't voluntarily acknowledged his relationship with the dead girl, and Lieutenant Manderson had had to dig up the information on his own. In apparently trying to convince the police of his innocence by impressing them with his belated candor, the copywriter had admitted that Helen Ann had tried to pressure him into marrying her by telling him she was pregnant. Thus, he had gotten himself into additional hot water by revealing a perfect motive.

Louis knew all this by the time he got Manderson's second phone call, early this morning. "We just talked to the boyfriend again. He won't change his story. So I'm asking you once more about the pregnancy."

Damn this lieutenant! thought Louis. *Is he going to hang this thing around my neck like an albatross?*

"She absolutely was not pregnant," Louis insisted, working irritation into his voice. "Why are you pressing this point so hard, Lieutenant? It's certainly a common enough lie for young girls to tell."

"Or maybe she had it aborted without telling him, after she saw she couldn't use it to make him marry her," said the detective.

"Yes, that's a possibility," Louis agreed. Had he

seized upon the explanation too hastily? Curse Manderson! The fellow was too sly and persistent. Why couldn't a dumber cop have been assigned to the case?

"The pregnancy proves motive," Manderson said. "I'm expecting some more information on this. When it comes through, I'll be in touch." Click. The phone went dead.

What other kinds of information could Manderson have been referring to? Or was he making idle threats? Not necessarily. No. There was the possibility that Helen Ann had gone to a doctor, and if it was a doctor close at hand—say, her family doctor—Manderson might succeed in tracing him and obtaining her medical records. These would verify that she had been pregnant. Louis would have to deny and deny that his autopsy had found any evidence of pregnancy, and keep putting forward the theory that she must have had an abortion. The police couldn't prove otherwise, unless they exhumed the body, which would require a court order. They weren't likely to go that far, Louis hoped. So it would be his word against their suspicions. But suspicions were enough to make his life more miserable.

It was the price he had to pay, ever since embarking on work that was far too daring and avant-garde for the world to openly condone.

They would never surmise that he had taken the fetus. They knew nothing of his experiments. He had been clever and careful in concealing the true purpose of the abortions, his pioneering studies, and his amazing results.

He was probably safe. Still, the pressure would be off entirely if the murder was solved. Then Manderson would leave Louis alone. Perhaps there would be some good news tonight. Maybe the copywriter would break down and confess.

But according to the TV commentator, there were no further developments in the Helen Ann Marx case. Lieutenant Manderson had not turned up any new leads. Was his talk about "more information" merely a ploy, after all? Or did he have something that he was keeping from the media?

While Louis sat worrying, the station credits rolled over newsreel footage taken earlier that week of Tiffany Blake in *The Nutcracker*. His attention was drawn, despite his agitated mental condition, to what he could see of her behind the white superimposed print. He recalled that some newspaper critic had called her "a blonde dynamo"—a cliché more suited to a roller derby queen than a ballerina. Reading the article, Louis had hoped he wasn't missing much by not going to see her perform. But judging from the news clips, she was really quite enchanting. It was such a pity that he had to stay away from all his old pleasures, but if he ventured into Heinz Hall, he would be a pariah, the mere sight of him eliciting shocked gasps and scandalous whispers from his former colleagues and friends. Once they had sought his company, his wit, his patronage. But they had not stood by him in his disgrace. With an angry jab, he shut the TV off.

In bed, he couldn't stop worrying about Lieutenant Manderson and the Helen Ann Marx case. Manderson was too smart. What if he found out that the fetus was stolen? What if he really did exhume the body? He was one of the most tenacious detectives on the force. What if he pursued this thing beyond all reasonable limits, and found out more than anyone else?

Louis considered hiding the results of his experiments in a safer place. He didn't want to go back to prison. He would rather die. He had lost his wife, his money, and his reputation. He couldn't stand to lose any more. Interfering with a criminal investigation was a violation of his parole. They would send him back for it; he would have to finish out the rest of his sentence, four more terrible, agonizing years. He would kill himself first. For a long time—it seemed like hours—sleep eluded him. He stayed awake tossing and turning, his thoughts tormented.

In his nightmare Tiffany Blake was on his operating table, but the operating room was a cell surrounded by steel bars. Tiffany's complexion was livid green, like that of a long-dead corpse, but she was still alive, and he was using a screaming electrical buzz saw to remove the top of her skull.

7 ❧

THE BEGINNING OF THE NEW YEAR SEEMED PEACEFUL enough at first, but then it was shattered by a horrible accident.

On the first Sunday after the holiday, Bryan slept until noon, and then had dinner with Julia at her grandparents' house. Julia's parents were both dead, killed in an automobile collision when she was only five, and so she had been raised by her grandfather and grandmother, Dominic and Theresa Valenti. To earn money to pay for her ballet lessons, she worked as a clerk in a hardware store on the South Side of Pittsburgh, near her grandparents' home. Dominic, now retired, was a dignified old-fashioned gentleman, spry and alert for his seventy-two years, who had worked most of his life in the nearby steel mill. He and

Theresa, having arrived in America poor and uneducated, thought it was wonderful that their granddaughter was going to marry a well-mannered college graduate who worked mostly with his brains instead of his hands. They bragged to the neighbors anytime Bryan's commercials appeared on TV.

Bryan liked having dinner on Sundays with the Valentis. He enjoyed their closeness and warmth. His own family—mother, father, and a younger brother—lived three hundred miles away in Philadelphia and he seldom saw them. But he was planning to go home for a few days soon after he got his work load cleared up, if a big snowfall didn't make the Pennsylvania Turnpike too hazardous. He wanted to exchange Christmas presents in person, if belatedly, with his mother, father, and brother.

Julia's grandmother made the best spaghetti Bryan had ever tasted. Usually she cooked meatballs and spareribs in the sauce, and the noodles were homemade. There were always tasty little side dishes, like fried eggplant, endive salad, and fried sweet peppers. Plus homemade bread. And red Italian wine that Dominic brought up from the basement. Theresa was frail and bent, her gray hair always in a neat bun. Bryan often wondered why the cooking and housekeeping weren't too much for her, but she hobbled around and got it done with a cheerful, no-nonsense smile.

After dinner, Dominic usually sipped wine and puffed on a strong black De Nobili cigar while watching television in his comfortable reclining chair. Sometimes he dozed off, the cigar going out in an ashtray or his mouth.

This particular Sunday, Bryan and Julia took the decorations off the huge, fat Christmas tree and dragged it out onto the front porch. Theresa joined in, moving around arthritically, packing away ornaments.

Her main concern was seeing that the manger and the baby Jesus were taken care of properly so she would have them next year to convey the true meaning of the holiday.

Julia was taking a week off from her job and from ballet rehearsals. But for Bryan, come Monday morning it was right back into the grind of the commercial film business. Around midnight when he was getting ready to leave, Julia asked him, "What are you going to do about Paul?"

"I don't know. Stick it out, I guess."

"Couldn't you hire someone to do the things he won't do?"

"Not really. It would push the overhead up sky-high. It's either get rid of him, or get someone to replace him. But maybe he'll shape up."

"At this late date it doesn't seem likely," Julia said. "But whatever you decide, I'm with you."

Bryan kissed her good night, and on the way home in his car he thought about his problems with Paul. Now that the wedding was coming up, he didn't want any unnecessary complications or hassles. He owed it to Julia to get his life in order as much as he could. But he owed something to Paul, too; in the beginning Paul had worked hard, but then disillusionment had set in. Maybe the real trouble was nobody's fault, just part of the grind of trying to succeed. Being partners with someone was like being married; you didn't run off and get a divorce just because everything wasn't peaches and cream.

But no matter how you cut it, Paul wasn't holding up his end. He hadn't the tact or the finesse to make substantial sales or develop good client relations. He could be an excellent craftsman when he saw fit to put out his best effort. But Bryan could get craftsmanship out of any number of freelancers whom he could hire for individual projects without having to shell out a permanent chunk of partnership profits. If Paul wasn't willing to live up to a solid commitment, then Bryan didn't really need him and would be better off on his own. If he could talk Andrew Blake or any other investor into backing a feature film project, he could write and direct and hire his own crew.

Bryan was unused to that kind of thinking, though, and didn't want to behave selfishly, even though Julia had told him that he worried more about other people than they did about him. No doubt she had an exaggerated estimation of his virtues because she loved him; but she also had a stake in his future and wanted him to make the right moves. He prided himself that he always put his fullest effort into something once he committed himself, even though others didn't do the same.

Wasn't it time he put his own future first? And Julia's? Now that she was tied to him, all the decisions became more difficult. It was easier to be noble if the only one who suffered was yourself.

Paul would have a tough time making it on his own. He'd probably flounder around as a freelancer, find out he couldn't pay his bills, and end up working for someone else. If so, he would hate it. He'd become twice as miserable and bitter as he was now.

It goaded Bryan that he felt responsible for Paul, even though Paul had ceased paying his dues.

Monday through Wednesday went by in a flurry of activity. In addition to filming a couple of public-service spots with a Pittsburgh Steelers linebacker as on-camera talent, Bryan and Paul had to attend to details like shipping the ballet footage out to be processed and riding herd on the lab people so the final print of the paint company movie would be pulled and delivered as promised.

On Thursday, they had an appointment to screen raw footage of *The Nutcracker* for Andrew and Tiffany Blake at the Blake estate. Adrienne Mallory and Julia Valenti were going to the screening, too, and they arrived at the film studio together, having come in Adrienne's car. But when it was clear that the presentation of the paint company film would run late, Bryan ducked out of the projection booth to explain that he and Paul would be tied up a while longer. Julia nodded and smiled, but she knew there must be some problem. She and Adrienne helped themselves to some coffee. They knew by now that it was always a critical time when clients were shown the final results of what they had paid for.

After a half-hour or so, everybody came filing out of the screening room. Disgruntled looks on their faces, the clients went straight for their coats and hats. As they stepped into the elevator, Bryan told them reassuringly, "Don't worry, this is only a trial print. I'll see that the lab corrects the flesh tones and burns in the supers better on the next one." The elevator doors shut and Paul pointed at his temple and made little circles with his index finger as the clients descended out of sight, where he obviously preferred them.

"Whew!" said Bryan. "Did you ever see people so picky? Three times they had to look at the damned thing!"

"The title of their dumb little flick is *Personality Paints,*" Paul told Adrienne. "We made it less dumb than it would've been if they hadn't hired us, but the agency flunky is taking all the credit for the improvements and blaming us for all the flaws."

"How typical," said Adrienne.

"We've gotta get a move on," said Bryan. "We're due at the Blakes' in less than half an hour. We're going to be late."

"So what?" Paul muttered.

"You can't take that attitude and expect him to put cash into a feature movie," Bryan admonished.

With cans of film and a sixteen-millimeter projector in the back of Bryan's station wagon, they headed out toward the suburbs. The roads were spotted with patches of ice, and Bryan had to drive carefully.

"Poor Nicolai," said Julia. "All those years of hard work to build something worthwhile here in Pittsburgh, and now he's going to lose his prima ballerina—plus the money that Andrew Blake contributes. He's been quite a patron of the company, no matter what anybody says about him. And look at the business he's given you and Paul, Bryan."

"Please, don't let's pretend he's a true patron of the arts," pleaded Adrienne. "We all know he wouldn't give Nicolai a dime if it weren't for Tiffany."

"His idea of art is a singing wiener," Paul said, referring to one of Blake's ideas for a Hot Dog Heaven commercial.

Everybody in the car chuckled.

"Bryan, what do you think? Will she go or stay?" Adrienne asked. "You've been interviewing her and getting close to her. Your opinion is worth more than anyone else's."

"I really don't know," Bryan answered, flashing a glance at Julia out of the corner of his eye to make sure she saw how extremely competitive Adrienne was obviously prepared to be.

"She's certainly the best dancer in Pittsburgh right now," Julia commented.

"Oh, I don't know about that," countered Adrienne. This produced a long moment of uncomfortable silence; which Bryan cut by saying, "She's very hard to talk to. One of the problems of making the movie has been trying to coax her into opening up. Our original plan was to tell the story with her own voice takes, but we may have to use a narrator, instead."

"Which will lose the feeling of intimacy," Paul explained.

"She's a real dodo, except when she dances," Adrienne complained. "I, for one, have my doubts that her father will let her go to New York. He watches over her like an old mother hen."

"Tiffany is over eighteen and legally her own boss," Paul said. "So let's hope she makes the right decision for herself—which is to go with Silvera."

Of course you're telling Adrienne exactly what she wants to hear, Bryan thought, wondering exactly what his partner saw in the Mallory girl. There was something cold and calculating about her. Her family was well off, though not in the class of the Blakes. Maybe Paul thought he could extract enough money out of her to get his sex satire produced. She was an intense dancer, driven by a will to succeed. But while Bryan could admire her technical ability, he always felt that she was smiling smugly at the audience, instead of forgetting herself in the dance.

Bryan knew that Julia would dance, even if she never got to go onstage. Knowing how much she loved ballet endeared her to him; the world was full of people who had no clear focus in life, no drive or ambition to give their lives meaning. Bryan liked people who were trying to accomplish something that could be beyond them. They were the only ones who had a chance to excel.

Sometimes he wondered how it would affect their relationship if Julia's career took off the way Tiffany's was on the verge of doing. Would they be torn apart by success, as seemed to happen to so many famous people?

Andrew Blake buzzed Tiffany on her bedroom intercom. "Let's go jogging before the film people get here," he suggested. "No ballet practice for you this week, but that doesn't mean we can let you go to pot."

He was kidding, but she chose not to laugh. During the past ten years he had often gone jogging with her, and until recently she had welcomed his company. But lately his presence impinged on her—she didn't need him playing watchdog, as if she couldn't be trusted to stay in shape on her own.

"What about the film people?" she asked, staving him off.

"If they get here while we're gone, they'll wait. I'm the one paying them, after all."

"All right, Daddy," Tiffany agreed reluctantly, wondering if he might try softening her up for another attempt at squelching the New York proposition. She had stayed angry at him long enough—since the fight at the club—and denying herself fresh-air exercise would be childish.

She got out of bed and stripped off her pajamas, turning this way and that in front of her full-length mirror, appraising the suppleness, flexibility, and shapeliness of her lithe dancer's body. She was physically attractive, her contours and proportions aesthetically pleasing; but she did not recognize this, not in a narcissistic fashion; rather, she used the mirror to evaluate herself as an athlete, a ballerina, who must scrupulously attend to any signs of weakness, flab, or disproportionate musculature. When the appraisal was finished, she got into her jogging clothes and went downstairs.

Mrs. Monroe, the black middle-aged housekeeper

and cook, offered to make her some toast and eggs, but she said not until she finished jogging. Her father was out on the patio warming up. She opened the sliding-glass door and joined him, beginning her stretching and bending exercises. There were patches of ice and snow in the yard. The sun was out, but the air was bitingly cold, invigorating.

"A good run will get our minds clear for settling the New York question," Andrew said, straightening up, his white breath streaming from mouth and nose.

"Daddy, there's nothing more to be settled," Tiffany replied curtly. "My mind is made up, and I'm going."

"Why so hasty?"

"There's nothing hasty about it. It's what I've always wanted but almost didn't dare dream it would happen. Besides, I've had three weeks to think it over. Arthur Silvera doesn't wait forever for anybody." She started off at a slow trot, making her father follow after her.

"I don't think you're mature enough to make this kind of decision," Andrew challenged, hastening to keep up with his daughter as they jogged around the side of the large graystone house and down onto the driveway. The three-mile jaunt they had measured some years ago by odometer led out into their Marlboro Park neighborhood, with its sparse population of elegant homes, vast well-tended lawns, and clean, snow-free driveways.

"I'll never *be* mature if I always live in your shadow," Tiffany argued, still trotting. "If I can make it in New York, I'll know I'm somebody special. That kind of achievement can't be bought with money. Whether I succeed or fail, it won't be because I'm your daughter. Can't you see how important this is to me?"

Blake huffed and puffed, not really hearing his daughter's viewpoint because he was concentrating so hard on how to argue her out of it. He couldn't understand why she was being so recalcitrant. He wanted to stifle her rebellion so she wouldn't leave him. The part of his life that wasn't wound up in his businesses was focused on her. She meant more to him now than ever—now that he had begun dreading the loneliness of old age.

The first mile of the jogging route led downhill, away from the fringes of the housing area, and at the bottom of the long hill there were some railroad tracks that Tiffany and her father had to cross before cutting through a patch of woods with a long winding biking and jogging trail.

"Speaking of money," Blake huffed, "you can't really make it in Manhattan on what Silvera proposes to pay you. Just two hundred dollars a week! You'll be a genuine starving artist. When you find out what it's like without Daddy's wallet around, the glamour of being on your own will wear off pronto."

Getting all this out while running caused Andrew to fall behind. Tiffany yelled back over her shoulder, hurt and angry: "You mean you don't intend to help me a little financially?"

Sensing he had found a weapon with which to discourage her, Blake pressed, voicing a threat he knew he didn't really mean: "If you persist in defying me when I only want what's best for you, I'll let you have a go at it totally on your own. Maybe you'll learn the value of my hard-earned cash if I cut you off from it entirely."

As they neared the railroad tracks, the red warning lights were flashing and Andrew stopped for the approaching train. But Tiffany, in an outburst of anger, dashed across just ahead of the locomotive, hoping to strand her father on the opposite side. At first there seemed to be time for her to make it. But her foot hit a patch of ice and—sickeningly—Andrew saw her falling, then trying to get up, but slipping again. He yelled, "Tiffany! Get up!" His words were drowned out by the train. She tried to roll as the engine thundered down on her, blocking her from view. Did she get out of the way in time by some miracle? Andrew had a desperate hope that the hours and hours of practiced agility had stood her in good stead. His heart pounded, his body full of useless adrenaline, as he stood rooted, horrified, car after car pounding through the intersection, brakes hissing loudly as the engineer tried desperately to bring the monster to a halt.

It was a short train, three or four boxcars, and when they cleared the crossing Andrew saw his daughter lying in a pool of blood, her mangled left leg severed at the thigh by the gigantic steel wheels, the lower part of the limb lying off to one side of the tracks. Andrew stood paralyzed—he couldn't move; it was like witnessing a nightmare. The crew from the halted train was scurrying around, gawking and muttering. One man looked at Tiffany and staggered toward some weeds and began throwing up. The engineer shouted in Andrew's face that an ambulance was on the way; he had radioed for it.

Suddenly, like a man possessed, Andrew sprang into action, leaping to Tiffany's side. She was unconscious and losing a great deal of blood. Andrew worked desperately, taking off his belt and using it as a tourniquet, tying it around his daughter's upper thigh. Then he dived into a snowbank, scooping up armfuls of snow to pack around the bloody severed limb, which he had laid onto his nylon jacket.

There was a line of cars stopped by the flashing lights, and one of the cars was Bryan Sinclair's station wagon. Badly frightened, Adrienne and Julia stayed in the car, but Bryan and Paul ran over to Blake and stopped in their tracks, stunned, not knowing how to help. Then, seeing what Andrew was doing, Bryan and Paul wordlessly helped gather snow, going through the motions of doing something, anything, but feeling numb and futile. Andrew wrapped the limb up, encasing it in snow as best he could, clinging to a forlorn hope of saving it somehow. "Oh, please, God, don't let her die," he said out loud.

After twenty or thirty long minutes, the ambulance came and Tiffany was loaded into the vehicle, with her severed leg laid down beside her. Bryan went back to the car, pulled it off the road, and sat with his arms around Julia, who was crying. Paul and Adrienne were sitting apart, their faces blank, their eyes glassy, in the aftermath of the accident. Dumbfounded, they watched the ambulance start pulling out, humping slowly across the tracks. Then the vehicle started gathering speed.

Siren wailing, Andrew Blake riding in back with his daughter, the race to the nearest hospital began. The roads were choked with morning traffic. The ambulance had to swerve in and out of lanes, sometimes narrowly missing oncoming drivers who didn't react quickly enough. During the wild, nerve-jangling ride, an ambulance attendant encased the severed limb in an inflatable plastic splint and placed chemical ice packs around it. Tiffany, still unconscious, was being treated for shock.

"What can they do for her?" Andrew asked in a weak, hopeless voice, his face ashen. The ambulance careened around a sharp curve, banging his shoulder against cold metal.

"Don't know," one of the attendants replied. "We radioed Emergency at St. Mary's to get ready for a victim of traumatic amputation. I've seen them sew fingers and thumbs back on—even a hand once—but never a leg. I guess it's possible, though. But if I were you, I just wouldn't get my hopes up."

"Assuming she lives," said the other attendant, unwittingly callous in his objectivity, "she's gonna lose the leg."

Oh, dear God, no! Don't let her die! Don't let her lose the leg! was Andrew's silent, desperate prayer.

8 ❦

FULL OF ANXIETY AND SELF-RECRIMINATION BECAUSE HE had provoked the argument that led to Tiffany's foolhardy attempt to beat the train, Andrew Blake waited in the emergency room at St. Mary's Hospital. If she lived, she would hate him forever; it would be his fault if she could never dance again. He had prayed that his daughter wouldn't go to New York; in his misery, it now seemed that his prayers had been diabolically answered.

He looked at his watch again. Half an hour since the arrival of the ambulance. What in the world was happening? Was Tiffany alive or dead? Why wouldn't someone tell him something?

He couldn't sit still, kept going to the water fountain, then to a a chair, then to the water fountain again, and

54

back to a different chair. All the chairs were of orange molded plastic. The walls were white. Lots of people stared at him—perhaps the news of his daughter's accident had been broadcast on the radio, or maybe they stared simply because he was the only one in a jogging suit. Some of the people in the emergency room looked ill and some didn't; some looked merely bored; others were in pain from assorted gouges, sprains, fractures, and lacerations. Andrew envied these lesser injuries and would have traded for one any day in exchange for what had happened to his daughter.

And there was nothing he could do. Money was of no use in this kind of predicament; this kind of emergency. If it was a normal illness, Andrew could buy the best care, medication, therapy. He could keep paying and paying willingly for as long as it took to make a difference. Sometimes money could actually buy health. But this time all the decisions had been left to chance. Rich or poor, there were no options. Whether she lived or died, it would depend on which hospital had been closest and which doctor was on duty.

"Andrew Blake?"

He jumped when his name was called. "This way, please," the plump middle-aged nurse told him, and he was led through a pair of orange metal doors into a white hallway. "First door to the left. The doctor will speak with you."

He entered a tiny office and shook hands with Dr. Mohamed, a short, fat swarthy man with heavy beard shadow, and black hairs that should have been trimmed growing out of his nostrils. He wore a stethoscope that flopped around on his belly, a stained yellow shirt, and a wrinkled white lab coat. His accent, possibly Egyptian, was very thick. Andrew listened hard, as it could be a matter of life or death for Tiffany. The first thing that he understood, with immeasurable relief, was that his daughter had been brought out of shock and her condition was now stable. The rest was more difficult to follow, but Andrew pieced it together after asking for repetition and clarification.

Dr. Mohamed said that emergency-room personnel had removed a shoe, sock, and part of a trousers leg from Tiffany's severed limb and put the limb in a basin filled with ice. It had thus been kept in good condition for a possible reattachment operation, known as a "reimplantation." However, St. Mary's did not have the staff or facilities for this procedure. If the leg were to be saved, paramedics would have to take Tiffany by helicopter to Belvedere General Hospital, on the other side of Pittsburgh. In the event that Andrew didn't give his assent to a reimplantation attempt, Tiffany's thigh would be cleaned and dressed just like any other amputation.

"How soon can the paramedics be here?" Andrew asked.

He was told that they couldn't come to St. Mary's Hospital because there was no place for them to land. Tiffany would have to be put into an ambulance again and driven to St. Mary's Church nearby, where there was a large empty parking lot that could accommodate a helicopter.

"Let's get started, then," Andrew said. He thanked Dr. Mohamed for saving Tiffany's life and for not closing his mind to the possibility of saving her leg.

"I am not promising anything," the doctor said in his nearly unintelligible accent. "Perhaps it will turn out that I am even wrong in holding out a false ray of hope."

"God bless you," said Andrew. "You've done your best for my daughter, and I believe you are a good man."

He was not unaware of the fact that in the last couple

of hours the word "God" had sprung from his lips more often than it had in the past fifteen years. He was not normally a religious man; in fact, if asked, he would have said he was an agnostic. But where his daughter was concerned, he would grasp at any straw. A part of him knew that when this crisis was past, however it turned out, he would return once more to being irreligious.

Nevertheless, after riding in the ambulance with Tiffany to the parking lot adjacent to St. Mary's Church, he entered the place of worship and said a prayer while waiting for the helicopter, his ears cocked for the sound of its descent. He thanked God for sparing Tiffany's life. And he promised sincerely that he would use his money to aid some needy charities, if the doctors would make her whole again.

Dr. Frederick S. Taylor, an orthopedist, headed the reimplantation team at Belvedere General. He was in his mid-forties, tall and stoop-shouldered, with black hair graying at the temples. The pallor of his complexion was due to his long intensive hours. His eyes were alert, though, and he looked kindly. And he was. Before each and every operation he reminded himself that he must always have reverence for the tissues of the human body. This would not be his first try at reimplanting a human leg; just three months ago he had reattached the left leg of a motorcyclist maimed in a highway accident, but, unfortunately, the stump of the right leg had been too mangled to reattach the severed limb. There were many factors governing the success of a reimplantation attempt: the cleanness of the cut, the quick refrigeration of the amputated part, and the timely restoration of blood flow; also, the age and physical condition of the patient were crucial. In Tiffany's case, these factors were in her favor. After consultation with two plastic surgeons and a specialist in blood vessel surgery, the other members of the reimplantation team, Dr. Taylor called the patient's father into private conference.

Growing used to the pressure over the length of time that had now lapsed since the accident, Andrew was as calm as could be expected at this stage. He was doing his best not to give in to panic, which might wreck his ability to make crucial decisions. Remaining level-headed in emergencies was one of the qualities that had made him a successful businessman. He now knew that Dr. Taylor was one of the most highly regarded surgeons in the eastern United States. Talking with him in his office, his demeanor and reputation inspired confidence.

The doctor explained that since the early Sixties, due to advancements in microsurgery, hundreds of fingers, hands, and arms had been reattached and functioned properly thereafter—he had himself performed dozens of these operations. "But, Mr. Blake, I must tell you that the human leg presents a more difficult problem. For a reimplanted leg to move and have sensation—not just to hang there like something dead—the sciatic nerve, which is the largest in the human body, must regrow from the site of the amputation down to the foot, a degree of nerve growth far greater than in other reimplantations. Surgeons in Australia and mainland China claim to have had some wonderful successes with reimplanting human legs, but it has only been tried a few times in the United States, and too recently to be sure of the long-term results."

Andrew sucked in a deep breath. He asked, "What's the alternative?"

"Well, the alternative would be to fit the amputated leg with a prosthesis—an artificial limb. This is not as awful as you might think. Prosthetic devices nowadays are quite sophisticated, both cosmetically and functionally."

The thought made Andrew cringe. "My daughter is a dancer," he said, his voice breaking. "If she lost that leg, it would kill her."

Dr. Taylor summed up the observations of his team of surgeons: "We've noted that Tiffany is in excellent physical condition. Although unconscious, she isn't in shock. The amputation was a relatively clean one—the remaining tissues don't seem to be mangled beyond repair. Thanks to your quick thinking at the scene of the accident, the severed limb is well preserved. If you give me the go-ahead, Mr. Blake, we're ready to try saving Tiffany's leg."

"What if you fail?"

"Then we can still clean the wound up and prepare it for a prosthesis."

After signing the necessary permission forms for the operation, Andrew went out to the emergency room waiting area and stood by a pay telephone, trying to decide what to do. Despite his anxiety and grief, he felt conspicuous in his jogging outfit. He decided to take a taxi home; there was nothing he could do to help while Tiffany was in the operating room. He would come right back after changing clothes. He'd have to break the bad news to his housekeeper, Elvira Monroe, if she hadn't heard it already on the radio. She'd be taking it pretty hard. The kindly black woman thought of Tiffany almost as a daughter.

A heavy wet snow had started, the sky clouding over since this morning, and the roads were getting more slippery. The snow plastered itself to the taxi's windshield and caked where the wipers pushed it aside.

Traffic was snarled up, thanks to the bad weather and the post-holiday shoppers hunting for bargains. Andrew again found himself praying for his daughter.

"What's the matter, fella?" the cab driver asked cheerfully. "Twist yer ankle joggin'?"

Andrew made no reply. The cabby had a thick, fat neck; pimples and blackheads clustered around black hair follicles. The man said, "All this physical fitness crap is bad news. Keeps the hospitals busy. Guys like you and me, we're too old for it. We should stick to bendin' our elbows at the saloon. You didn't wrench yer back, did ya?"

"I'd rather not talk about it if you don't mind," said Andrew. But he regretted being curt and told himself he'd make it up with a big tip. He had the superstitious feeling that good behavior on his part while Tiffany was under the knife might help avoid disfavor from whatever forces presided over the outcome. The cabbie would have to wait while he ran into the house for his wallet—then for sure Mrs. Monroe would know something was horribly wrong. Of course, she'd be worried sick by now, anyway, since he and Tiffany had not come back from jogging.

Why did the details surrounding accidents and deaths always seem so picayune and unreal?

He remembered when his wife, Alice, had died. Tiffany had been almost too young to understand. Alice had worked hard and had done without a lot of nice things during all the years Andrew was struggling, establishing the businesses. She had loved him and stuck by his side, looking toward the future. But there wasn't to be a future. Just when he was getting ahead and their lives would have gotten easier, she became incurably ill with leukemia. Andrew had tried to give Tiffany everything; everything money could buy; everything he couldn't give to Alice. What had he wanted money for, in the first place? To buy the nicest possible lives, full of happiness and comfort, for himself and his wife and daughter. Why had it been his jinx to be struck by tragedies beyond the reach of the supposedly almighty dollar?

He could say honestly that most of the trappings of success didn't mean much to him. His professional, and even his personal acquaintances, his so-called peers, were a lot of insufferable bores or overbearing egomaniacs. Some, like Hoffberg and Snyder from the bakery, were sycophants; they danced when Andrew pulled their strings. The few people he respected—Nicolai Artov and Bryan Sinclair, for example—he had met outside his normal circles, and somehow he couldn't get close to them. Money didn't help, especially when he tried to use it to control them. Andrew only respected those his money couldn't control; yet, he tried to use it to control everybody. He had a deepseated fear, a phobia, that if he didn't keep people tied to him by the power he could wield over them, they would see no reason to give him their love, respect, or loyalty. His relationship with his own daughter had been plagued by this weakness. She was the only person in the world, other than his wife, whom he had ever truly loved. And today, to his sorrow and despair, he might have destroyed whatever love she felt in return.

Tiffany had been given Demerol to wipe out pain, antibiotics to prevent infection, and a diuretic to cleanse her kidneys and reduce the risk of renal failure. Now she was on the operating table, anesthetized, powerless to do anything to help herself. It was all up to the surgeons.

The operating room team—four doctors, a circulating nurse, scrub nurse, and anesthetist—had recovered from the quiet awe that always came over them when first confronting a case that was particularly gruesome and challenging. A few wisecracks had followed, not out of irreverence, but because of the necessity for relieving tension. Then seriousness and esprit de corps had taken over.

In his surgical mask and gloves, Dr. Taylor said a small private prayer. Once the operation began, the procedures were of necessity mechanical, objective, controlled, almost as if there wasn't a human being on the table. Still, Dr. Taylor always tried to remember the human element. He did not believe that sophisticated technology was the be-all and end-all of his profession; he tried to leave room for the possibility that a psychic bond might be established between physician and patient—that a patient's will to live and desire to be made whole might affect the outcome of an operation.

He and his operating team had discussed and mentally rehearsed what had to happen. After the bones in the two parts of Tiffany's leg were matched and set, the surgeons would have to identify, match, and stitch back together the separated blood vessels, nerves, muscles, and tendons. The sciatic nerve would have to regenerate from the site of the rejoining to the end of the limb, growing only one millimeter a day, or an inch per month. Many of the blood vessels and nerves were less than one-twentieth of an inch in diameter, and would have to be operated on with miniature surgical forceps, scissors, and needles, the surgeons peering down through suspended microscopes allowing magnification up to twenty times.

Dr. Benton, one of the plastic surgeons, worked on the severed limb. He trimmed away mangled flesh and bone and, using long sutures of different colors, carefully tagged the ends of the sciatic nerve, femoral and saphenous veins and femoral artery so they could be readily located later. The other plastic surgeon, Dr. Palermo, trimmed and tagged the blood vessels and nerves of Tiffany's upper thigh. In doing this work, Dr. Benton and Dr. Palermo relied on color plates of human anatomy showing nerves and blood vessels in meticulous detail, because each individual is different, and when the vessels and nerves were joined, they would have to be matched precisely.

Dr. Taylor and the blood vessel specialist, Dr. Sanchez, used a drill to remove the marrow from the inter-medullary canal of Tiffany's thigh bone. Then they inserted a ten-inch stainless-steel rod into the marrow cavity, pushing it all the way up the thigh bone and into the hip, where they anchored it. Next they tapped the lower end of the steel rod into the remaining three inches of thigh bone in the severed leg. The rod would provide structural support for the reattachment.

The blood vessels were flushed out with an anticoagulant solution, and large doses of liquid antibiotics were administered. A blood sample was taken and sent to the laboratory to make sure the proper amount of oxygen was entering Tiffany's bloodstream. Already the operation had been in progress for better than two hours.

Dr. Sanchez began suturing together the ends of the severed blood vessels. The needles he used were finer than human hair, gripped with tweezer-like holders; the prolene sutures were gossamer in texture and strength and very slippery; when the doctor tied a knot with them, he had to scrutinize it under the microscope to make sure it was tight because he could not feel the tension; if he tugged on it, it would break. All the while, he could not even see his hands, only the magnified tips of his needles and forceps and those of Dr. Palermo an inch away. Double viewing pieces on the operating microscope enabled both doctors to work together on the blood vessel surgery. They perspired profusely under the strain, and from time to time the circulating nurse would wipe their brows. At one point Dr. Sanchez accidentally ran a needle through his glove; the needle was discarded, a new suture was gotten, and the circulating nurse removed the damaged glove for the doctor and put on a new one.

When the blood vessel surgery was completed, three hours had passed. Anxiously, Dr. Taylor checked the clock. Had the severed limb been without blood too long? Or might improperly repaired blood vessels block circulation? Repeatedly he pressed Tiffany's calf—and a thrilling moment occurred. The grayish-blue lifeless limb slowly began turning warm and pink. A cut on Tiffany's toe began to bleed. The limb was alive and being nurtured again. Wordlessly, the nurses and doctors congratulated each other, their eyes registering satisfaction and hope.

Dr. Sanchez rejoined the two ends of the sciatic nerve and the other nerves of Tiffany's leg, operating under the surgical microscope and working from the inside of the leg outward. The nerves had fibers not only for sensation, but also to stimulate muscles; it was therefore essential to join sensory nerves with sensory nerves and motor nerves with motor nerves, or the leg would not be capable of performing both functions.

The tendons were matched, realigned, and sutured with black silk. To do this properly, the doctors again consulted detailed anatomy charts. Then they reconnected the major muscles of the thigh and knee, the quadriceps and hamstrings. All the muscle repair work was accomplished using heavy chromic catgut. This part of the operation was not nearly so delicate as the nerve and blood vessel microsurgery. Muscles and tendons could be expected to heal quickly, within four to six weeks. Regeneration of nerves and return to function would take much longer—from six months to a year.

Finally, after more than seven hours on the operating table, Tiffany's surgery was over. Her damaged leg had been splinted, not placed in a full cast, since it would have to be watched closely throughout the healing process. Very carefully, all four doctors and three nurses lifted her from the operating table to a recovery bed. Then, having done all they could for her, the surgeons took off their sweaty and soiled gowns and gloves and discarded them. "I'll write out a list of instructions for recovery room and intensive-care people," Dr. Sanchez said to Dr. Taylor. "You come and check later in case you want to add anything."

While Tiffany was in the recovery room, Dr. Taylor called Andrew Blake to his office to explain the results. There was good reason to suppose that all would go well from here on out, but Tiffany would still face more surgery. In six weeks an exploratory operation would ascertain how well the sciatic nerve was regenerating. Scar tissue would be removed and some of the suturing would be refined. It might be possible to facilitate regrowth of the sciatic nerve by grafting fibers taken from a less important nerve in Tiffany's other leg. And she would receive skin grafts from her right thigh to cover the surgical incisions.

"But will she dance again?" Andrew asked. "Is there any hope of total recovery?"

Behind his desk, Dr. Taylor tightened his lips and leaned forward, extreme tiredness showing in his face. In a dry, resigned voice he said, "She won't be able to dance, I'm afraid. You must realize that when the train wheels ran over her, a three-inch section of her thigh was totally destroyed. The reimplanted limb will be shorter than the other leg. Tiffany will have to wear a lift in her shoe, but she'll be able to walk and run and control her own movements. We'll have saved her from the far worse handicap of total amputation and the use of a prosthesis. Mr. Blake—" The doctor stopped, seeing that Andrew had broken down, crying. "Mr. Blake, even if Tiffany has to give up dancing, she still has a future, a life to lead that can in many other ways be rewarding. You've got to pull yourself together so you can encourage her, give her all the love and understanding she needs. Otherwise, this unfortunate accident will cripple her emotionally, as well as physically."

Andrew looked up, his face streaked with tears. "God help me, Doctor!" he blurted out. "What happened is my fault, and I'll never stop blaming myself. Taking dancing away from Tiffany . . . to her it will be worse than taking her life."

Watching television that evening, Dr. Louis Augenstein leaned forward in his chair when the news came on about Tiffany Blake. The commentator blathered on and on, naïvely calling what Dr. Taylor and his team had done "a miracle of medical science." Louis snorted derisively. To him, Tiffany's operation was an outright failure. Her left leg was *three inches shorter* than her other leg! This was not a success—this was a miserable, pathetic, grotesque flop!

Louis knew Dr. Frederick Taylor and even worked with him once. The man was a highly competent orthopedic surgeon, but he didn't know what Louis knew. Louis had the key that could open his eyes, expand his effectiveness a million times, rendering him truly capable of helping the Blake girl. But Louis wasn't going to tell. His knowledge belonged to him alone; if they didn't approve of how he got it, he would keep it for himself. Let them flounder in their ignorance, since they seemed to prefer it that way. They were fools groping in the dark. It was the world's fault, not Louis Augenstein's, that Tiffany Blake and millions of others had to remain maimed, mangled, and deformed—physically and psychologically.

Tomorrow Louis would buy the local newspaper so he could clip out items pertaining to the Blake girl. Articles on her accident, her operation, as well as reviews and advertisements highlighting her accomplishments as a ballerina would become part of his file. Actually, her story was more moving, more dramatic, than that of the Boston cellist; there was a heightened poignancy about youthful promise cut short. *Yes, "cut short"—thanks to Taylor and his ignorance!* thought Louis with a smug grimace.

He went to bed, the lack of news on the Helen Ann Marx case bothering him less than it would have if he had not been mulling over, almost savoring, the ramifications of what had happened to Tiffany Blake.

9 ❧❧❧

IF HE HAD IT TO DO OVER AGAIN, ANDREW BLAKE WOULD do all in his power, not to thwart his daughter, but to help her become a great ballerina. Too late, he saw that she would be happy no other way. He had lost his only chance to keep her love and respect. If only he had let her go to New York! It would have been a small sacrifice, compared to what he was suffering now. Besides, the glamour and excitement of the move might have worn off after a few weeks, a month, even a year, and she would have come back to him in one piece—instead of a hopeless cripple.

His feelings of guilt and remorse were increased, rather than diminished, by the irony that Tiffany didn't seem to blame him for losing her leg. She blamed herself—her own impetuousness, her own blind anger.

It wasn't a healthy reaction—lashing out at no one but herself. She was being a martyr. It was pitiful evidence of how totally her ego had been destroyed. Whatever pride, whatever satisfaction she had ever felt, came from her accomplishments as a dancer. In her young life, she had not given herself to any other endeavor of any importance. She had nothing else to live for. In order to rally spiritually and emotionally, she would have to muster the courage, not only to accept her injury, her handicap, but also to develop new interests, new outlets dynamic and challenging enough to replace her total commitment to ballet.

To someone who didn't know Tiffany very well, her stoical behavior in the hospital, in the weeks following the accident, might have passed as bravery. But her father knew better. At first he thought she was in a kind of shock, a possible prelude to a complete breakdown. But as the weeks went by, and the breakdown never came, he saw that she was keeping it bottled up. It was ravaging her insides. She never even cried much, not in his presence, and he began to wish that the anguish and the tears would spill forth, cleansing the deep inner wounds that needed to be purged. Her lack of responsiveness in the face of what had happened was torture for him. It ate at him, tore him apart. He would rather that she cursed him and beat him with her fists—he was the one responsible for wrecking her life.

Although she did not overtly go to pieces, she did not say anything to let him off the hook, either. It was clear that she wanted him to suffer. In one of her rare outbursts at the hospital, she quietly and bitterly said, "You're probably happy it happened. Now it will be almost impossible for me to ever leave you." Stunned, he did not reply to this, and she did not apologize. Her words stuck in his craw, tormenting him.

He realized that in her mind she was not his daughter

any longer, but his prisoner. Her morale was at such a low ebb that she couldn't imagine making a life on her own—a road that was open to her as much as to any other amputee, more so because of his money, which could help her get started in anything that might interest her. Right now she felt that if she couldn't dance, her life was over. Andrew wished fervently that he could make her whole again, to give her a free and open choice as to whether or not to leave him, and then if she decided to stay her decision would be worth something. It would mean that she loved him. The ordeal of her terrible accident had wrought a change in him, it had taught him something; but like much knowledge, it had come too late, after the price had already been paid.

There was no second chance. Or was there?

Perhaps the notion of making Tiffany whole again was not entirely outside the realm of possibility. In his anguish and grief, Andrew clutched at the idea; it wormed its way into his brain. There were dozens of successful kidney transplants. Heart transplants. Why couldn't human limbs be transplanted, too?

Over a business lunch with Bert Snyder from the bakery, Andrew found out that Snyder's wife had a valve in her heart replaced by a valve taken from the heart of a pig. "That was over two years ago," Snyder said. "Without the operation, she wouldn't have lasted six months. Now she'll probably outlive *me*." He chuckled wryly. "Don't know whether the doctors deserve a medal or a kick in the ass."

"If they can do that, why can't they do other things?" Andrew mused out loud.

While they followed up lunch with a couple of dry martinis, Snyder confessed that as a young man he had wanted to go to medical school, but his father had pushed him into the bakery business. "I've always been fascinated with surgical procedures and possibilities. Read up on it a lot, too. Tricks they're doing nowadays are marvelous . . . fascinating . . . like what they did for my wife and your daughter. But the future is even more promising. They're learning all about genes and chromosomes and so on—the so-called building blocks of life. Research that may unlock the secret of aging, and of death itself. Think of it, Andrew! One of these days, people won't have to die. Their bodies won't wear out. And if anything gets damaged, it'll simply be replaced—either from an organ bank, or from an animal, or from an inventory of synthetic man-made parts that work as well or better than what nature originally provided."

Snyder sipped his martini, letting his gaze follow the smooth, sexually alluring stride of a pretty cocktail waitress crossing the crowded dining room on her way to the bar. Turning back to Andrew, he said, "Looking at that makes you *want* to live forever, doesn't it? But old codgers like you and me aren't going to be around to see the great discoveries that are on the horizon. We may be the last generation to have to die—unless we pay to have our old, tired corpses frozen in liquid helium. Then, probably, nobody would bother to thaw us out."

Andrew didn't laugh. He found the discussion more intriguing than funny. Eyeing Bert Snyder soberly, he asked, "How far do you think they are from being able to do limb transplants?"

The man from the bakery weighed his answer carefully, a flash of insight telling him that he should not be the one to dash Blake's hopes utterly. The Hot Dog Heaven account might hang in the balance. "I really don't know," he said, being tactful and evasive. "I'm only a knowledgeable layman and I can't pretend to know everything, especially concerning any very recent developments. Why don't you ask your doctor? I do know this—he's one of the best in the business."

That afternoon at Belvedere General Hospital, Andrew got up the nerve to broach the subject to Dr. Frederick Taylor. At first the doctor appeared startled. And his answer, when it came, was not encouraging. In fact, it was calculated to destroy hope, what he regarded as false hope, altogether—so it wouldn't distract from Tiffany's rehabilitation. His words were firm and irrevocable: "You're distraught, Mr. Blake, and so you're clutching at straws. It's not the best way, or the sanest way, to cope with this tragedy. I'm afraid the notion of a limb transplant is quite farfetched at the present time, even though some experiments with animals have been done along those lines. We haven't been able to overcome the problem of tissue rejection, the same phenomenon which causes the failure of most heart transplants."

"I'd contribute money to research," Andrew argued desperately. "I'm talking about lots of money, all I'm worth—if it would help you or anybody else to discover something new, something that might prevent my daughter's life from being ruined."

"I wish I could help you," said Dr. Taylor, shaking his head ruefully. "But I can't perform miracles. I can only work within the limits of my profession. What you're asking is beyond those limits. I've done the best I can for Tiffany, and the results so far *are* a kind of miracle, considering the shape she was in when you brought her here. Try to be thankful for it, Mr. Blake. Please."

But in his tortured frame of mind, Andrew found it impossible to accept Dr. Taylor's advice. Instead, he became obsessed with the idea that his daughter might eventually benefit from some revolutionary new medical discovery. Perhaps his thoughts wouldn't have been warped in this direction, if Tiffany had been making progress in accepting her destiny. But she was doing little to help herself. And seeing her languishing in her hospital room, Andrew became more and more despondent, and more fanatical in his quest for a miracle.

Instead of giving his attention to his business enterprises, he began poring over medical journals and books and magazines, technical and non-technical, hoping to discover just what level of scientific knowledge had been reached and if a breakthrough might possibly be on the horizon. He told himself that his research would pay off handsomely if only he could learn of some institute, or some lonely genius, whose work looked promising. Then he would pour on enough money to get what he wanted. Look at the space program that put Americans on the moon—it proved that money was the catalyst to transform theoretical speculations into accepted facts, dreams into realities. What else was money good for?

Much of what he read stirred glimmers of hope, tantalizing his imagination. He learned that through Kirlian photography, a process discovered in Russia, scientists had succeeded in photographing the "aura" of a missing limb—that is, the shape of the amputated arm or leg appeared in ghostly form on the photographic plate, as if the organism actually retained a "memory" of its missing part. Could this phenomenon, this biological memory bank, have something to do with the ability of certain low forms of life, like starfish, to regenerate portions of their bodies which had been torn off? Could higher forms of life, even mammals, be somehow stimulated to grow back their missing limbs? Apparently some doctors thought so. They were using electricity to stimulate the regrowth of damaged bones, muscles, and nerves. Plastic surgeons in Britain were using muscle grafts to aid patients suffering from facial paralysis, the grafted tissue activating cells from which entirely new muscle fiber developed. This sort of thing was a long way from regrowth of an entire human limb. Nevertheless, in a laboratory experiment that perhaps heralded things to come, a possum was able to regenerate part of its missing foot and three toes.

Blake had no idea that medical science had come so far. Much of what he read was startling, even bizarre. For instance, at Cleveland Metropolitan General Hospital, one of the world's leading neurosurgeons had performed actual head transplants on monkeys; the heads lived for several days on their new bodies, although they were incapable of movement because of the severed spinal cords. But brain-wave measurements had proved that thinking was still taking place. All the heads and bodies eventually died because of tissue rejection, the same phenomenon which, according to Dr. Taylor, was an insurmountable barrier to a limb transplant for Tiffany.

In a magazine of popular science, Blake read an article predicting that one day the problem of tissue rejection would be solved, that it would be possible to use aborted fetuses as "cultures" for growing fingers, hands, arms, and legs to be supplied to persons who suffered the loss of their own limbs by accident or disease. The article went on to discuss the moral issues that would have to be debated before this procedure could be put into widespread use.

Blake made some investigation into the area of prosthetic devices and artificial organs, but what he found was disappointing. Although technology had accomplished wonders, so far all the man-made legs, arms, heart valves, pacemakers, kidney machines, heart and lung machines were woefully inefficient and clumsy compared to the functioning of the human body. Science-fiction fantasies like bionic men and women had no relationship to what might become scientific reality in the near future. It was futile to hope that within Tiffany's lifetime there would ever be available to her a prosthetic device that could function in any reasonable similarity to the sophistication of a human limb.

The only real hope was a transplant. Theoretically, a donor limb could be supplied to Tiffany—the muscles, bones, ligaments, blood vessels, and nerves joined to her own by surgical methods identical to those employed to save her amputated leg. For a transplant operation to succeed, though, the problem of tissue rejection would have to be overcome. A suitable donor would have to be found. To Andrew Blake, this did not seem out of the question. People who were terminally ill often donated hearts, eyes, kidneys, and other organs to be used by the living. Why not a new left leg for Tiffany? He could encourage a donor with a huge cash payment to her survivors, provided a transplant operation were truly possible.

After mulling it over and building up the courage, he got Dr. Taylor alone in the privacy of his office and tentatively presented his speculations. The doctor got the point immediately. He had hoped that his last talk with Andrew had brought him around to facing reality. He said as much, to which Andrew responded defensively, "I assure you, I *am* facing reality. I've done some very careful research. I'm trying to find a way to help my daughter. You'd do as much if she were your own."

Dr. Taylor tried to be patient, reminding himself that the poor man had gone through quite a shock and deserved sympathy. He told Andrew, "I wish it could be otherwise. But a transplant will not work because no way has yet been found to combat the human body's own defense mechanisms. Tissue rejection results when an organism produces antibodies to fight off invasion by a foreign substance. An organism recognizes as foreign, and will reject, any living matter not precisely of its own biological composition."

"But yet heart and kidney transplants *have* worked," Blake argued stubbornly. "I think you're afraid to try to help my daughter."

"Be reasonable, Mr. Blake. I've helped her the only way that's possible. Another surgeon might not even have tried the reimplantation procedure. The methods we presently have for combatting tissue rejection fail dismally in a majority of cases. The successful ones you've read about usually take place when tissue rejection is not a problem, as in the case of identical twins."

"There are chemicals, like the cortisones, which inhibit tissue rejection."

Taylor took a deep breath. "Yes, I see your problem, Mr. Blake. You've got a layman's smattering of knowledge about these matters, and you're driving yourself crazy with wild hopes and speculations. You want your daughter to be able to dance again? She'd never be able to while her body was being ravaged by the side-effects the cortisones produce—everything from tumors, cysts, and ulcers to softening and weakening of all the bones and muscles."

Normally a kindly, soft-spoken man, the doctor had not meant to come on that strong. But Blake needed to be shocked onto the right track. He wouldn't be able to help Tiffany as long as he continued to chase pipe-dreams.

His face red with anger, Andrew said, "Maybe you're afraid to experiment, Taylor. Maybe you could find some way to help my daughter if you had more imagination and guts."

After Blake stomped out of his office, Dr. Taylor sat

for a while, thinking the situation over. The truth was, his pride was wounded, despite the fact that he had trained himself not to expect gratitude. Over the years, the times he had been thanked for a successful operation could be counted on the fingers of one hand. But when he did something wrong, real or imagined, he got the brunt of it. Like any doctor nowadays, he lived with the realization that anything he did or didn't do could result in a lawsuit. His own inner satisfaction over the quality of his work, a life saved or made more bearable, was the reward with which he usually had to content himself, while taking comfort in the thought that most patients were probably appreciative, even if they didn't express it.

He feared that the situation with Andrew and Tiffany Blake was developing dangerously. He didn't like the direction it was taking. It gave him a funny feeling that he couldn't quite put his finger on. The patient's father, more than the patient, seemed to be in need of psychiatric counseling. Yet, Dr. Taylor dreaded mentioning any such thing to Andrew Blake, who, to put it mildly, would never be receptive. Tiffany's operation *had* been a success, and there was every chance that she would recover emotionally, as well as physically, once the initial trauma wore off. Given more time, she should be able to come out of it. Her father was the main obstacle. His attitude was counter-productive. He, more than his daughter, was refusing to accept and adapt to new realities.

Tiffany was intelligent, atrractive, and there were things she could do other than ballet. She would have to pull herself together and reorient herself. She was young and her life was ahead of her. Like other victims of similar misfortune, she would have to learn not to feel sorry for herself. She would reach a point, psychologically, where the will to survive would assert itself. She would put tragedy behind her. At least Dr. Taylor hoped so. He wanted Tiffany to be happy—otherwise, his own efforts, though they may be technically marvelous, would be next to worthless from a human standpoint—the only standpoint that truly mattered.

Dr. Louis Augenstein subscribed to a clipping service so he would not miss any items pertaining to Tiffany Blake. Although he thought it sublimely ridiculous and ironic that she would end her life as a cripple, deprived of his own superior knowledge, he was still deeply interested in the healing and mending process because the basic surgical aspects of her operation were so similar to what he could have done for her with his secret knowledge. Over the past few weeks, he had built up a fat file.

Due to Andrew Blake's position in the community and the attention Tiffany had received while she was still able to dance, her story was broadcast on local radio and television and headlined in the newspapers. There was also considerable national coverage, because the public at large mistakenly believed that Dr. Taylor and his cohorts had pulled off an extraordinary achievement. *Time, Newsweek,* and the wire services all ran feature articles and follow-ups. Most of the reporters, in their ignorance, treated Dr. Frederick Taylor as a hero—a real-life superman in surgical mask, gown, and gloves.

All this made Louis feel sick. If the world only knew: Taylor was just another runner-up, and *he*, Louis, was the real star. But they were not ready for him to come forward and reveal himself.

Louis was feeling secure and self-satisfied lately. For almost a month, he had not heard anything from

Lieutenant Manderson. The murderer of Helen Ann Marx had not been caught. The ad-agency fellow had not confessed. And there didn't seem to be any new evidence. Louis knew Manderson would have pounded on his door by now if he had found a doctor who could testify that the dead girl had been pregnant. Manderson's earlier threat must have been a bluff. The detective had nothing to go on, no justification for a court order enabling him to exhume the body.

So Louis went about his daily routine, working at the morgue and hating it, but outwardly portraying the diligent, scrupulous pathologist. If he bided his time, the Helen Ann Marx case would blow over. There were plenty of unsolved murders on the books, and this would be just one more of them.

Shocked as she was over Tiffany's accident, and the horror of being practically an eyewitness, Adrienne Mallory knew she couldn't afford to dwell on it. She had to put it out of her mind and concentrate on her own future. On the day that it happened, back at Paul's apartment she and Paul had somehow ended up making love, vigorously and passionately. There was no reason to feel guilty about this. Paul had pointed out that it was an affirmation of life, just as during wartime people were drawn to each other sexually and emotionally in the midst of death and destruction.

Afterward, Adrienne had almost fallen asleep when she heard Paul murmur, "Well, I guess the ballet movie will be scrapped now." He was thinking out loud and his comment was rhetorical; he didn't expect an answer, probably hadn't even expected to be heard. Nestling snugly against him, Adrienne didn't open her eyes or alter the soft rhythm of her breathing. Drifting deeper into slumber, her lips formed a slight smile as she realized it hadn't taken him long to make the transition from concern for Tiffany to contemplation of how the accident might affect him.

Paul's self-interest did not bother Adrienne. Squeamish, ineffectual persons might consider it ruthless, distasteful, but to her and Paul it was merely practical. They were both alike in that way. They had a level-headed determination to succeed. The strongest and best people had it; it was an extension and refinement of the survival instinct. Feeling sorry for others was all well and good, but you couldn't dwell on it, couldn't let it get the best of you, especially when no amount of anguish and gnashing of teeth could change what had happened to them.

Life must go on. Survivors must be strong enough to maintain their fortitude in the face of tragedy and despair.

Now, Adrienne realized, either she or Julia would be prima ballerina of the Artov Ballet Company.

Some weeks after the accident, Bryan and Julia were having coffee with Nicolai when he said of Tiffany, "What amazed me about her was that she had such a strong need to dance. I saw this in her from the first, before I knew that her father had money. He doted so much upon her, almost anything could have been hers for the asking. But she wanted the dancing. It made her feel . . . alive and fulfilled. We all need something to give us that feeling."

"She was difficult to work with," Bryan said. "I wasn't getting much out of her, yet I didn't think it was because she didn't like me. I came to respect her while we were making the movie. As you say, she could've taken the easy way out. But she wanted to excel at something, maybe to prove she really deserved everything she could have had for nothing."

Julia spoke up, chastening: "My God, we're speaking of her in the past tense, as if we've already written her off."

They fell silent, thinking about it. Bryan took Julia's hand, telling her, "You're right. Maybe she'll channel her energies in another direction."

"What about the movie?" Nicolai asked. "Will Blake pay you?"

"I guess he'll pay for what we've done so far," Bryan responded. "At least our out-of-pocket costs. Maybe I can still put something together to help you, using the footage that doesn't involve Tiffany."

"It would be deeply appreciated," said Nicolai, smiling. "We vain and foolish artists must go on through all adversity, though a blow like this makes us fear that our so-called noble aspirations are frail and trivial."

"Not as frail and trivial as the Roth Auto commercial I'm filming tomorrow," said Bryan. "Mr. Roth is having a 'Get Ready for Easter Sale,' and he's going to be on camera himself, in a rabbit suit, hawking used cars."

"Oh, gosh, I hope you and Paul can keep from cracking up," said Julia, laughing.

10 ❧❧❧

ANDREW BLAKE ENTERED TIFFANY'S HOSPITAL ROOM AND
tensed up immediately because Elvira Monroe was
there. Two weeks ago, as the result of an argument that
was his own fault, he had fired his housekeeper, who
had been with him for twenty-three years. He wanted
to ask her to come back but was too proud. For his own
good, she had tried to tell him he was drinking too
much, and he had lost his temper. He hadn't had the
nerve to tell Tiffany what had happened. He hadn't
hired anyone else in Elvira's place, and the house was
getting to be a total mess. It was lonelier than ever with
both his housekeeper and his daughter gone. And his
drinking, if anything, had gotten worse. He knew it,
but he didn't want anyone saying it to his face.

Lately he was getting into arguments with everybody—not only with his housekeeper and his secretary down at the office, but with people like Snyder and Hoffberg from the bakery, who didn't have the gumption to fight back, and certain clients and customers who did. Some recent episodes had been bad for business. His foul temper was losing him money. He often repeated to himself, "To hell with everybody!" But deep inside he regretted his actions and feared that he was going to pieces. Still, he continued to drink.

Before leaving for the hospital, he had had a few belts of gin, and he didn't want Elvira to smell it on his breath. She smiled sheepishly and said hello as he came in. He mumbled a greeting in return, and wondered if Tiffany had been told about the firing. He suspected not. Mrs. Monroe was not a vindictive person. And she wouldn't want to hurt Tiffany if it could be helped. So she would probably avoid mentioning the incident, or put it in the kindest light possible in case it came up.

Trying to cover his uneasiness, Andrew bent and kissed his daughter on the forehead, hoping she wouldn't get a whiff of the gin on his breath. She accepted his kiss unresponsively. He sat down in an uncomfortable straight-backed chair and scanned the table of contents of a *Reader's Digest* he had bought in the hospital gift shop after noticing that it contained an article on regeneration of human fingers. He found the correct page and started reading while Tiffany and Elvira chatted. They had a rapport which made Andrew jealous, and at the same time it rubbed in what a mistake it had been to lose his temper to the point of asking the housekeeper to leave. Tiffany would never forgive him once she found out he was to blame.

The *Digest* article told of an English physician specializing in emergency medicine who had discovered that when children accidentally severed any of their fingertips, the best treatment was none at all. If cleaned and covered with a clean bandage, the finger, including the nail, would grow back within twelve weeks, the new fingertip appearing as if nothing had happened to it. But there were three requirements for regrowth: the patient must be under twelve years old; the cut must be above the crease of the first joint; and surgeons must keep hands off the injury. Any operation performed on a finger or thumb destroyed its ability to grow back.

Well, so what? The article contained nothing that would help Tiffany in any way. More and more, it seemed to Andrew as though any scientific advance that could be of benefit would come years in the future, too late. She'd be too old to dance. He snapped the magazine shut, leaned forward, and placed it on her night table, telling her, "I brought this for you to read."

"I asked you for *Newsweek*, not *Reader's Digest*," she replied petulantly.

"I'm sorry," he said meekly. "I'll go back to the gift shop and get it."

"No, don't bother."

There it was again. That attitude in her voice which said he wasn't really part of her life anymore; she didn't want anything from him if she could help it.

"It's okay, I don't mind," he said. He got to his feet, fidgety and needing a drink.

Elvira glanced at Tiffany, then Andrew, disturbed at their lack of closeness. "I guess I'll be going, too," she apologized. "I have to get supper on the table for my husband."

"I'll walk you to the elevator," Andrew offered, his eyes meeting hers, trying to tell her he had something to say in private.

Elvira put on her coat and hugged Tiffany and kissed her good-bye. Both women were crying. "I'll miss you," Tiffany said through her tears. "Have a good time and write to me from Florida."

So she *had* said that she was leaving, Andrew realized with a jolt, wondering what kind of light she had put it in.

"I will, honey," said Elvira, dabbing at her eyes with a tiny balled-up handkerchief.

Andrew led her past the elevators, to the smoking lounge at the end of the hall. Luckily no one else was in there. He didn't want eavesdroppers. "I'd like you to come back and take care of us," he said earnestly, as he and Elvira came into the lounge.

Self-consciously, she looked down at her shoes, then back up at him.

Before she could speak, he told her, "I'm sorry; it was my fault we argued. I guess the pressure got to me."

"Mr. Blake, I know you didn't mean any harm. But I'm getting up in years and it's high time I retired, anyhow. When you told me you didn't need me anymore, it made up my husband's mind about something I'd been trying to talk him into. We had gone around and around about it for a long time, and now he's gone ahead and taken his pension. The two of us are going to Florida to live close by our youngest daughter."

"Well, I hope you'll be very happy," Andrew said, his voice dry and husky. "Does Tiffany know why you're leaving? That is . . ."'

"I didn't tell her that we quarreled, Mr. Blake. I figured I was as much to blame as you were, after I thought about it. I should have minded my own business."

No, you had a right, he thought; *you weren't just hired help; you were part of the family*. But he had never told her he felt that way, and he didn't own up to it now. He couldn't make the words come out. So instead he said, "Please write to me when you get settled in your new home. You have pay coming to you. And I'd like to send a little something extra to show my gratitude."

"Sure, I'll stay in touch. I'll be thinking about you. But you needn't send me anything I don't have coming to me, Mr. Blake. Just my wages and letting me know that you two are getting along is all the payment I need."

He hugged her, the first time he had done so in all those twenty-three years. Tears ran down her face, and she blotted at them with her little handkerchief. He escorted her to the elevator. There was a long uncomfortable wait before a car came. Andrew felt sorry to see her go, sorrier than he ever knew he would feel. But he was relieved that Tiffany wouldn't blame him for it, because she hadn't been told the details. Elvira Monroe was one more person he had driven away. He was alienating all his friends and business associates; he realized it, but he couldn't stop himself. He was losing control, as if he had a subconscious urge toward self-destruction. After what he had done to Tiffany, nothing seemed to matter very much anymore. He had a blind, futile drive to try to help her, but in his heart he realized the situation was hopeless.

He knew that he was an object of pity—not fear, not respect, but simple pity. It was why people stood for his moods, his outbursts of temper, as much as they could before finally giving up on him. Because he had given up on himself.

He waited for another elevator and went down to the gift shop and bought a copy of *Newsweek*. The racks full of magazines reminded him that issues of *Dance Magazine* were piling up at home. He hadn't brought any into the hospital, and Tiffany hadn't asked for them. What was the point? She was never going to

dance again. Reading or talking about dancing would
only hurt her.

When he got back up to his daughter's room,
Adrienne Mallory and Markian Teslovic were there.
Andrew didn't enjoy seeing them—they would only
remind Tiffany of things that were best forgotten.
"Where's Paul?" he asked Adrienne, after saying hello
rather coolly.

"Oh, we broke up," she replied matter-of-factly.
"I'm going with Markian now."

Andrew raised an eyebrow. "How nice for you," he
remarked pointedly, wanting Adrienne to know that *he*
knew what her game was. She could talk herself into
being in love with whomever could do the most for her
at any given moment. Paul could no longer help her
career, now that the ballet movie wasn't going to be
made. But Markian, the principal male dancer for
Nicolai Artov, might help her worm her way into the
position of prima ballerina.

Andrew sat down and leafed through the *Newsweek*
while the young people carried on a conversation.
Markian was a quiet young man, dark, wiry and not
very handsome; he threw in a comment or a shy smile
here and there, while most of the babble was between
Adrienne and Tiffany. Andrew kept an ear cocked,
hoping nothing would be brought up that would make
his daughter feel terrible. At first it seemed that
Adrienne wasn't going to be as catty as usual, since
Tiffany was no longer competition for her. But then—
intentionally, it seemed to Andrew—she let a remark
slip about an upcoming Heinz Hall performance. She
immediately caught her breath and acted as though she
hadn't meant to say it—but the damage was done.
Inwardly seething, Andrew pretended to be reading
but watched his daughter out of the corner of his eye,

expecting her to break into tears. But she handled the moment quite nicely, managing a brave little smile and an almost offhanded declaration that she had been thinking lately of trying for a career as a set and costume designer.

"Oh, of course!" Adrienne shrieked. "I'll bet Nicolai would let you work with him!"

"How's he doing?" asked Tiffany.

"Hasn't he been here to see you?"

"Oh, yes, of course. Several times. But he's so busy . . . I don't expect him to come here every week. Hospitals are depressing."

"Well, since you don't seem to mind talking about it," said Adrienne, pausing, as if waiting to be contradicted, "I might as well tell you that we're getting ready to do *Giselle*. Naturally, Markian will dance Albrecht. And the part of Giselle is up for grabs between me and Julia."

"Oh, I'm so happy for you," said Tiffany.

"I was afraid that Nicolai might bring in an established star from New York," Adrienne disarmingly confessed. "But apparently he's not going to. He believes there's plenty of good talent within his own company, and he wants to use *Giselle* as a vehicle to prove it."

"Either you or Julia could dance the role wonderfully," pronounced Tiffany.

In a pig's eye! Andrew thought, laying the *Newsweek* on Tiffany's bedside table and slipping the *Reader's Digest* into his jacket pocket. He decided that he didn't want Tiffany coming across the article on limb regeneration—it might upset her. As far as he was concerned, his daughter was twice as talented as Adrienne or Julia. Yet, they would be getting all the glory from now on. Neither would have stood a chance of dancing *Giselle* if they had to go up against Tiffany. If Tiffany was well. If the world was always fair and just and beautiful.

It broke Andrew's heart to see his daughter forcing herself to put on a brave front for the likes of the Mallory girl—a fickle, malicious opportunist. Rather than taking any sort of hope in Tiffany's tentative voicing of career aspirations in set and costume design, Andrew was convinced that such sentiments were spurious. It was the first time Tiffany had said anything of the kind. Obviously, she had to affect an air of resiliency in front of Adrienne, who could well afford to prattle on and on, puffing up Tiffany's false hopes as if they could really amount to something, and then going home gloating over her own good fortune, her unimpaired physical condition. *She* was the one who deserved to lose a leg, Andrew thought, with a sudden burst of malice, and then felt ashamed for thinking of it. But if it had to happen to anyone, he rationalized, it should have been Adrienne. Unlike Tiffany, she didn't have a talent worth mourning. And neither did Julia. Before Tiffany became a cripple, the Mallory and Valenti girls had fancied themselves as her rivals, but they couldn't hold a candle to her. Again and again, when the chips were down Tiffany had beaten them both out for top honors. And neither of them ever got an offer from the New York National. They hadn't even been scouted. Silvera hadn't so much as noticed them.

At home in his desk drawer, Andrew kept a letter addressed to Tiffany that had come from Arthur Silvera a week or so after the accident. In a dignified but poignant way, the letter expressed condolences and regrets, lamenting the "enormous potentiality that is now lost." Andrew had cried while reading it, but it had also made him proud. Someday, perhaps, he could show it to Tiffany. No matter what else happened in her life, she would always have proof that she had been recognized and wanted by one of the world's greatest ballet masters.

After her father and her two visitors from the ballet company had gone, Tiffany lay in bed thinking, trying to ignore the intense pain that had been with her constantly, ever since her accident, no matter how much pain-killer the nurses gave her. Under the covers there were the mocking outlines of her two legs, one considerably shorter than the other, one foot sticking up where it wasn't supposed to be. When sufficient healing had taken place and the splints were removed, she would have to wear a thick built-up shoe and steel brace to begin learning to walk again. She almost didn't want to try. She almost wanted to die. But the will to survive—that stubborn irrational force woven into the cells of every human being—was tenacious enough to keep the "almosts" in those two thoughts.

She would go on, she realized, despite the awful repugnance of being a cripple. The only thing more repugnant was death—for the time being—although it might become, at some point, her best option. If it got to the time where she couldn't stand it, she told herself, she could always commit suicide. But, at heart, she knew she would never do it. She would not take her own life; she didn't have it in her. The same drive that had caused her to excel as a dancer was part and parcel of the will to go on living—a blessing and a curse in her present circumstances, preventing her from taking the easy way out. She would go on existing, even if part of her didn't want to.

Although she was still feeling profoundly sorry for herself, the truth was that she had already begun groping toward emotional recovery. In this, her father had not given her enough credit. He was imposing his own guilt concerning the accident upon her. And he thought that his daughter couldn't possibly rally against the fate that had befallen her, because he was unable to do so himself.

Tiffany didn't really blame her father for what had happened—he had tried to coerce her, but in this he was only being himself. She was the one who had tried to beat the train. He had not pushed her under the wheels, though it was true that if he had not provoked the argument, the accident never would have happened. Tempting as it would have been to blame him for everything, Tiffany was taking it out on him, not because of the accident itself, but because the accident had crystallized the realization that had been forming in her mind ever since the opportunity with the New York National had presented itself. Her father's love was domineering; it had made her his prisoner for all of her young life—and she would remain under his thumb forever if she could not rise above being a cripple.

As a matter of fact, Tiffany had been serious in mentioning to Adrienne the possibility of a career in set and costume design. She had surprised herself by coming out with it. And once voiced, the notion had taken on some life, some impetus. Now, alone in her hospital bed, she considered it, and admitted to herself that the idea had been lurking in the back of her mind, unexpressed. Even if she was a cripple, she knew that she would still remain involved in the ballet world. She only feared becoming a freak, a sort of Hunchback of Notre Dame, a clumsy clubfooted person hobbling about backstage, amongst all the beauty, grace, and mobility personified by those who could still dance.

That night in the hospital, sleeping in a delirious stupor of pain and pain-killing drugs, she dreamed that the *Nutcracker* prince came to her bedside and kissed her, healing her with his love, making her whole again and giving her the ability to dance wonderfully. But in the midst of a beautiful *pas de deux* in the Kingdom of the Sweets, the prince was suddenly transformed into the Rat King and Tiffany awoke struggling to crawl away, dragging a swollen, ponderous left leg that had become a huge ball and chain made out of her own flesh.

While Tiffany's dream was turning into a nightmare, her father was at home in his study, sipping straight gin on the rocks and reading a magazine article entitled "The Future of Microsurgery." The part of the article which interested Andrew the most dealt with scientists' latest attempts to control the human body's immune system and its tendency to reject transplanted tissue. Subjecting the lymph glands to radiation was a new technique which had been partially successful, stopping the lymph glands from producing thymocites—the white blood cells responsible for rejection. Unfortunately, however, this method also killed off other types of white blood cells needed to combat infection, so that patients upon whom it had been tried had a very low resistance to disease and a high mortality rate. What was needed was some sort of drug which would attack the thymocites selectively without interfering with the other types of white blood cells.

If the rejection phenomenon could be controlled, the article speculated, living organs could be obtained from donors on a much wider scale than was now possible. "In point of fact," stated one noted microsurgeon, "the donor problem is already improving, as more and more doctors advocate the concept of 'brain death,' whereby a patient can be declared legally dead even if his heart is still beating. In the not-too-distant future, we may view as commonplace not only the transplantation of hearts, kidneys, and corneas, but also external cadaver parts like arms and legs. New methods of preserving donor organs have made it possible to keep the organs alive and in good condition for as long as three or four hours, and to 'harvest' them from as far away as five hundred miles. A spare-parts bank for human components may be as normal to society in a decade or so as an auto-supply store for our cars is to us today.''

Reading over and over some of the paragraphs, as if he could milk additional scientific progress out of them, Andrew Blake nursed another glass of ice-cold gin before getting ready for bed. Without the gin, he would have had a tough time falling asleep. Ever since the accident, he suffered from insomnia. Much as he wanted to sleep at night, he was afraid to dream. When he went to bed drunk, he didn't dream, or at least he didn't remember doing so. And whenever he went to bed sober, he spent half the night tossing and turning, and then nine times out of ten he had a recurring nightmare of Tiffany lying under the wheels of a train, and he was trying to get to her as she beckoned and screamed, the stump of her leg pumping blood, the severed limb in his arms; he knew he could put it back on if he could reach her in time, but it was like trying to run through quicksand. He kept getting more and more tired and couldn't get any closer to his daughter.

As a lover, Markian was a disappointment. Adrienne reflected upon this as she drove home from his apartment, after an erotic interlude that was less than satisfying. She had managed to reach an orgasm of sorts, but it was only a shade above point zero on the Richter scale. The likeliest explanation, in her mind, was that Markian was a latent homosexual. If so, it was a pity for him to be at war with his own nature, and a shame for him to be adding weight to the belief already held by the general public that most male dancers were gay.

The problem with Adrienne was that she was so preoccupied with rating the men she went to bed with that it prevented her from having any insight into her own shortcomings. She was acquisitive, demanding, and selfish. She did everything imaginable to pleasure a man in bed—out of pride in her own ability, coupled with desire to receive a wide range of favors in return for her own uninhibited efforts. Just as she was technically a very fine dancer, she was a proficient bed partner, a sexual athlete. This was fine and dandy with a man like Paul Smith, who, like Adrienne, found the best sex in the long and varied and energetic interlockings of strong and healthy bodies—the epitome of physical sex with the emotions left out of it, or relegated to a secondary status. On that level, Adrienne was an excellent performer, a delight to go to bed with, the kind of woman who would "screw a man's brains out."

As lovely as this had first seemed to Markian, in the final analysis it wasn't enough to fulfill him. The truth was, he wasn't gay at all. He was—that overworked word—sensitive. He wanted to be, if not in love, at least loving, tender, subtle. His body wasn't merely an attractive machine, operating for and of its own volition; it was the vehicle of his emotions. And when those emotions weren't truly reciprocated, he sensed something wrong—and it turned him off. He was beginning to realize the basic shallowness of his new girl friend.

In the meantime, however, Adrienne would get what she wanted out of it—all the help that Markian could give her in perfecting her dancing and winning the coveted position of prima ballerina.

Adrienne's attitude about her rival, Julia Valenti, was that Julia was cute and charming in a naïve way, but certainly no match for a real woman. Bryan Sinclair could be taken away from Julia anytime Adrienne put her mind to it. The fact that Bryan was engaged to Julia didn't thwart the possible challenge, but merely made it more interesting. At the moment, however, since the ballet movie was on the shelf, there wasn't much to be gained by seducing Bryan, except Bryan himself, who, admittedly, was quite talented and reasonably handsome—tall and well built with dark, wavy hair, and regular, if unremarkable, facial features. His most appealing quality was that he seemed professional, and he radiated self-confidence. But he lacked the overt streak of hardness and meanness that Adrienne equated with sexiness and ballsy determination. He and Julia deserved each other. They were both "nice people" who would probably always be also-rans, edged out of wealth, recognition, and power by those who were quicker to seize advantage.

Paul actually had been more nearly perfect for Adrienne than any of her other lovers, and in many ways she missed him. He was probably not as innately talented as Bryan Sinclair, but he had a stronger, more desperate greed and ambition—a will to succeed even if he had to hurt someone to get what he wanted. It was impossible, Adrienne thought, to get to the top without stepping on other people, so if you didn't have the guts to do this, you were probably a loser. She considered herself a realist—a practical, not an immoral, person. She and Paul were cut out of the same mold. One way or another, she expected, they would probably get back together once she dumped Markian. For the time being, Markian was serving his purpose as a dance, if not a bed, partner.

Adrienne parked her red Fiat in the spacious driveway rather than pulling it into the four-car garage, and mounted the wide stone steps and curving flagstone walkway to the front porch. The lawn and the exterior of the large brick house were brightly illuminated by the porch light and the gas lamp on a post at the top of the steps leading up from the driveway. When she turned her key in the lock and pushed the door open, she heard the strains of a McDonald's jingle and, taking her coat off, went downstairs to the plush family room where her father was watching the late-evening news on television.

"Hi, honey. Join me for some hot chocolate?" Jim Mallory said, smiling sleepily at his daughter.

"Sure, Daddy. Stay right there. I'll make it."

"Thanks. But be sure to wake me when it's ready. Don't just let me be, if I happen to doze off."

"Okay."

She pivoted and climbed the shag-carpeted stairs to the kitchen. Jim Mallory followed her with his eyes, appreciating the time spent in her proximity. Like most fathers and daughters, they didn't do enough things together. He wanted to share her life, perhaps more than she wanted him to. He wondered about her romances, her successes, her failures, if any. But he knew better than to probe too deeply or aggressively. He loved his daughter. But there were areas—sexual matters, for instance—in which she would never confide in him and never seek his advice, and this, he figured, was as it should be. She probably wasn't a virgin anymore, but he didn't want to hear about it.

He sometimes had the uncomfortable idea that perhaps he had taught Adrienne to be too aggressive, too unfeminine. Perhaps he had infused in her too much of his pragmatic approach to life, too many of his hard-nosed business principles. But he wanted his children to be survivors, not weaklings, so they could protect everything he had built up for them. He had taught his two sons and his daughter not to take any crap from anyone and to go after whatever they wanted in life—hook, line, and sinker. This wasn't being dirty; it was just being tough. You had to be tougher than the other guy, or he'd screw you.

He didn't doze off and was wide awake watching the weather report when Adrienne brought in the hot chocolate. At moments like this, he felt he was making a reasonable attempt at being close to his daughter, without being pushy. He usually asked her how her ballet dancing was coming along, and that was how he opened the conversation this time, after she sat down at the coffee table, having changed into her robe and pajamas. He didn't really hear her answer, since he was thinking how much like a little girl she looked, all ready for bed. And one ear was cocked to catch the weather report, to see if rain might further delay his company's work on a shopping center under construction and behind schedule. However, he rationalized, the important thing was just for him to show he was interested; she probably didn't want him to pry too much, anyway.

Adrienne knew that her father hadn't listened to her. He seldom listened; on a conscious level she thought that his habit of not listening had stopped bothering her. Part of her drive to succeed came from a desire to please him, though. She wanted to prove she was worthwhile, so that maybe he'd pay attention to her and love her. She didn't realize that she already had his love but he didn't know how to show it.

11 ❮❮❮

BRYAN SINCLAIR AND PAUL SMITH WERE FINISHING
taking the camera and lighting gear off the elevator and
storing it in the equipment room adjacent to their small
shooting studio. Before they were done, someone on
the floor below pounded for the elevator, which they
had on "hold" during the unloading procedure, so
Bryan pressed the button, letting the elevator go. In
the meantime Paul made a pot of fresh coffee on the
Mr. Coffee machine. He and Bryan sat down to discuss
the day's work. They had spent the day filming the
Roth Auto commercial, featuring Mr. Roth himself in a
rabbit suit. Car dealers were notorious for "acting" in
their own TV commercials, since they rarely had big
advertising budgets and could save talent fees and
residuals by not hiring union actors. Bryan and Paul

had made several of these types of spots starring the dealers and/or members of their families in situations that ranged from the inane to the bizarre—but this was the first time anyone had dressed up like a rabbit.

"The gig today kept reminding me of a scene from a Fellini film," Paul said, stirring his coffee. "What a way for grown men to earn a living."

"We're getting two thousand bucks for the job," Bryan pointed out. "So long as Roth pays us, I don't care if he wants to impersonate Humpty Dumpty."

"*I* do!" Paul snorted. "I have *some* sense of dignity!" He drummed his fingers rapidly on the receptionist's desk, behind which he was sitting.

"I have a sense of my *own* dignity," said Bryan. "Roth is the one who made a fool of himself. We merely recorded the deed for posterity."

"That's one way of looking at it," Paul admitted. "Still, I don't like cavorting around all day with someone in rabbit drag."

Bryan laughed. Although he would have preferred filming something else, he didn't find the Roth Auto commercial all that trying. The toughest part was keeping a straight face behind the camera. Mr. Roth made a silly-looking rabbit, with portly jowls, a red bulbous nose, and the heavy kind of beard that looks like five-o'clock shadow even when it's freshly shaven. Also, springy plastic rabbit whiskers stuck on with spirit gum, that kept slipping. And long fuzzy ears stiffened with wire that spronged off the wall above the doorway when Mr. Roth tried to enter the showroom without ducking. All these details would give Julia some good laughs when Bryan picked her up after ballet practice tonight and took her to dinner. On impulse, he asked if Paul would like to come along and bring Adrienne.

"I'm not dating her anymore," Paul replied in a flat tone of finality.

After an uncomfortable moment, Bryan said, "I'll unload the exposed footage and send it to the lab tomorrow. It should be back in three or four days. Meantime, do you want to get the sound takes transferred and mark the slates? Then I'll do the synching."

"Sure, I suppose so," said Paul without enthusiasm. "Who's going to do the final edit?"

"Do you want to?"

"Not particularly."

"I'll do it, then. It's only half a day's work. Nothing fancy. It can only be cut one way."

Paul shrugged disinterestedly and drummed his fingers on the desktop. "Anything else to discuss?" he asked, obviously hoping there wasn't.

"Yes, there is one thing," said Bryan. "I've finished a first draft of a murder mystery involving a ballet company. I'd like you to read it and give me your opinion."

Paul looked up with a startled expression, his eyes flashing. "You mean a screenplay? Or a novel?" If Bryan had a property in any stage of development, this would reduce the chances of one of Paul's own properties getting produced.

"A screenplay," said Bryan. "I'm pretty happy with it. I think it may be salable."

Paul leaned forward, and spoke accusingly. "You told *me* that if I wrote something along those lines you'd try to get it financed. Now you've gone and done it yourself. What's the big idea, Bryan?"

"Have you written anything?"

"No, but—"

"Do you have an outline? Or any ideas on paper?"

"Not yet."

This was as Bryan had thought. Paul wasn't taking the ball and running with it, yet he could still become upset when someone else did. "Look, Paul, the concept of basing a feature movie on Nicolai's company was something I thought of myself. When I visited my folks after Christmas I had some time to relax and I started writing. I got it about halfway written in a few days of heavy effort, and finished it little by little since then. It's not my fault you didn't do anything with the idea. But I'd like you to work on the film if I can raise the money. Actually, some of what we've already shot could be used as environmental stuff."

"If Blake gives his permission," Paul squelched. "He owns the footage." Eyeing Bryan, Paul leaned back and twisted the ends of his mustache.

"He hasn't paid for it yet," said Bryan.

"He'd better," Paul countered. "We need the money. And once he pays for it, he owns it. My guess is, he'll never release any of the material relating in any way to Tiffany."

"You may be right," Bryan agreed reluctantly. "But in any case, we have the screenplay now. And it's a viable property."

"We'll see," Paul intoned skeptically.

"Try to be openminded," Bryan warned. "If you don't want in on the project, I'm going to try to do it anyway. I've already spoken to Nicolai, and I have his full cooperation."

What Nicolai's full cooperation meant was not lost on Paul. Beautiful dancers, elegant sets and costumes. A vast rehearsal studio for behind-the-scenes ambiance. And colorful, exciting performances in places like Heinz Hall. All these ingredients would be perfect for giving a low-budget movie a classy, high-budget look. If the script was any good, Bryan might really be onto something.

The thought made Paul jealous.

He realized that the publicity surrounding the Artov Company because of the things that had happened to

Tiffany Blake was a definite asset. It would make a movie involving the ballet company a more attractive investment than most movie projects would be to stodgy money sources. And it would help sell tickets at the box office once the movie was released. Bryan Sinclair would never come right out and admit that these crass considerations had had any part in his thinking. But to Paul it was perfectly obvious. And the net result, whether Bryan had arrived at it consciously or unconsciously, filled Paul with envy.

"You're welcome to join us for dinner, if you like," Bryan offered, as he and Paul rode down on the elevator.

"No thanks, I'd be a third wheel," Paul said. "I'll grab some Kentucky fried chicken on my way home. Then I'll stay in tonight and read your script. I'll let you know what I think of it." He made an effort to sound congenial, masking some of the animosity he had shown earlier. He had the script tucked under his arm. If it stood a chance of being produced, he didn't want to exclude himself from any involvement, even if he'd rather work on a project totally his own. He would try for an important credit—producer, for instance, or at least co-producer—provided Bryan didn't intend to hog all the worthwhile credits for himself.

In his apartment that night, Paul started to read the script, entitled *Beautiful Victims,* hoping that it wouldn't be any good. It dealt with a series of brutal murders that appeared to be the work of a sex maniac. The only thing tying the murders together at first was the fact that all of the victims were young ballerinas belonging to the same ballet company and vying for the position of prima ballerina. Thus, a possible motive could be conjectured—the maniac, in his demented way, might be out to advance the career of one particular girl. But, instead, in a surprising plot twist halfway through the screenplay, it was revealed that there was indeed method to the killer's madness, only he wanted to *kill* one particular girl, not help her. And a large inheritance was at stake. Grudgingly, Paul had to admit that Bryan was building a great deal of suspense with a simple premise that could make an effective, highly exploitable low-budget movie. Paul wished he had written it himself. It wouldn't win any awards, might not impress the critics, but it had all the proper elements going for it at its level of production: affordability; optimum use of readily available sets, locations, and costumes; strong plot with plenty of sex and violence—all against a backdrop of beauty, grace, and excitement.

When Paul was two-thirds of the way through the script, reading in bed, the telephone rang. Groping for the receiver, he dropped it and had to retrieve it from the floor.

"Hello."

"Mr. Paul Smith?"

"Speaking."

"Oh—Mr. Smith. This is Dr. Bernard Augenstein. Remember me?"

"Yes, of course." At first, Paul didn't actually remember. The clipped nasal quality of the phone voice seemed familiar. Then it came to him. Two years ago he had produced a documentary film for the Right to Live Foundation, presenting moral and ethical arguments against abortion. In one of the state prisons, he had interviewed Dr. Bernard Augenstein, a convicted abortionist. Bernard had a brother, Louis, serving time, also. Louis had declined to be interviewed. But Bernard had given cooperation of sorts, appearing on camera in order to state some opinions which were largely self-serving. Paul didn't blame him for that, although much of what the doctor had to say had been useless from the point of view of the Right to Live people and had not found its way into their finished documentary. Although his statements could possibly have been used as an example of the callousness of certain advocates of legalized abortion, the Right to Live Foundation had vetoed this notion on the grounds that Bernard Augenstein's opinions contained a certain amount of warped logic that could be misinterpreted by an unsuspecting public.

"I came across your name," the doctor was saying, "in an article about the Tiffany Blake case. Apparently, you were on hand at the scene of her accident. Such a terrible thing!" He paused, as if feeling Paul out for a reaction.

"Yes, very unfortunate," Paul said. "I know Tiffany very well. I also know her father."

"Ah, is that so?" The doctor sounded pleased. He went on, almost bubbly. "I told my brother, Louis, I told him there couldn't in all likelihood be two Paul Smiths in the film business in town here, despite the commonness of the name 'Smith.' I told him it had to be you who was mentioned in the article. And so I decided to try to get in touch."

"Why?" It was a sharp, pointed question, directing the doctor to come to the point. Paul was wondering what he was going to be hit up for. Could be something as simple as a character reference. A plug for an ex-con. But if the guy once had a practice, he must have more than a few former patients who could vouch for him.

After a long pause, the doctor answered in carefully composed sentences. "My brother and I would like you to provide us with some intelligent evaluations—your opinions, really—as to how Andrew Blake and his daughter might respond to a certain delicate proposition we are prepared to lay before them. If you could

104

be instrumental in helping us consummate the deal we have in mind, it would be beneficial to both the Augensteins and the Blakes, and you could earn yourself a great deal of money."

Paul couldn't help being intrigued, even though his gut reaction was that he was probably talking to a crackpot. He got an inner chuckle out of the fact that this Bernard Augenstein obviously didn't realize that Andrew Blake and Paul Smith hit it off like Eskimos and suntan lotion. "I'm interested," he heard himself saying. "Fill me in a little."

"I'd rather not go into the actual details over the telephone. Could we meet someplace tomorrow evening?"

"Okay. Where?"

"By the fountain in Point Park. At six o'clock, if that's convenient."

"That will be fine."

"See you tomorrow, then. And thank you. You won't regret meeting with us."

After hanging up the phone, Paul wondered: Were the two doctors, ex-convicts, going to propose something illegal? It certainly seemed so. They didn't want to take a chance on the phone being tapped, and they wanted to meet out in the open, where there was little chance of being tailed or bugged. In any case, it wouldn't hurt to hear them out. Nothing illegal in that.

At Louis Augenstein's apartment on the other side of the city, Louis faced his brother, who had just got done talking on the telephone. "Do you think the young man will show up tomorrow?"

"I believe so."

"What if he doesn't?"

Bernard didn't know what he was expected to say.

"You'll have to approach him again," Louis told him,

"or else think of some other way to get to Blake. I want to feel him out first, before sticking our necks out. The narrow escape I had with Lieutenant Manderson and the Helen Ann Marx case has convinced me that we must take immediate steps to re-establish ourselves, for self-protection. We're too vulnerable. We need to acquire a great deal of money. Why should we go on living so miserably when we possess knowledge that the world will pay fortunes for . . . even if it has to be done on the black market?"

"You're right, Louis." Bernard nodded. "You've always been right. Even when you got us in trouble."

Bryan and Julia had agreed, once she brought the subject up, that they had stayed away from the hospital too long, and so they went to visit Tiffany. They were surprised to find her reasonably cheerful. On previous visits she had seemed morose, downright despondent. But now she even talked with a degree of enthusiasm about getting involved in set or costume design.

Andrew Blake, however, wasn't too effervescent about anything, including his daughter's tenuous plans for rehabilitating herself. In fact, he seemed rather determinedly gloomy and not entirely sober. Nevertheless, Bryan found an opening and made mention of the bills he and Paul had incurred on the unfinished ballet movie. "I have more important things on my mind than an unfinished movie," Blake rebutted with heavy sarcasm. "Just be patient and we'll get those expenses taken care of for you. What's the matter, Bryan? Don't you think I'm good for the money? Or would it pain you to get stung in the pocketbook just because Tiffany had a nasty little accident?"

Stunned, Bryan didn't quite know what to say or how to defend himself, when he didn't feel that he had said anything that needed defending. After all, he and Julia were going to be married soon, and they had to have money to live on. But Blake seemed to feel that the whole world should suffer, just because of what had happened to Tiffany.

Leaving the hospital after cutting their visit short and saying some awkward good-byes, Julia remarked to Bryan, "I always used to secretly feel close to Tiffany because she lost her mother and I lost both my parents. We had that much in common. Not that we were really friends or anything. I don't think she really made friends with anyone."

"The way her father shoots his mouth off, it's a wonder anyone comes to see her," said Bryan. "I'll bet he always scared her friends away, even before her accident."

"Bryan, don't forget he's been under a terrible strain," Julia cautioned.

"He'd better get himself together. The way he is right now, he's no good to anybody. He didn't even give Tiffany any encouragement when she was coming out of her shell, trying to make a few plans for the future."

"He probably thinks her plans are pathetic. He can't get over how everything has come crashing down for her."

"You're probably right. But he'd better find a way to shake that attitude. Tiffany is okay. She's obviously going to bounce back, if he'll let her."

After the hospital visit, Bryan took Julia home to her grandparents' house, and Theresa served them coffee and sweets while Dominic sat in his old favorite armchair, chewing on an unlighted cigar. They talked of the upcoming wedding and the plans of Bryan's family of coming into town for the occasion. After a brief honeymoon at the seashore, Julia would move into Bryan's apartment. The two of them had been putting in a lot of time lately, getting it ready. But both of them were so busy, and so little had been done. Bryan was working on an air force training film. When the actual filming got under way, he, and Paul Smith, and some crew people would have to go to an air-science research center in Vermont for few days to photograph the operation of an aircraft missile launching system.

Recognizing the light in Julia's eyes when she looked at Bryan, Dominic knew the two young people really loved each other, and he believed and hoped that they would be happy together. Because he approved of Bryan and liked him, Dominic stifled his anxiety over the amount of time Julia spent alone with her fiancé in his apartment, "getting it ready." These days it was nothing unusual for young couples to have sex before they were married, and perhaps it was no longer a sin, or soon wouldn't be in the eyes of the Church, just as eating meat on Friday used to be a sin and now wasn't. If Julia was no longer a virgin, it was because she loved Bryan and he loved her. Thankfully, the wedding would be over soon, before there could be a scandal. Best not to talk about these things with them. Best only to say a prayer for them every day. Julia was raised well, and therefore with God's help she would do what was good and proper, or else, even if she didn't, maybe she wouldn't be punished too badly for it.

12 ❦❦❦

LATER THAT WEEK, ON A FRIDAY, ANDREW BLAKE arrived at his office building at ten o'clock in the morning, in a foul mood. Mrs. Simms, his secretary, handed him a package in a plain brown wrapper. "The reason it doesn't have any postage on it," she explained, "is because it didn't come in the regular mail. A man came by an hour ago and insisted on leaving it for you. I don't know if he's some kind of nut, or what. I asked him if he had an appointment and he said he didn't want to meet you personally—not quite yet, anyway. His exact words were: 'Please see that Mr. Blake gets this. He's terribly concerned about his daughter's well-being, and so I'm absolutely certain that what's in here will interest him. I'm equally certain he'll be getting in touch with me once he looks it over.'"

Having thus delivered her spiel, Mrs. Simms—a chubby, freckled, middle-aged lady who prided herself on her efficiency and attention to detail—stood in the hallway with her arms extended, waiting for Andrew to take his package. Glowering at her as if she was party to some kind of lunacy, he snatched it from her and marched down the corridor in a huff which diminished as he began to get curious about what might be under the plain brown wrapper.

Unwrapping the package in the privacy of his office, he extracted from a cardboard box and held in his hands a book entitled *The Horror of Treblinka*, by Dr. Louis Augenstein. Clipped to the dust jacket was a handwritten note which said:

Dear Mr. Blake:

I can help your daughter as no one else can. *Believe me!* Read this book and then get in touch with me through Paul Smith, who will vouch for my credentials. *Do* read the book first. It will facilitate our establishment of a rapport.

Sincerely,
Dr. Louis Augenstein

Intrigued, Blake turned the book over and over, wondering what it could mean to him. His curiosity got the best of him and, putting business aside, he began reading *The Horror of Treblinka*. It turned out to be a long personal account by Dr. Augenstein, a Polish Jew who was forced to perform experiments on human beings, living and dead, while he was an inmate of the concentration camp Treblinka during the final two years of World War II. The doctor under whom

Augenstein worked, while enjoying temporary freedom from the gas chamber, was Dr. Adolf Barkema, a colleague of Josef Mengele, the notorious Nazi "Angel of Death." The experiments at Treblinka were related to those carried on by Mengele at Auschwitz. Mengele was fanatically absorbed in investigating the phenomena of twin births and congenital deformitories in human beings. The mission assigned to him by the Führer himself was to discover ways in which the reproduction of the "master race" might be increased by multiple births. At the same time he documented and collected organs and skeletons of Jews who were physically deformed (hunchbacks, clubfoots, diabetics, etc.) so that these specimens could be exhibited in Nazi museums—the proof to future generations of Aryans that the Jewish "race" had been "degenerate" and needed to be destroyed.

As a corollary to Mengele's diabolical work, Major Adolf Barkema at Treblinka performed experiments on pregnant women and their fetuses—in an attempt to discover why fetuses are immune to most diseases while carried in their mothers' wombs. The fetuses aborted by Dr. Augenstein, working under Barkema, were dissected in a special laboratory at Treblinka and carefully examined as scientifically as possible. Sometimes whole fetuses or organs of special interest were preserved in formaldehyde and sent to the Institute of Biological, Racial, and Evolutionary Research in Berlin. Such specimens were always stamped "War Material—Urgent" and given top priority in transit, even in the last years of the war, when the transportation of troops and guns might have been thought of primary importance.

Reading *The Horror of Treblinka* that morning in his office, Andrew Blake was both fascinated and repelled. It was a grisly narrative by an eyewitness to, and participant in, a nightmare of human cruelty and perversion. What could any of it possibly have to do with helping Tiffany? Louis Augenstein, a man forced to perform experiments on pregnant women and unborn babies, saved his own life by taking life from others in the name of science, and he rationalized his behavior by telling himself that even if he had refused to operate, to dissect, someone else would have. Wasn't aborting those doomed to the gas chamber actually an act of mercy? This Dr. Augenstein constantly told himself to preserve his sanity, such as it was, while he went about his miserable undertakings. And then, at the end of the war, a survivor of horrors almost beyond description, he vowed never again to practice his calling, never again to take up the tools of the surgeon. The last paragraph of his book was a summation of his belief that his right to do good, to serve mankind, had been aborted in the Nazi concentration camp.

But, before he laid the book aside, an idea began to dawn on Andrew Blake—a germ of an idea that excited and repulsed him as it titillated his imagination: What if Augenstein had discovered something crucial through his macabre experiments? With thousands of unwilling human beings to work on, instead of rats or guinea pigs, could the doctor have made a breakthrough denied to conventional medical researchers? Stirred by such speculations, Blake locked the book in a drawer of his desk and went down the corridor to talk with his secretary. "Did the man who left that package give his name?" he asker her offhandedly.

Mrs. Simms was surprised by her employer's kindly tone, something unusual of late. "Yes, Mr. Blake," she said, anxious to please. "He told me his name was Louis Augenstein."

"An elderly fellow?"

"No . . . young . . . but bald on top. He had gray
sideburns and baggy eyes and he was tired and pale
looking. I'd say he could be about thirty-five years
old."

"Thank you, Patricia," Blake said.

Back in his office, he puzzled over the information
Mrs. Simms had given him. According to the book he
just read, Louis Augenstein was in his early thirties in
March, 1944, when he was imprisoned at Treblinka.
That would put him in his seventies now. So it couldn't
have been Dr. Augenstein who had dropped off the
package.

Warily, Andrew mulled over the possibility that this
whole business with the book was a come-on, a setup of
some sort—the first stage of a con game. Somebody
was going to try to bilk him out of some money by
offering a miracle cure for his daughter.

Andrew unlocked his desk drawer and for the third
or fourth time re-read the note that had come with the
book. It mentioned Paul Smith. What in the world
could Bryan Sinclair's film partner have to do with this?

After some time spent deep in thought, Andrew
Blake looked up Paul Smith's home phone number,
dialed the number, and listened impatiently through
eight rings, but nobody answered. He decided not to
call Paul at the studio. He didn't want anyone to
overhear this conversation.

In his room at the Stanford Chapman Home for the
Aged, an old man sat in a wheelchair, his eyes
unblinking and staring, apparently focused on something very distant. A plump young nurse with peroxide-
blonde hair peeked in on him, catching sight of his
flaccid genitals, which were in plain view through the
yawning slit in the front of his green hospital pajamas,
and came into the room briefly to tug at the flap of his

robe, remedying the involuntary "indecent exposure." She expected no response from the patient and received none. He had recently suffered his third, and worst, in a series of strokes which had rendered him speechless, immobile, and totally helpless. Still, who could say, the nurse wondered as she left the room, what if anything went on in his mind?

He was Dr. Louis Augenstein, the author of the book called *The Horror of Treblinka*. He had two sons, Bernard and Louis, who seldom came to see him. He sat silently like a living mummy all day long, day in and day out, tortured by his thoughts, or rather by their endless repetition, a phenomenon over which he had no control, any more than he could control his urinary tract or his bowel movements. Wasted away to a near-skeleton, as if he was fated all along to end his life resembling an inmate of a concentration camp, he was weak and ready to die, anxious to die, and yet could not manage even to sleep—a paradox which did not entertain him.

Morning and night he relived Treblinka, which as a younger man he had tried to exorcise by writing down his experiences. But the writing did not make the images go away. If only he could think of something else! After all, the horrors that he witnessed, experienced, and performed had no real meaning for him anymore; for years he had worked at erasing them, blotting them from his conscious mind every time they intruded. Why must he keep seeing and hearing those same events again and again, as if his disembodied mind had become the unthinkingly dull but morbidly efficient receptor of powerful signals straight from Hell . . . ?

It was important to discover at which stage in the development of the fetuses the immunities were lost. For this reason they had to be aborted at scheduled, precisely timed intervals during the pregnancy cycle. Some were delivered alive, some of the premature and all of the full-term ones, and then immediately killed by Dr. Barkema by means of an injection of chloroform into the heart. The mothers were always taken straight from the delivery room to the gas chamber and the crematorium. Sometimes, rather than being gassed, they were dispatched by Obersturmführer Bachman, who claimed not to be bothered emotionally or psychologically by the task of shooting soft-nosed bullets into the backs of the necks of thousands of victims. Bachman and his SS cohorts called this "tumbling a few Jews." One day he "tumbled" eighty in a row, then came to the infirmary and complained of not feeling well, although he could think of nothing he had eaten which should have upset him. Dr. Augenstein, in charge of treating the SS in addition to his duties in the experimental laboratory, told Bachman that the headaches, indigestion, and high blood pressure he had evidenced lately were probably due to extreme nervous tension because of his "duties" in the execution chamber. At this, the Obersturmführer got very angry, saying, "Your diagnosis is obviously incorrect. An Aryan doctor would know better. It doesn't bother me to kill one man or a thousand for the Reich. If I'm upset, it's merely because I drink too much."

Many such ironic, macabre, nightmarish, impossible-but-true visions kept repeating themselves in Louis Augenstein's disembodied mind. He saw himself using human flesh to cultivate bacteria in an incubator . . . dissecting limbs and organs of born and unborn children . . . boiling tiny human corpses in an iron caldron till the flesh separated from the bones, then bleaching the bones and assembling the skeletons and mounting them for the edification of the Nazi "scientists" at the Institute of Biological, Racial, and Evolutionary Research. Did these research specialists, whose letters expressed over and over again their gladness to be receiving so many wonderful specimens, know that the subjects they were studying had not died natural deaths? Did they assume that these were the "normal" casualties of wartime? Did they care?

Were they all warped and demented in some strange way, like Dr. Adolf Barkema, the harsh and scrupulous servant of the Institute, who demanded that laboratory charts, studies, documents, and reports must always be kept religiously up to date, and in elaborate, painstaking detail? His fanatical devotion to his work was living proof of the hell on earth that could be produced when science was divorced from morality.

Never, before the advent of the Nazi concentration camps, had there been such a vast reservoir of human beings, alive and dead, at the disposal of scientists avid to learn all they could about medicine, biology, physiology, and the pathology of disease. The thousands of "political prisoners"—mostly poor Jews and Gypsies— were ideal guinea pigs for the frontiers of knowledge being probed by the diabolical and ruthless machinery of the Third Reich. Never had the organizational might and the resources of a modern technological state been turned wholeheartedly to such a purpose.

Day after day the "freight" arrived—the thousands of human beings unloaded from jam-packed boxcars to be "selected" by Major Barkema for either immediate death, or slave labor and eventual death, or experimentation and then death not by gas, bullet, or starvation, but by an injection of chloroform into the heart.

Louis Augenstein always believed that he would die in the camp, too; it was only a matter of time and he, too, would share the fate of his subjects. That was why he did not feel guilty much of the time. He even had a few chances to alleviate suffering, by passing out tranquilizing pills to those who were doomed. Once he was even able to actually save the lives of a mother and her young daughter, by whispering to them to volunteer for a "selection" he had heard Dr. Barkema say was being sent not to the gas chamber, but to Italy to work in a munitions plant. Perhaps they actually survived the war, although many of the slaves laboring in Nazi war factories were starved and beaten to death as a matter of routine.

It was Louis' good luck, or his curse, to be still alive when Treblinka was liberated in 1945. He came to America and never practiced as a doctor again. He could not bring himself to do so. But he fathered two sons, whom he raised to be doctors so that they might carry on with clean conscience the good, healing work he himself ought to have done.

But the curse of the concentration camp was not finished, and it reached out to claim the sons, even after thirty long years of trying to make sure the horror and misery stayed buried and did not repeat itself.

If only—Dr. Louis Augenstein thought, in a spasm of lucidity rare for him since his third stroke—*if only I had destroyed the files of Dr. Barkema instead of keeping them as a constant reminder of my unworthiness and guilt.*

13 ❧❧❧

THE BEST DANCERS, THE ONES WHO HAVE REAL PROMISE, are totally unaware of each other at the practice barre. As jealously as they might be competing on one or more levels—for roles, for praise, or even in some instances for the same lovers—those who cannot put extraneous issues out of their minds for the long, sweaty, grinding duration of their ballet classes are probably doomed not to ever join the ranks of the truly accomplished professionals. It takes that much concentration to reach the pinnacle.

Though Adrienne and Julia were separated by only three other people in the company, who were also concentrating and straining, they paid absolutely no attention to each other. They gave no clue that they were rivals; each was in a world of her own, not seeming to care what the other was doing, not taking the time to be distracted by a hasty check on the other's correctness of timing, movement, or position. For each girl, the only things that mattered in the vast rehearsal studio, with its gym-like odor and brightly pervasive fluorescent lighting, were the judgments rendered by the walls full of mirrors and the uncompromising instructor, Nicolai Artov, who moved from person to person, occasionally praising, but more often correcting mistakes of execution, to the accompaniment of tape-recorded classical music.

Julia knew, and tried always to remember, that ballet class ideally should be a process of discovery and discipline. The rigorous exercises, performed scrupulously, would result in a slow accumulation of strength and technique. One had to practice and practice, till correctness became second nature. Mistakes had to be weeded out—because a mistake repeated often enough could become second nature, too, defeating one's ultimate purpose. The dancer's job was to aspire and perspire, training to the limits of endurance, cultivating proper classical form and weeding out bad habits. When technique became so ingrained that it was almost automatic, only then could one reach for the moments of magical inspiration that sometimes happened onstage during a performance. The seemingly effortless grace, ephemeral beauty, and spontaneity that thrilled audiences was the culmination of years and years of relentless physical and mental preparation.

When practice was over, Julia knew that she had had a good class. They weren't all good—some days she might feel she could do a hundred pirouettes, and other days two were a struggle. But this class had been one of

119

the good ones. Her mistakes had been few; she felt right about herself. She was tired, but she knew the exertion was good for her; after she took her shower, she'd feel tingly, alive, exuberant.

In one corner, Adrienne and Markian were holding hands, talking animatedly to one another. An outsider observing them might have thought their appearances too messy to inspire any sort of romantic interplay. Their faces were sweaty, their tights drenched, their hair plastered in ringlets on their foreheads. Julia said hello as she passed them, and puzzled once more over how easily Adrienne had ditched Paul and taken up with Markian. She would not have been able to switch her own loyalties so readily. When she gave herself to any cause or any person, it was completely, risking everything. Her decisions were made carefully, but once made, they were irrevocable. She had committed herself so deeply to Bryan that she could not imagine being without him. On a rational level, she realized that life might bring changes in them both, that they were not necessarily immune, any more than others were, to the forces which caused separation. But on an emotional, or instinctive, level, she automatically discounted the possibility. If they changed, they would change together, for the better. She would see to that, and so would Bryan.

"I had a good class today," she told him proudly when she stepped off the elevator at the film studio. She was meeting him there so they could go around the corner to a little bar for a late-night sandwich and beverage.

"Glad to hear it," he replied, smiling. He gave her a welcoming kiss. "Want some coffee? Help yourself. I have a few more shots to splice together, and I'll be right with you."

"Keeping a straight face?" she teased, laughing,

because she knew he was editing the TV spot starring Roth, the auto dealer, as a huge rabbit.

"I would've been done two hours ago if I hadn't wasted so much time cracking up," he told her, exaggerating.

She sat and leafed through a magazine in the reception area while he went back into the editing room to finish working. She could hear voice and music tracks playing back and forth for twenty minutes or so on the Moviola, and when the last shots were slugged in, Bryan called her to come and watch the edit. Sure enough, a big pseudo-rabbit came on screen and talked enthusiastically, if unprofessionally, about the great used-car bargains that could be had from the Easter Bunny at Roth Auto. For some strange reason, though, it wasn't as funny as Julia had expected. It was more bizarre and demeaning than it was hilarious. In fact, she found herself not laughing.

"I feel sorry for Mr. Roth," she announced when the spot was done playing.

"Why?" asked Bryan, as he pressed the button to rewind. He turned off the volume so the tracks wouldn't screech over the sound heads.

"Well . . . obviously he doesn't know he's making a fool of himself. And nobody bothers to tell him."

"We tried selling him on other concepts, but he just doesn't listen. He's bound and determined to be a victim of his own bad taste. That doesn't make him any different from a lot of our other clients. I've grown used to it, I guess. I don't know if that's good or bad."

"Did Paul like your script?" Julia asked, changing the subject because she knew that the newly written screenplay was Bryan's first chance of getting into feature-film production.

"I don't know if he's read it yet," Bryan answered as they walked out to the elevator.

"You mean he hasn't said anything?" Julia was incredulous. "He's had it for over a week!"

"Well, he's been busy. And I think breaking up with Adrienne upset him more than he's willing to admit."

"I didn't think he cared that deeply about her."

"He wasn't in love with her. My guess would be that he's never been in love with anyone. But he does hate to be dumped."

"What a strange partner you have, Bryan!"

At the bar and grill on the corner, they each ordered a bacon-burger and a draft beer, and Julia told Bryan that one of the dancers in the company seemed pretty sure that Tiffany would be brought home in a few weeks. Apparently a series of skin grafts had been completed, and the regrowth of her sciatic nerve was proceeding well.

"What that doctor did for her was marvelous," Bryan said, "but not quite marvelous enough."

Suddenly Julia turned morose, coming down on herself, saying that even if she got the part of Giselle, or if Adrienne did, they wouldn't have gotten the opportunity were it not for the fact of Tiffany's terrible accident.

"So what's that supposed to mean?" Bryan snapped. "That you don't deserve it?" She didn't answer. He went on. "Nonsense, Julia. You know perfectly well that you can be an excellent Giselle. You're improving rapidly and—who knows?—you may soon be dancing better than Tiffany. If you get the part, you'll have earned it. Nicolai is no fool; he's not out to sacrifice his reputation—he does what is best for his company. Besides, if Tiffany had not been injured, she would probably have gone to New York to join the National, so this opportunity was coming your way, anyway. I'll bet Adrienne isn't wasting any time looking backward. Concentrate on competing with *her,* not on feeling guilty about Tiffany, because what happened to her wasn't your fault."

"I'm working pretty hard," Julia defended. "I told you I had a good practice today."

"Yes, but don't let anything undermine your confidence. Don't be your own worst enemy."

In his office at Blake Enterprises, Inc., Andrew Blake awaited the arrival of Dr. Louis Augenstein. It was late at night, long past regular working hours, and he was alone in the building. He knew what to expect, thanks to his conversations with Paul Smith. He was expecting not the author of the book *The Horror of Treblinka,* but that man's eldest son.

In deciding to meet with Augenstein, Blake had not relied entirely on information gleaned from Paul Smith, although what the filmmaker had to say corroborated what Andrew was able to find out on his own. After reading the *Treblinka* book, he had gotten in touch with a friend, Bill Perry, who was business editor of the largest of the city's two major newspapers. From the paper's morgue, Perry had obligingly dug up quite a file on the Augensteins. There was an interesting connection between the father's work in the concentration camp and the crime that the two sons had been sent to prison for. Under the Nazis, Louis Augenstein had been studying aborted fetuses, trying to discover why they were immune to certain diseases; and his two sons, Louis and Bernard, had been convicted of performing abortions illegally. Could the sons have been trying to further the scientific work their father had started? Could they have discovered something about tissue rejection? The notion had Blake excited, but he almost didn't dare hope. In the back of his mind, though, he knew that he would give these Augensteins almost anything they wanted, if he became convinced that they could help his daughter. On this wild, thin chance, he had agreed to a meeting.

Meanwhile, Louis was standing on the corner down the block from Blake Enterprises, trying to mentally prepare himself for the confrontation. He and his brother, Bernard, had quizzed Paul Smith thoroughly to ascertain whether Andrew Blake was likely to react favorably to a proposition that would cost him a fortune and would simultaneously put him in deep jeopardy because it was not legal and, moreover, in the judgment of most people it was highly immoral—which, of course, was poppycock. The Smith fellow, himself a crass, brazen individual, insisted that Blake was so "hung up in guilt" over what had happened to his daughter that he would probably go to almost any lengths to redeem himself in her eyes. However, if this evaluation of Blake's temperament proved to be wrong, Louis would be divulging his secrets, the results of his experiments, and would get nothing in return but contempt. If the experiments became public knowledge, even if the results were mocked and disbelieved, Lieutenant Manderson might put two and two together and realize that here was a crazy motive for what could have happened to a fetus found inside Helen Ann Marx; this might enable him to get an exhumation order.

When the night bell rang, Andrew went to the front door of the building and let Louis in. They shook hands, eyeing each other appraisingly. Then Andrew ushered Louis down the semi-darkened corridor and into his private office. He sat behind his rich mahogany desk while Louis sat in a leather chair. He did not offer coffee or a drink. He wanted to get down to business.

"Obviously you're a successful man," Louis remarked. "This room is quite elegant, and tastefully decorated."

"I can't take credit for that myself," Andrew stated. "I have no interest in furniture, drapes, and so on. I'd rather turn the job over to an interior decorator."

"Still, you selected a good one."

"Thank you. Actually, my daughter made the selection and most of the final decisions, based on the decorator's recommendations. She's talented in other ways besides dancing. But dancing means the most to her."

"What will she do if she can't dance anymore?"

"There's no *if* about it. Her reimplanted leg is three inches shorter than the other one. You knew that, didn't you?"

"Of course. And I wasn't meaning to be cruel. You see, Mr. Blake, I don't think it's out of the question for Tiffany to perform again—if she accepts my help, and if she works very hard to rehabilitate herself thereafter. It may take a couple of years, but the situation is far from hopeless."

"Explain yourself."

Drawing a deep breath, Louis began to elucidate at length. "From reading his book, you already know what happened to my father. He encouraged my brother, Bernard, and myself from the time we were youngsters until we went to medical school and became doctors. We both graduated with honors and went on to become highly regarded in our specialty, which was orthopedic surgery. But we both had an insatiable drive to experiment, to learn more, to perhaps one day make some kind of dramatic discovery. We became intrigued by what could have been the meaning, the ultimate outcome, of the *in vivo* experiments Father was forced to participate in at Treblinka. Could any good at all, in terms of scientific advancement, be projected out of so much human suffering? One day I discovered that my father had kept many of the most important documents from Dr. Barkema's laboratory, and I prevailed upon him to turn them over to me and Bernard. Some of what we learned was so intriguing that we began to discuss ways that we might carry the Nazi research to its logical conclusion, without harming anyone, without subjecting unwilling human beings to pain and suffering and trauma. Finally, we hit upon an idea. We considered the risks, in light of the legal statutes at that time, and we decided to go through with it. Our abortion clinic was set up, not only because Bernard and I believed in the right of every woman to decide whether or not to have children, but also because the unwanted fetuses could be used to further our studies." Louis paused, allowing what he had just said to sink in. Then he asked: "Do you believe in abortion, Mr. Blake?"

"I'm not against it. But I have certain reservations."

"Do you believe that the fetus has legal rights? A soul? Do you believe that it is a *person*—the same as you and I?"

"Not really. No."

"Bernard and I may have broken a few laws," said Louis, looking to Blake for understanding. "But it sounds to me as if you would agree that we did nothing immoral. Yet we were punished. And the world still doesn't know what we were on the verge of, and what we have since brought to fruition."

Louis stood up, in his fervor. Andrew didn't interrupt him but listened with rising excitement. Leaning over the mahogany desk, his eyes flashing with triumph, Louis shouted, "The answer was in the amniotic fluid!"

"What answer?" Blake responded timorously.

Louis fixed him with a lingering stare, then sat back down in the leather chair. He lowered his voice to a dramatic half-whisper. "The secret of transplant rejection. Bernard and I have discovered it. And the antidote."

"You can't be serious," Andrew said slowly, as if he disbelieved, but something already told him that Dr. Augenstein was telling the truth.

"The answer was in the amniotic fluid," Louis repeated, lingering over each word. Then: "We've developed a serum compounded of extracts of this fluid, plus certain of the cortisones, and hormones manufactured in the mothers' bodies during pregnancy. Our serum neutralizes the antibodies which cause a patient to reject any limb or organ not of his or her very own biochemical makeup. If a donor can be supplied, Mr. Blake, your daughter can be given a brand-new and wholly functional left leg."

Louis sat back but did not relax, knowing he had reached the critical point of his presentation. Now he had exposed himself; he was vulnerable. How would Blake react? Surely he must realize that implicit in the offer that had just been made was the suggestion that the missing limb must somehow be supplied—and there was no way of doing so legally. The operation itself would have to be kept secret. No hospital could sanction such a surgical procedure, involving not only a donated body part, but also a strange new serum that had never been tried, tested, and approved by the ruling bureaucracy—the A.M.A., the F.D.A., and other professional and governmental associations and agencies—all anxious to disbelieve and condemn any results that had not been obtained under their auspices, their paralyzing restraints, their stultifying obstacles.

For a long time, Blake thought everything over, weighing the implications. Then he asked, almost musingly, "Where would we get a donor?"

Louis purposefully replied very evenly, as if they were discussing something quite ordinary. He didn't want to jar Andrew Blake, but to ease him gradually into some new modes of thinking. "A cadaver recently dead, or someone alive and willing, perhaps a person suffering from a terminal disease. Mr. Blake, finding a suitable donor would be up to you. Let me be frank with you at this beginning stage of our association, as regards monetary matters. We'll have to set up our own facility for doing the operation, and that will cost several hundred thousand dollars. In addition to that, Bernard and I must have two hundred thousand apiece for performing a transplant and seeing it through to a successful outcome. And we intend to keep the operating equipment for our own use once you've paid for it."

After a long period of contemplative silence, Blake said, "Tiffany may as well be dead as crippled. In fact, I'm afraid she's degenerated psychologically to the point where she may even be suicidal. She tries to hide her feelings from me, but she can't. I know her far too well. I'd do anything to make her whole again, Doctor. *Anything*. And what happens to me afterward is of no consequence."

"Bernard and I are the only ones who can really help you," Louis replied, solidifying his position.

"Why wouldn't you take this discovery of yours, this fantastic serum, to a medical foundation? Surely they would reward you. You'd become famous. You might even get the Nobel Prize."

Louis scoffed. "The fact is, Mr. Blake, that society has no understanding, no *respect*, for our achievement because of the way the results were attained. They'd condemn us, despite our enormous potential benefit to mankind. Bernard and I only wanted some great good to finally come out of what our father suffered—out of the Nazi torturing and murdering. But we've already been treated as criminals, and locked up in jail for four years with the lowest type of human trash you could think of. Do you know what it's like, Mr. Blake, to be beaten and sodomized in a prison cell by a gang of brutal sex-crazed fellow inmates?"

Louis glowered across the desk at Blake for long seconds, as if expecting an answer, but Andrew averted his eyes. He was embarrassed.

Louis cleared his throat. "No, Mr. Blake. The world has lost its right to profit from risks taken and effort put forth by me and my brother. Nothing can make up for the humiliating, degrading, soul-sapping years of confinement. But our aim now is to acquire enough money to live out our lives in peace and comfort—and to carry on our work, in the hopes that someday it might be appreciated. If society remains as narrow-minded and repressive as it is now, it would be best for us to take our secrets to the grave with us."

In a low, tremulous voice, Blake said, "You indicated that we'd need an operating room and equipment."

"Bernard and I will tell you what to buy. May I suggest setting it up someplace where there is absolutely no chance of being bothered? The basement of your home, perhaps. We'll want to be close to Tiffany at all times."

"What about staff?"

"Bernard's wife, Doris, is a wonderful operating room nurse and anesthesiologist. She'll work with us, as she has all along, through the experiments and everything else. We three possess all the expertise that is necessary. Once we get the equipment into place, the operating microscopes and so on, we'll practice microsurgery on the tiny blood vessels and nerves of laboratory animals, to make sure our skills are at the optimum for Tiffany."

"And Paul Smith? He knows what you're proposing, doesn't he?"

Louis shook his head with a wry grimace of regret. "I'm afraid he pried more out of us than we wanted him to know. At first we thought we could get away with telling him very little. We only wanted to gather some insight as to how you might react, what sort of person you are, before we took the risk of exposing our secret. We offered Paul Smith five thousand dollars. But as soon as he became aware that we intended doing something not exactly legal, he wanted more money."

"Where does it stand now?" Blake asked, aggravated.

"It's not so good," Louis admitted. "Once we got involved with him, we realized that he had enough information to figure out the rest eventually, after the fact—that is, after the operation had been performed. So we think we're going to have to give in to what he's asking."

"How much does he want?"

"Fifty thousand dollars."

Blake whistled. "He doesn't go light, does he?"

Louis said nothing, hoping that the whole deal wasn't ruined. It was true that Paul Smith was a problem. But after all he had been through in prison, Louis didn't blame himself for being too frightened to approach Andrew Blake directly.

"Did you intend paying the fifty thousand out of your own share?" Blake probed. "I mean you and your brother."

Louis nodded affirmatively.

After several more seconds of contemplative silence, Blake said, "We've got to involve him more. Make him part of this thing, so he doesn't blackmail us. He's got to know his own ass will be in a sling if he talks. Then you can pay him the fifty thousand."

"I think he wants to use the money to help finance a movie he has written," Louis interjected.

"Oh, well, he's crazy about movies," said Blake disparagingly. "I think he'd do just about anything to get his name up on a piece of celluloid. Whatever he makes will probably flop, though; in my view, he's not one-tenth as talented as he thinks he is."

Louis asked, "Realistically speaking, Mr. Blake, do you think this Paul Smith will present an obstacle?"

Blake thought about it. And after thinking, he said, "No, I don't really think so. I think we can take care of him."

Louis began to catch a glimmer of what Blake meant, and he shook his head approvingly.

"One way or another," Blake added, "I think we can make sure that Paul Smith doesn't cause any long-lasting problems."

"I never got to see your daughter perform," Louis remarked, changing the subject, smiling slightly. "But I used to admire the ballet. And I can assure you that I'm looking forward to seeing her onstage, where she belongs."

Andrew Blake made eye contact with the doctor. So much about the man seemed weird, incongruous. He had an aura of refinement, of culture, upon which had been superimposed the hard, cynical lessons of the penitentiary. Was he a savior or a madman? Andrew wanted desperately to believe that he was more of the former than the latter, for Tiffany's sake.

14 ⋘

AFTER SEVERAL POSTPONEMENTS THAT PUT IT A MONTH and a half behind the original schedule, the filming in Vermont on the movie about the air force missile-launching system was set up for the first week of May. On the night before Bryan's departure, he and Julia spent an evening together at his apartment, enjoying a dinner of wine, steaks, and salad, and afterward they made love. Then they lay in bed talking of the wedding, which was coming up in June, and the presentation of *Giselle*, which was still scheduled for the last week of May. So far, Nicolai Artov had refrained from announcing any decision concerning who, between Adrienne and Julia, was to dance the title role.

"He's letting it go right down to the wire to get the most out of both of us," Julia complained.

"It's a good strategy," Bryan teased, nuzzling her forehead as she nestled against his bare chest.

"He's a genius and a slave-driver," Julia said without real annoyance, because she liked Nicolai too much to feel really annoyed with him.

Bryan told her, "You've got that part in the bag. Don't be so uptight about it. Adrienne is the one Nicolai's egging on, making her think she has a chance so she'll try harder."

"She *does* have a chance! You should see her dancing. The extra practice with Markian is paying off. I—"

The ringing of the phone interrupted her, and although she was closest to it, she waited for Bryan to reach across her and pick it up.

"Oh, hello, Paul," said Bryan.

Julia lay patiently still and listened while her fiancé and his film partner went through a checklist of production details, airline schedules, and so on, regarding the Vermont filming. She already knew what the job entailed, because Bryan had told her, and it sounded like something out of science fiction. It was to be a sales film for a remote-control device that pilots could wear in their helmets, which enabled them to sight in on and destroy a target by pressing a button and launching a homing missile that would go straight to the target the pilot had been looking at when he hit the button. Neither Bryan nor Julia had had any idea that the air force possessed weapons so sophisticated, or that they were so common that they weren't even classified "Secret," or that they were being offered for sale on a wide scale to foreign countries—which was why the film was being made. It was a good-paying job from a large advertising agency, and Julia was proud of Bryan for landing it.

Just as Bryan thought all the details were cleared up

and was about to say good-bye, Paul asked, "By the way, will you be talking to Julia?"

"Yes, she's here now. Why?"

Paul cleared his throat. "Uh . . . I was talking with old man Blake earlier today. I took a notion to haggle him about payment for the ballet footage. He finally agreed to put a check in the mail."

Bryan was surprised that Paul had taken the initiative to chase down an overdue account. It wasn't like him. He usually confined his efforts to the "creative" side of the business.

"What else did Blake have to say?" Bryan asked.

"That's what I was going to mention. I got the distinct impression from him that Tiffany is feeling pretty damned miserable and would like Adrienne and Julia to drop by and say hello. Her old man wouldn't come right out and say it, mind you, but it was pretty clear that Tiffany could use some cheering up. She's home, you know."

"Yes, I heard."

"Look, Bryan, I'm not the one to ask Adrienne for any favors at the moment. But I do feel sorry for Tiffany. And I was hoping maybe Julia could get together with Adrienne, not letting her know the idea came from me, and maybe they could phone Tiffany and go out and pay a visit. Julia will have a little time on her hands with you out of town. Why don't you ask her if she thinks she and Adrienne can do a good deed together, maybe tomorrow night or the night after?"

"Okay. I'll ask her."

"Good . . . good. Tell her to give the Blakes a call when she has it together with Adrienne. Apparently, Tiffany likes visitors sometimes, but she doesn't like to be taken by surprise. She has to psyche herself up quite a bit first."

"Will do. See you in the morning, Paul. I'm aiming

to get to the airport a half-hour early. Want to join me for breakfast there?"

"Sure. So long, Bryan."

As soon as he hung up the phone, Julia jumped on top of Bryan and kissed him. They made love intensely and languorously, trying to make it tide them over till he came home again.

15 €€€

Two days after Bryan left for Vermont, Julia and Adrienne arranged to drive out to the Blakes' house in Adrienne's car, after ballet practice. They took their showers and put on skirts and blouses but left their hair up in buns rather than taking time to wash and dry it. It was already late and nearly dark out when they met outside the locker room and descended the stairs to the sidewalk. They had to hurry because Tiffany was expecting them. She'd understand, though; Nicolai had held the class overtime, as usual.

Today's session had been devoted to rehearsal of *Giselle*, Adrienne and Julia each having a turn at dancing a *pas de deux* with Markian. Julia felt that she had not done her best, while, in contrast, Adrienne had been in top form. She felt it only right to say so as they crossed the street in front of the studio and got into Adrienne's shiny red Fiat, tossing their gym bags full of sweaty ballet clothes into the rear of the auto.

"Thank you," said Adrienne, glancing at herself in the rearview mirror and checking her lipstick. There was barely enough light to do so.

Down the block from the studio, which was in a rundown section of the city where the rent was cheap and there weren't enough decent stores to make busy sidewalks, a man parked in a tan Chevy hatchback kept his eyes on the red Fiat and its occupants. He had been there for an hour, waiting for the young women to appear. He had been getting bored and restless and had smoked half a pack of cigarettes, despite the fact that he had been trying to cut down. Now he was glad to spring into action. He started his car engine, flipped on his CB system, and spoke into it, establishing contact with his two partners.

Adrienne started the motor and turned on the headlights, then pulled away from the curb into sparse traffic. The tan hatchback pulled out behind her. The man driving knew he didn't have to be too careful tailing; these two pretty young things weren't suspecting anything. The job should be a piece of cake. He would rather have tailed them walking than driving— they both had nice legs and firm, shapely buttocks, which he had appreciated while watching them cross the street; only now their attributes were hidden from view inside the Fiat.

Stepping on the accelerator, Adrienne said, "I thought you did well, also—much better than I, in fact. Oh—I wish I knew which one of us Nicolai is going to pick!"

"Probably you," said Julia.

Lately Adrienne had come to believe this, too, but she was not about to admit it. She wanted to lull her competition into a false sense of security. "Honestly, I think you have it made, Julia! If it weren't for the extra help I'm getting from Markian, you'd be even more of a shoo-in than you are already." This was her way of acknowledging the extra help and downplaying it at the same time, thereby discouraging Julia from thinking of it as an unfair advantage. "How are the wedding plans coming along?" she chatted. "Have you heard from Bryan?" The more Julia got engrossed with talking about Bryan and the wedding, the less concentration she would be able to put into *Giselle.*

"He called me when his plane got into Burlington. That was Monday. I probably won't hear from him again till later in the week, when the job's finished and he's ready to come home." Julia smiled in the darkness. "I hope he remembers to bring me some maple syrup."

The car passed under a streetlamp and Adrienne glimpsed her passenger, briefly illuminated, out of the corner of her eye. She decided, rather smugly, that Julia was very pretty, no denying that, but in a youthful, too innocent way. Adrienne, three years older, tried to project a spicier, more insolent beauty combined with sexiness, so that she could have her way with men, rather than vice versa. It did not occur to her that this quality might be the opposite of what would be required in *Giselle,* a ballet about an innocent peasant girl of the Romantic Period, who, deceived by her lover, Count Albrecht, dies of a broken heart. Neither did it occur to Julia that her own ingenuousness, coupled with fine dancing ability, might be exactly what Nicolai was looking for.

The man in the tan hatchback spoke into his CB. "I've been sticking pretty close all the way. No chance they'll get wise. I'll cue you when they get within a quarter-mile of the crossing." He lit another cigarette.

He shouldn't smoke, but the trouble was that the job was too damned easy to occupy his mind. He wouldn't even get to handle the women. That was the other guys' end. They'd probably have themselves a ball. The only thing that could be said for this gig, or at least his own part of it, was that it was easy work and good pay.

"Doesn't it bother you that Bryan might meet a strange girl when he's so far away?" Adrienne teased. She laughed to indicate she was kidding, but she hoped she was furnishing Julia with something else to worry about—in case she hadn't thought of it on her own.

"Bryan loves me," Julia replied simply.

The simple confident truth of it made Adrienne jealous. Love doesn't last, she scoffed inwardly, but that didn't make the feelings of envy go away. Although she lived in a pragmatic way, espousing for herself a philosophy that she imagined was practical and realistic, and considering people like Julia weaklings, that didn't stop her from feeling a void sometimes that could have been filled by some of the values the weaklings had.

To counteract her pangs of emptiness, she fell to dwelling upon how much she wanted the part of Giselle. She envisioned her father and mother and oldest brother coming to Heinz Hall with all their friends to see her. They would be proud of her at last, for something that she did on her own, without their support. She would be the center of attention, surrounded by the lavish scenery, dramatic lighting effects, beautiful music, and an entourage of lesser dancers from the corps de ballet, to which Julia Valenti would be relegated.

Julia was recalling a silly dream she had had last night and wondering if she should tell Adrienne. It was funny, but also embarrassing. She decided not to tell it, but remembering it almost made her laugh aloud. In the dream, the entire ballet company was rehearsing in the nude, which was outrageous in and of itself, but the hilarious thing was that she was trying to hide in a corner, not because she was ashamed of being naked, but because her legs weren't shaved. She recognized the imagery as a subconscious representation of her fear of not doing well, of making some horrendous blunder in front of everyone. Bryan was right. She had to try not to be her own worst enemy. Her self-doubts could be self-defeating.

The red Fiat was climbing a hill over the crest of which, at the bottom of the downgrade, lay the railroad crossing where Tiffany Blake had had her accident. Pleased with himself, the man in the tan hatchback spoke into his CB, delivering his final message. Then he turned around and headed for home, anxious to pop open a can of beer and watch the last couple of innings of the baseball game on television. Once or twice, without success, he had tried to catch the score during the intervals between CB transmissions, and now, on his way home, he listened to the game on the radio. That afternoon he had phoned his bookie, placing a bet, which, if it panned out, would double the money he had just made by tailing the two good-lookers from the ballet studio.

Coming down the long, curving hill, the headlights of the Fiat made strange dancing shadows out of the leafy foliage on both sides of the road. Then suddenly they spotlighted a white van that was stopped at the bottom, in front of the railroad tracks. Its side and back doors were wide open, but there didn't seem to be anybody inside the vehicle; yet, the taillights were on and the engine was running. Adrienne saw the exhaust smoke as she began applying her brakes and came to a screeching, angry stop. She and Julia glanced at each other, panicky, wondering what to do, now that their way was blocked on a stretch of dark, lonely road by an apparently abandoned vehicle.

In a fit of exasperation, Adrienne laid on the horn, although there appeared to be no one around to honk at. Julia laughed and started to wind her window up.

Just then the car doors were yanked open by two men wearing nylon masks and brandishing guns. Julia saw the one on her side first, and her laugh turned into a scream.

"Shut up, bitch!" the man barked, jabbing his weapon cruelly into Julia's ribs, his voice muffled by his amorphous face-covering.

Adrienne was staring wide-eyed at the second man, doing her utmost to remain calm. "What do you want? Money?" she managed to say, but her voice cracked and the man emitted a harsh laugh.

Julia bit her lip, trying not to cry out in pain. It was a hopeless situation. Neither Julia nor Adrienne could fight back. The two attackers easily overpowered them, menacing them with big, ugly pistols, forcing their heads back against the car seat and pressing chloroform-soaked rags over their mouths and nostrils, so that they became weak and nauseous, and in the midst of nausea they both quickly lost consciousness.

Dominic Valenti was sitting at the kitchen table over a half-finished cup of coffee when the phone rang, startling him. He glanced at the wall clock, as if the time might be a clue as to who was calling. Nine o'clock. Maybe it could be Bryan, hoping Julia was home. Dominic picked up the receiver and said hello softly enough not to wake up his wife, who was upstairs sleeping.

Nobody answered.

A little louder, Dominic said, "Hello? Who is-a there? Bryan?"

"Mr. Valenti?"

"Yes. Who is-a this?"

The voice on the other end of the line, hoarse and whispery, definitely did not belong to Dominic's future son-in-law. Without any exact reason for it, the old man became afraid.

"Never mind who this is," the voice said. "Just shut up and listen. Your granddaughter won't be coming home tonight. But if you do exactly what you're told, she won't be hurt. We are holding her prisoner, along with Adrienne Mallory. Two cute ballerinas. I'm sure you'd like to have them back. We'll release them both for two hundred thousand dollars. Jim Mallory will pay. He's the moneybags, not you. We'll be in touch later to give him further instructions. He knows this. Don't go to the police. We told him, and we're telling you. If anybody in either family brings in the police, both girls will die."

Click. The line went dead.

Dominic stood there stunned for a few seconds, staring at the receiver as if it were a snake that might bite him. Then he hung it up. Immediately it rang again, making him jump. The first time he said hello, nothing came out and he had to clear his throat and say it again.

"You didn't call the police, did you?" Jim Mallory blurted out, in a tremendous panic over his own daughter's safety.

"Eh?" mumbled Dominic. He was so shook up he couldn't think clearly.

"The *police!*" Mallory shouted. "You didn't call them, did you?"

Dominic took an additional few seconds gathering in

his faculties, then answered in his Italian accent, which always became worse when he was rattled. "No, Mista Mallory, I didda not."

"Whew! That's a relief. Listen, Valenti, we've got to do exactly what the kidnappers tell us—nothing more, nothing less. We can't afford to take foolish risks. I'm prepared to pay the ransom they ask and more, but I don't want Adrienne—or Julia—hurt."

Even through his panic, Dominic noticed that the concern for Julia seemed to be an afterthought on Jim Mallory's part. This increased the old man's fear. He was poor, Mallory was rich, and he knew that people with money stood the best chance of coming out on top in this world.

"Promise me you won't call the police," Mallory demanded.

"Sure. I p-promise," Dominic stammered, feeling browbeaten but not knowing what to do about it. He needed time to collect his thoughts. He didn't know how to deal with criminals.

"We have to do exactly what the kidnappers say," Jim Mallory insisted. "It's the only way we'll ever see Adrienne and Julia alive. I have to be sure you agree on this, Mr. Valenti. Back me up, and I'll shell out all the necessary cash. They know you can't afford to pay, but I can. Your granddaughter's safety depends on me."

Dominic gave his word to do what Mallory wanted, but Mallory needed more than one reassurance before he finally got off the line. He even said at one point that he would take care of Dominic—meaning financially— if things turned out all right. Bewildered, the old man cradled the phone. Why did the kidnappers take Julia, if Adrienne was the one they wanted? And why wouldn't they simply kill Julia, since she wasn't worth hundreds of thousands of dollars to them?

He couldn't handle this terrible situation. He

couldn't think straight. From under the kitchen sink, he got the bottle of anisette, poured himself a double shot, and gulped it down, but it didn't help. All he got out of it was the strong licorice taste; it didn't settle his nerves at all. Maybe he was too old. Or perhaps he loved his granddaughter too much to be objective when she was in such extreme danger.

Finally, he knew he had to wake up his wife and let her share his grief. Climbing the stairs slowly, his mind muddled and his bones aching more than they usually ached, he found himself wishing that Bryan was home. He didn't know how to get in touch with his future son-in-law. Julia had the Vermont number in her purse. Dominic thought that perhaps the younger man might be able to understand what was happening and figure out the right thing to do.

Julia came out of the doping effect of the chloroform with a crashing headache, painful bruises, and an extremely foul taste in her mouth. She had no idea of where she was or how she got there. Her ribs hurt where she had been poked with the barrel of a pistol. Her mouth was gagged and her eyes were taped shut. Her wrists and ankles were tightly bound. She was lying on her side on a cold, gritty concrete floor.

What was she going to do? How was she going to get out of this? What were they going to do to her? She had no answers, and she fought down the effects of rising panic as she realized her total helplessness. Where was Adrienne?

As if in answer, Adrienne screamed and cursed—Julia recognized her voice—mixed with the sounds of a wild thrashing struggle that was going on a short distance away. Adrienne was fighting with someone!

"Goddamn you!" a man groaned. Then there was the sound of a fist smacking into soft flesh. Adrienne whimpered. The man grunted and hit her again. This time she did not cry out.

Julia was shocked into high-strung terror as the nearby struggling noises evolved into something else—something quieter and more sinister. Julia cringed in mind-boggling horror, tortured by ugly visions of what must be going on.

On a dirty furniture pad in the dingy dark warehouse where the two women were being held, Adrienne Mallory was being raped. Surgical tape was glued tightly over her eyes, but her gag had slipped loose in the struggle. Barely conscious, she whimpered and moaned under her attacker. His powerful blows had weakened her, eliminating her will to resist. She, who was so accustomed to having her own way with men, had to endure the sweat and stink of this strange man as he grunted and cursed, driving his unwanted flesh into her.

Julia tried to shut the sounds out, but she couldn't. She was afraid that she would be next.

The sounds of the rapist continued in the darkness.

Bryan and Paul didn't get back to their motel till almost ten o'clock, after a long day of filming and then dinner and a two-hour production meeting with their client, Riley Morgan, of Morgan Associates in Pittsburgh, and two of the people from the air-science research center in Burlington. One of the main topics of discussion was whether to go for a finished print on film or to edit on videotape. Film would be cheaper and tape would be faster, a consideration that wouldn't have come into play if the numerous postponements of the shooting schedule hadn't put the deadline in jeopardy. Even though the delays hadn't been their fault, Bryan and Paul were going to have to swallow the extra costs, and Paul was upset about it.

Bryan invited his partner to have a drink in the cocktail lounge of the motel, and he explained that Riley Morgan had told him in private that even though the agency couldn't go for additional billing on this particular job, they'd make it up in the future. This meant that they'd goose up the budget on the next job that they hired Bryan and Paul for.

Paul wasn't buying it. "We've heard that story before," he groused, slamming his beer bottle on the table. "What usually happens is they hire someone else on purpose, so they never have to tack on what they figure they owe us."

Bryan knew this was true, but there was nothing he could have done about it. "I know, but I couldn't call Morgan a liar," he defended. "I had to play along with him. If I'd have gotten feisty, for sure we'd never get any more work out of him."

"Are we going to lose money on the gig now?" Paul asked, unmollified.

"We should come out okay," Bryan told him. "Actually, I padded the bid a little in the first place, because I was anticipating this sort of thing. We should still make decent bread out of it."

Paul relaxed a little, hearing this, and Bryan wrote on a cocktail napkin, running down the figures for him. By the time they had another beer apiece and went over plans for the next day's shooting, he seemed satisfied. They said goodnight to each other in the corridor outside their adjacent rooms. The wake-up call was for six-thirty; they were meeting the crew and the client at seven in the lobby.

Now it was close to eleven o'clock at night, and Bryan wondered whether or not to phone Julia. She might be in bed already. The ringing of the telephone might wake up Dominic and Theresa. Sitting on the edge of his bed in shorts and T-shirt, Bryan dialed the motel operator and requested a six-thirty wake-up. He set the alarm of his travel clock and placed it on the nightstand for back-up. Then, looking at his watch and thinking of Julia, he decided to dial the Valentis' number, long distance.

Dominic answered on the first ring, his voice shaky. At first Bryan was going to apologize for waking up the old man—but then he sensed something wrong on the other end of the line and he asked immediately for Julia. Dominic didn't answer right away and Bryan began to panic. "Mr. Valenti, what's the matter?" he asked worriedly.

Trying not to cry, the grandfather nevertheless emitted a choking sob. Then Bryan heard Theresa's crying in the background. "She's notta here," Dominic whimpered. "They havva taken her . . . I don' know whatta to do. . . ." He stopped rambling abruptly as he failed to suppress his tears.

Truly alarmed now, Bryan shouted into the phone. "Mr. Valenti . . . please . . . what's happened? *Tell* me!"

After some cajoling and comforting, Dominic pulled himself together and explained clearly what had occurred. Flabbergasted, but trying to react logically, Bryan said that he would get the first plane available—which wouldn't be till tomorrow morning—and come home. Paul Smith could handle the filming on the air force job. Also, Bryan told Dominic: "I think the police should be brought into the case, but you don't have to make any decision yet. Wait till I get there and we can talk it over. The best hope may be to get Jim Mallory to stall somehow on delivering the ransom, by making the kidnappers give us proof that the two women are still alive, and pray that the police can rescue them before something bad happens."

But Dominic said, "I givva to Mallory my word notta

to call the police. He tol' me he's gonna pay the filt'y scum who took Julia. I donna know what is-a the right t'ing to do."

"Listen, don't do anything yet. Let me think this over. I'll be there on the first plane I can get tomorrow morning."

"T'ank God," Dominic said with a note of relief in his voice that Bryan suspected was unwarranted.

"Is he coming?" Theresa whispered anxiously in the background, her breath bated.

Bryan heard Dominic reassure her. After he got off the line, he immediately called the airport and made flight reservations. Thinking for a few minutes, he then called Paul's room and told his partner that he was suddenly feeling very ill, possibly with appendicitis, and he was flying home in the morning. If the story sounded fishy, he didn't care. Maybe Paul bought it, though, because he was very solicitous and reassuring about taking over the job on his own tomorrow.

Bryan spent a long, sleepless night, waiting till he could get on a plane and go home to do whatever he could to try to save Julia.

Still worried that she might be raped, Julia lay bound and gagged on the cold, dirty concrete floor, her eyes taped tightly shut. She could hear Adrienne crying softly from somewhere not far away. The only good thing about the crying was its evidence that Adrienne was still alive.

From time to time there had been footsteps, the sounds of the rapist moving about inside the warehouse. At one point Julia had heard the noise of a chair scraping across the floor, a beer can popping, and a loud belch.

Suddenly the rapist spoke to Adrienne. "You might as well stop bawlin', honey. I know you really liked what I done to ya. Your friend over there—Julia—I bet she wouldn't cry if I did it to her. Maybe I will, too. Bet that'd make you real jealous, wouldn't it? Heh-heh! If you two wasn't all tied up, bet I could have you scratchin' each other's eyes out over Big Tony." He chortled, terribly pleased with his own sense of humor.

Julia cringed. Much as she hated being tied up, the bonds represented security for the time being. As long as her ankles were lashed together, she could not be raped.

The chair scraped and clattered to the floor, and Julia heard Big Tony's approaching footsteps. He stood over her, moisture from his beer can dripping on her leg. Through her fear, the cold wetness reminded her that she was awfully thirsty—a strange thought to have in the presence of so much danger.

"How about it, little ballerina?" the man teased in his gruff voice. "Would you suck on me real nice if I took your gag off for a while? Or would you scream bloody murder?"

Julia's heart was beating wildly, the adrenaline of fear and revulsion coursing through her. *Oh, please, keep this animal away from me!*—her mind cried out silently.

Just then there was the grating, screeching noise of a large steel garage door being lifted, and a vehicle of some type drove into the warehouse.

"Oh-oh! Boss is here," said Big Tony. "Our fun will have to wait till later. Heh-heh! Bet you're disappointed, huh?" Tipping his beer can up and guzzling, he walked away, his footsteps going in the direction of the vehicle that had just entered.

Thankful for the reprieve, Julia tried to clear her mind enough to try to think of a possible way out of her predicament. But there was no way. The situation seemed truly hopeless.

Adrienne had stopped crying.

Doors were slamming as somebody got out of the vehicle that had just come in.

Julia stiffened in a sudden spasm over a bad cramp in her calf, the result of lying on the cold concrete floor for so long.

16 ⋘

AT HOME IN HIS CHEAP RENTED APARTMENT NOT FAR FROM the steel mill where Dominic Valenti used to work, Bernard Augenstein was having a discussion with his wife, Doris. They had been living here, scrimping on what Doris made as a nurse, ever since Louis and Bernard were paroled. Bernard had been unable to get a job, or had not tried hard enough because he was so demoralized. He didn't envy his brother the job at the morgue.

"Well," Bernard told Doris, "Louis is of the firm opinion that Andrew Blake is going to give us the chance we've been hoping for."

"When will we know for certain?" asked Doris. She was a stout, rather severe-looking woman, forty years old. Too old, she thought, to go on supporting her husband. She had remained loyal while he was in prison, but enough was enough. If Louis and Bernard could pull off the deal that was on the horizon, they all could look forward to a life of comfort, which they fully deserved. It was cruel of the world to try to punish them for being geniuses.

"We expect to know something in a matter of days," said Bernard, purposely keeping the edge off his enthusiasm. "It seems that Mr. Blake is fanatical in his desire to see his daughter cured. The cost is no deterrent to him. Neither are the risks."

"Then perhaps we should have asked for more money."

"Yes, perhaps. But we are getting enough. After all, how much can one use?"

"You're not ambitious enough," his wife stated. But she really wasn't angry with him this time.

Bernard, a pale, slender fellow in his late thirties, took his wire-rimmed eyeglasses off and dangled them by the stem as he gazed across the coffee table at his wife, his eyes watery and unfocused because of his nearsightedness.

"What's on your mind?" she asked finally. "Bernard, if something's bothering you, please tell me."

"What if the serum doesn't work?"

"Of course it will," she answered quickly.

"Of course," said Bernard, not to upset her. "Don't mind me, Doris. I merely brought it up as an academic possibility."

Doris shot him a hard, probing look. "Bernard, if you have any serious doubts about the serum, now is the time to say so. None of us wants to go through with this if there is a substantial margin for failure."

Bernard pursed his lips sardonically, after hooking his glasses behind his ears and pressing them into place at the bridge of his nose. "Substantial margin?" he asked rhetorically in his soft nasal twang. "Who can say what the true margin is? We're pioneers in this, after all. In our favor is the fact that the recent skin grafts we tried on each other worked perfectly. And, of course, before Louis and I went to prison, the limb transplants on animals were largely successful. This gives us a good solid basis to go on. But undoubtedly, if we were operating in an orthodox research program, funded adequately through conventional channels, we would have to advance more cautiously and deliberately, through intermediate stages step by step, before trying what we've proposed to Mr. Blake."

Doris thought this over before asking, "What does Louis think? Is he confident about going ahead?" She already knew that Louis would have a bolder attitude than her husband had just expressed, but she wanted to hear it to bolster her own faith in the undertaking. She didn't want to be dissuaded from it. Her sights were already firmly set on what they were going to get out of it.

Bernard's eyes twinkled bemusedly. "You know Louis as well as I. Louis is always confident. He says that ultimately we're going to be more highly regarded than Louis Pasteur or Jonas Salk."

"I thought he was only interested in the money at this point in his life."

"Not really. He vacillates. He still has some of the old 'Savior of Mankind' syndrome in him. What Louis really wants, I'm sure, is to set up a research foundation in South America—where he can pursue his medical theories outside of the Establishment."

"It would be ironic, wouldn't it?" said Doris, sitting back, contemplating.

"What would?" asked her husband.

"If Louis ended up fleeing to Paraguay or maybe Brazil, like Mengele and Barkema."

Lying in bed that night, Bernard considered his relationship with his younger brother. Louis was always the dominant one; he had the fire in him, the spark of genius that had gotten them both into serious trouble. He was consumed by pride in what he could do with his medical training, his ability and daring. Some people would have said that he liked to play God. And, in a way, they wouldn't be too far wrong.

Bernard remembered an incident that had occurred not long after Louis finished his internship. Under nearly impossible conditions, he had saved a woman's life on the operating table, when almost any other doctor, even the most experienced, would have lost her. But Louis rose to the occasion. A tremendously fat black woman had been brought by ambulance to the emergency room, her abdomen gaping wide open from a jagged knife wound, so that all the blubber and guts were visible. Louis tried and tried, but he couldn't get a clamp on an artery that kept gushing blood—the vessel was too slippery, the wound too deep, blubbery, and messy. Finally, he just stopped trying and told the rest of the operating team, "We'll just have to let her bleed." When she lost enough blood, the woman went into shock, as Louis realized would happen, and her bodily functions slowed down, including the bleeding, and Louis was able to get a clamp on the artery. Then he successfully treated her for shock and saved her life. His quick thinking had hit upon the only method that could possibly have worked, and he was proud of himself for it. Later, boasting about the episode, he said half-jokingly, "So I've got a new trick now, Bernard. I let them get within an inch of death, and then I bring them back."

Louis was so avid to learn more and do more as a doctor that he allowed his marriage to disintegrate. His pretty young wife, Angela, who had stuck by him through medical school, eventually started to crumble under the strain. She had expected their lives to get easier once Louis graduated and went to work in a hospital, but she hadn't counted on her husband's extraordinary zeal for his profession. She hardly ever saw him, as he worked fifteen- and twenty-hour days, eager to operate every chance he could get, and volunteering whenever possible. The work load seemed to make him happier, while Angela got more and more despondent. By this time they had two small children who hardly realized they had a father. And then Louis was called upon to fulfill his military obligation, and got sent to Vietnam as an army surgeon.

He enjoyed the war as much as some soldiers who love killing; only Louis loved *fixing*. The new type of combat used by United States forces in Vietnam, with its quick evacuation of casualties by helicopter, saved the lives of thousands of men whose wounds would have proved fatal in previous wars. Louis operated on these men when they were near death. Under that kind of pressure he had often to come up with intricate, ingenious ways of saving them and patching them back together. There was a satisfying thrill in being able to wire, splice, splint, and stitch bones, nerves, muscles, and organs that were horribly, seemingly irreparably, shattered. Hundreds of paraplegics, amputees, and others with damaged, partially functioning brains and bodies had Louis to thank for their ability to go on living.

Louis was so in love with the challenges that he decided to take a second tour in Vietnam, but when he told Angela she filed for divorce. In an attempt to win her back, he didn't re-enlist, but his wife left him anyway, and moved to a different part of the country with the two children. As blind to their needs as Louis may have been when they were legally together, the fact that his family would leave him was something he couldn't understand or forgive.

Now he had his anger over his loss, plus all of his former zeal, to drive him. As a civilian surgeon, he plunged himself into his work, putting in hours upon hours at the operating table and rising quickly to a position of pre-eminence in his orthopedic specialty. This didn't satisfy him, though. Nothing ever seemed to satisfy him. Soon he was talking about having his own clinic, with his brother as a partner. And at about that same time, his ambition was being kindled to new heights by his discovery of the files smuggled out of Treblinka.

Bernard wondered what his own life might have been like if he had not allowed his younger brother to draw him into the daring but forbidden experiments . . . if he had insisted upon operating the clinic legally. But there was no stopping Louis. He kept arguing that it would be worth it, but then he grew careless about the screening procedures that should have followed each female patient who wanted an operation. He didn't count on ending up in prison for his troubles, dragging his older brother along with him, and throwing the clinic into bankruptcy.

The roof caved in after Louis induced delivery of a thirty-one-week-old fetus and the mother's uterus ruptured and had to be removed. Performing an induction on someone so young was too big a risk. She was sixteen, pregnant out of wedlock, and prior to the operation she had signed papers to the effect that she understood that the fetus was deformed (which it wasn't) and she wanted it aborted. Louis had suggested the lie to the parents, but when the girl's mother discovered that removal of her uterus meant she could never have another baby, she went to pieces. She told her story to the district attorney, who kept digging till he found several more women willing to testify against the Augenstein brothers. The case made such a big splash it ensured his re-election.

It could have been worse. Doris wasn't indicted, only because the prosecutor couldn't dredge up enough evidence to prove her involvement in the illegal abortions. Most fortunate of all was the fact that nobody got wise to the clinic's scrupulously guarded secret—that the fetuses had been used for experimental purposes.

Sometimes Bernard didn't know why he allowed himself to be swept along by his brother's wild schemes. True enough, Louis was brilliant. But the trouble he got himself into over the Helen Ann Marx incident was further indication of his impetuousness, which hadn't been tamed. He could have gone back to prison, and might yet if Lieutenant Manderson ever exhumed the body. No doubt about it—Louis really needed a grand success with Tiffany Blake so he could get his life in order once and for all. Even if he didn't go to South America, at least he might have enough money to pay off the right people, in case he ran afoul of the law again.

17 ⋘

As soon as he got out of the white van, Sammy Triglia went around and hit the button causing the steel door to descend automatically and slam shut, raising dust motes off the concrete floor. They danced in the uneven glare of naked light bulbs dangling at wide intervals throughout the warehouse. Nothing was presently being stored there. Down at one end was a stack of empty wooden pallets.

Sammy was wearing a gray sharkskin suit, shiny black shoes, and a red tie on an off-white shirt that he considered extremely dapper. His black hair, thinning and receding on top, was lightly greased and combed straight back, since there wasn't enough of it to employ the "dry look" to advantage. Sammy was considering buying a toupee or a weave-job or even a hair transplant as soon as he got paid off for this latest caper. His Italian mama always made such a fuss over his gorgeous head of hair, before he lost it, that he grew up convinced that all the girls were dying to run their fingers through it. It gave him enough confidence to score pretty often. Now he figured only a decent hairline stood between him and serious handsomeness. He was thin, wiry, and dark with a hook nose, deepset black eyes, and a too-small chin that gave his face a weak appearance and emphasized his dome-like forehead.

Big Tony Fallon, a huge oaf of a man with rotten teeth, sallow complexion, and a ponderous beer belly, waddled toward his partner, glad to have somebody to talk to after several hours spent guarding the two captives. Big Tony crushed his empty beer can in his hands and plunked it into a steel drum as he crossed the warehouse.

Sammy walked carefully, not wanting to get a coating of dust on his shoes and pants cuffs, and scanned the two women lying on the floor about ten feet apart. The brunette looked pretty much the way he had seen her last, but the redhead's face was now badly bruised and her frilly pink panties were balled up beside her on the furniture mat. He shot an appraising stare at Fallon, whose baggy brown trousers and yellow knit shirt were smudged with grime from the struggle with Adrienne.

"Have yourself a little fun while I was gone?" Sammy jibed.

Big Tony chuckled lewdly. "Why not? Fringe benefits."

"I don't know if the boss would like you messin' with 'em," Sammy grumbled. Actually, he was jealous. He would love to have had a turn on the brunette, but he had too much pride to force himself on a broad—this attitude still persisting from the days when he had been able to get laid rather easily.

"Boss never said not to," Big Tony defended.

Bound, gagged, and blindfolded, Adrienne and Julia lay still, listening to everything going on around them, conscious that whatever they heard could have a bearing on their fate.

"Well, so you got laid, so never mind," said Sammy. "We gotta get humpin'." He caught himself. "No, not *your* way." He and Tony both laughed at the double entendre. "I mean, we have to move out already. We gotta put these two in the back of the van."

"Where we takin' 'em?"

"You'll see when we get there."

"Wise ass. One of these days you're gonna forget once too often that I'm bigger'n you."

"You're also dumber. Come on, take hold of her ankles. Earn your pay for a change."

Julia felt herself being rolled over onto her back and hoisted by the ropes around her wrists and ankles, then carried across the floor and put into the rear of an uncarpeted van, the ice-cold metal putting instantaneous goosebumps on her bare skin. She shivered uncontrollably. In a little while Adrienne was deposited beside her. Their bodies touched, and she could feel Adrienne shivering, too. But there was some comfort in being close to each other. Within a few minutes, the steel door made its grating noise as its motor lifted it, the van's engine started, and the vehicle backed out of the warehouse, headed for some unknown destination.

It was impossible to figure out where the van might be going, without knowing where it had been. Julia kept trying to sense something that might provide a clue. Once moving, the vehicle didn't stop or slow down much, as it would have had to do on busy city streets with traffic lights and stop signs. For a long time the rate of speed seemed to be constant and fairly rapid. One of the men up front rolled down a window, and the resultant rush of wind wasn't unbearably cold; so it was probably daytime—something Julia had already presumed, although she had no way of telling how long she had been unconscious. She tried to convince herself that the blindfolds were a good sign—if she and Adrienne were going to be killed, the kidnappers wouldn't be so careful about concealing their identities.

Julia assumed that the motive for the kidnapping was money, so Adrienne must be the main target. Her family could afford to pay a great deal. Sex hadn't been the primary motivation, judging from the conversation between the two men, but obviously either was capable of rape. Poor Adrienne. Julia felt the other woman's arm resting against the small of her back and she wanted to turn around and hug her and give comfort, but of course her bonds frustrated and prevented the impulse.

Terrifying as the basic circumstances were, it was doubly frightening to Julia to realize all the unknowns. She and Adrienne couldn't possibly know all the forces at work, how the people close to them were reacting, and how much real jeopardy they might be in from moment to moment. Bryan might not even know anything was wrong. She hadn't expected him to call until the end of the week. Thinking of how much she loved him, Julia tried to face the possibility that she might not ever see him again.

In the cab of the van, Big Tony cleared his throat to get Sammy Triglia's attention, then gave him a wink.

"There's a nice patch of woods over there," Big Tony said, for the benefit of the girls in back. "What say we pull in where the van won't be seen and take turns humping the two broads? The redhead showed me a hard time. I have a hunch the brunette would treat me a lot nicer."

"Sure," said Sammy, going along with the gag. "I know a better place, though, down the road. We might as well have our fun before we turn 'em over to the boss. I noticed they both got nice asses and legs."

"Which one you want first?"

"The brunette."

"I'll flip you for her."

"Okay."

Tony and Sam stopped talking at that point, knowing that Adrienne and Julia would be waiting, terrified, for the van to pull off the road. Actually, the more Sammy toyed with the idea, the more he wanted to go through with it. One of his peeves was that people like Tony, coarse and stupid, took what they wanted out of life, while people like himself, more intelligent and refined, went around horny all the time.

Julia stayed frightened, but as time went on and the van didn't actually stop anywhere, her fears eased up somewhat. Her body was so cramped and cold, it was almost impossible to concentrate on anything else after a while, even the fear of rape. In the warehouse her muscles had eventually gone numb, but now the bouncing and jostling of the van on the road kept every little ache and pain alive.

Adrienne was thinking about revenge. Having been raped once, she could endure it again. Painful as it had been, *hateful* as it had been, she'd survive it. Her father would pay these bastards what they wanted. She'd be set free. If they intended to kill her, they'd have done it already. So they must be figuring on letting her go. And while they thought they were safe and were spending the ransom money, her father would hire people to track down the animals. Not to put them on trial. But to treat them to a nice, slow death. If her father or her brother wouldn't do it, she'd do it herself.

18 ⋘

DOMINIC AND THERESA VALENTI WERE UP EARLY AFTER A miserable sleepness night. The old woman made scrambled eggs, toast, and coffee, but most of it went untouched. She went about the kitchen mumbling and saying prayers to herself while Dominic paced and worried, trying at times to sit in his leather armchair but always failing to stay there for long. The hours went by very slowly.

"Bryan will be here soon," the old man said for the third or fourth time. "He musta be onna his way." Again he took out his pocket watch and stared at it.

"He will know what to do," said Theresa. "And maybe God will help us."

She crossed through the living room, moving arthritically, and Dominic heard her slippers on the stairs. She was going up to their room to kneel by the bed and say the Rosary. He had tried many times to convince her that a crippled old woman didn't have to kneel in order for God to hear her, but she went on praying on her knees, same as always.

Dominic dragged out his pocket watch again and it seemed that the hands hadn't moved. When he paced in the living room, he stared at the gold watch he had gotten for his retirement from the mill; when he was in the kitchen, he kept looking at the clock on the wall with its plastic face and electric pendulum. He had no real idea when Bryan was coming; he only had his faith that somehow Bryan would have managed to get on an early plane.

He leaned on the piano and looked at a picture of Julia as a little ballerina, eight years old. He had never understood how a little girl could know so passionately that she wanted dancing lessons, but Julia was crazy about ballet from the first time she saw it on television. She never outgrew it, as Dominic had expected. He let her have her way, paying for the lessons he could barely afford, till she got the job in the hardware store when she started high school. He would never have allowed her father to do anything so expensive. Except he wanted her father to study the violin, but as a young boy he never listened.

Dominic's eyes watered and he collapsed into his armchair. He wiped his eyes with his sleeve and tried not to think of the old memories. He got up and walked into the kitchen again. Something he hadn't thought of before popped into his mind, and he wondered about it without knowing why it was bothering him. Adrienne and Julia had to have been kidnapped shortly before or after they had a chance to visit Tiffany Blake. Dominic considered calling Blake to ask if Adrienne and Julia ever arrived there. But, his hand on the phone ready to dial, he realized it would be a mistake, for it would give away the fact that the girls were missing.

Dominic felt helpless. He didn't like the idea of standing by and doing nothing while his granddaughter's fate was decided by evil men. Unable to control his mounting anxiety, he telephoned Jim Mallory and asked if there had been any further word from the kidnappers.

"You didn't go to the police, did you?" Mallory instantly shot back.

"No, I didda not," said Dominic, "because I givva you my word. But Bryan t'inks maybe you are wrong."

"Bryan? Who's that? Your son-in-law? Well, what does *he* know? You shouldn't have told him anything. He has no business meddling in this." Mallory got more and more worked up and became stern, bullying. "Look, Mr. Valenti, we have to play this thing *my* way. Money talks. My daughter is the central figure in this drama. I haven't heard anything more, but I'm sure I will. They know I have the hard cash. For God's sake, don't let Bryan talk you into doing anything rash! I'll pay the ransom and get your granddaughter back for you in one piece."

"She's notta wort' any money to them," Dominic lamented in a meek voice.

"I know, but Adrienne *is*. That's why she's the key to Julia's safety, as well as her own. Trust me in this, Mr. Valenti, *please*."

"I wait to talka to Bryan," Dominic answered. "Then we talka to you some more before we make uppa our minds."

"Listen to me, Valenti! If Bryan has any doubts, promise me you'll have him call me right away!"

"Sure, that's whatta we gonna do. We gonna keepa in touch," Dominic promised before saying good-bye.

Jim Mallory was a nervous wreck. Cold and calculating as he could be in business dealings, this danger to his daughter had him totally flustered. He was coming apart at the seams, and now old man Valenti sounded flaky enough to make a crazy move and get both girls killed. And his son-in-law, or future son-in-law, was a real jerk—wanting to go to the police right off the bat. If the kidnappers wanted money, that's what you had to give them. You had to play the game their way. It was the best chance of getting Adrienne back alive. And the other girl, too, for that matter.

Mallory had not told his son, Jimmy, the one who helped run the construction company, anything about what had happened to Adrienne. He had told only his wife. He didn't want to alarm anybody unnecessarily, even family members. Their long faces would give away the fact that something was wrong. He had called in sick with the flu; that was an excuse he could play for a week or more, if need be. Christ! He hoped this thing was over before then; otherwise, he didn't know if he could take it. He went to the liquor cabinet, poured himself a big glass of bourbon, and sank into an easy chair in the family room, next to the telephone. Under his breath, he cursed Dominic Valenti—if the old man hadn't been on the line tying it up, maybe the kidnappers would have called.

A big, square-jawed man with wiry iron-gray hair and a ruddy complexion, Jim Mallory usually looked and felt in command of every situation; most times he projected that aura even when he was slightly unsure of himself. This was the big exception. The strain was showing through. His wife, Sarah, seemed more under control than he did, and that irked him. She was usually the shrinking violet. But then, when he thought about it, he recalled that she had always been unexpectedly good in any emergency involving the kids. Some kind of mother's instinct came to the fore, enabling her to do the right thing at the right time. When Adrienne was three and almost got drowned in the swimming pool, Sarah revived her with mouth-to-mouth resuscitation—and Jim Mallory had to eat crow because he had poked fun at Sarah's C.P.R. classes, just as he had mocked her classes in yoga, Chinese cooking, ceramics, and numerous other fads she'd taken up and dropped from summer to summer. The latest thing was a gardening course.

Usually Mallory wouldn't have valued his wife's opinion. But this time her mother's instinct agreed with his own hard common sense. She, too, felt that the best way was to keep mum and make the payoff without notifying the police; they could be called in after Adrienne was safe.

Through sharing this crisis with Sarah, Mallory felt closer to her than he had in months, maybe years. She seemed to have her wits about her this time, and agreeing with him was part of it. When the phone still didn't ring after a long wait, he went out through the sliding-glass door and onto the patio to join Sarah as she tried unsuccessfully to take her mind off the pressure by transplanting some potted flowers that didn't really need it.

She was sitting on a bench in front of a redwood picnic table with newspaper spread out to collect spilled dirt from the flowerpots. Shiny metal trowel blade flashing in the sun, she looked up as her husband approached. Her face was made up, her hair recently set and dyed auburn, and she was wearing a bright flower-print smock and green denim jeans with a leather label on the hip pocket, all of which contrived to give her a youthful look till Jim got closer and saw her baggy eyes, puffy from crying. She was a nice-looking woman, but she didn't turn Jim on sexually anymore. "Any word?" she asked, though she already knew the answer by the look on his face.

He shook his head no.

"We're bound to hear something by and by," she said as if reciting a credo.

"Yes," Jim agreed, sitting down opposite her and sipping his bourbon. It stung his throat and he wished he had put ice in it. "Want some?" he offered, hoping to get rid of it.

"Not this early in the morning," said Sarah, without censure. Wearing plastic gardening gloves to protect her fingernails, which were always manicured and painted, she patted the soil around her transplant, a bright red tulip. She was keeping busy, going on with the little things as normally as possible, as if that might have an effect on bringing everything back to normal.

Again Jim marveled at her composure, knowing she was as torn up inside as he was. By way of contrast, he thought of his young mistress, a girl barely out of her teens, who went to pieces if she got her hair wet. Times like this made him value Sarah's companionship and the twenty-five-year span of their marriage, which had taken them through plenty and given them a lot in common. The mistress would dump him if he lost all his money. But Sarah would stick, no matter what happened. Jim couldn't quite say that the feeling he had for her was love any longer; it wasn't that passionate. But whatever it was, it got stronger in a crisis.

Sarah stopped patting the soil around her tulip. "We'll get our daughter back," she said staunchly. "I feel that in my soul. Don't ask me how, but I feel it."

169

"Then I'm sure there's something to your feeling," Jim Mallory said, wanting to believe in a mother's instincts.

Theresa Valenti continued to pray the Rosary. She knelt beside her bed, her calves numb, pain shooting up from her knees through her thighs and into the small of her back. God would recognize her suffering and her humility. He would answer her prayers in His own way, according to His superior wisdom. If He took Julia, cruel as it might seem, there would be a Divine Purpose to it that mortals could not understand.

Downstairs, Dominic kept pacing back and forth from living room to kitchen, averting his eyes from the picture of Julia on the piano, looking first at his pocket watch then at the wall clock, worrying and waiting for Bryan, who represented hope.

In his study nursing a tumbler full of gin, Andrew Blake was having a contemptuous reaction to an article in the morning newspaper about a punk artist in New York who had chopped off two of his own fingers in order to protest his lack of recognition by the "art establishment." He had refused to let surgeons reattach his severed fingers, saying, "Like Vincent Van Gogh, I know that you have to sometimes do something far out in order to get the world's attention. My hope is that now people will lend an ear to the plight of the starving artist."

Here I am, thought Andrew, *doing all I can to help Tiffany, and here this nut is, going around giving away pieces of himself.*

At the Stanford Chapman Home for the Aged, Louis Augenstein was arguing with the plump young nurse with peroxided hair who was supposed to be taking care of his father. Louis and Bernard had purchased a black-and-white TV set for the room, in hopes that the patient might get some enjoyment out of it, even though he had no outward responses. But now the set was missing.

"I don't know where it is. I've looked in all the rooms," the nurse said, not very concerned about the matter. "I don't think he could understand any of the programs, anyway," she added, as if this excused the theft of the television.

Louis was extremely angry. "All right!" he snapped. "You either find that TV set and bring it back to this room before I leave here today, or I'm going to write a letter to the governor about the way you treat these old people, allowing their belongings be taken from them right under their noses, when they can't even protect themselves."

This shook the nurse up sufficiently that she brought Louis downstairs to the office, where he argued the matter some more with the home's director, a mousy little man named Smythe with a liberal coating of dandruff on the shoulders of his brown suit. Again Louis threatened to write to the governor, and in the end Mr. Smythe promised reluctantly to either locate the television set in question or purchase and install a new one. "This time we'll chain it down so it can't be removed." He smiled, exposing nicotine-stained teeth. "If you are going to write any letters, Dr. Augenstein, you should ask the powers that be why my state funds that I'm supposed to get are so meager and always so late. I'm understaffed and it's impossible to look after so many patients."

"We pay you enough," Louis said, not giving the man any leeway. "You ought to be able to do a better job than you're doing." He pivoted and walked haughtily out of the office.

In a show of attention and efficiency, the plump young nurse had now chosen to start making up his father's bed, so rather than chase her out, Louis wheeled the old man down a long corridor into a lounging area where patients might smoke, read, or simply take some sun. There were a couple of card tables with chess and checker sets and worn-out decks of cards, and a magazine rack full of battered, out-of-date magazines. No one was in the lounge at the moment but Louis and his father, which suited the younger man perfectly. Anxious to provide whatever marginal comfort he could in a place like this, he stopped the wheelchair in a spot where the sun was slanting in bright and warm through a dirty window with dusty side curtains.

The old man was immobile, expressionless, almost lifeless; yet, futile as it seemed, the son felt a deep inner need for communication with his parent. Standing and looking down at his father, Louis delivered a monologue which was an attempt to unburden himself to an audience which may have been absent.

"I don't know if you can understand me or not, Papa, or even if you're hearing me. I want you to know that I've always honored and respected you, even when you've believed otherwise. You became bitter when Bernard and I decided to go against your wishes by making use of the files you kept for Dr. Barkema. But the fact is that we've been trying to build something worthwhile out of your suffering. And we're on the verge of succeeding!

"We want to vindicate you, to make you proud. We want to create good out of evil. Our ambitions are not unholy, but noble.

"Maybe the world will never understand. But I want you, of all people, to be for us instead of against us. And believe me, my deepest wish is that you live long enough to see your life justified, by our transformation of human misery into medical advancement!"

Louis fell silent, looking into his father's glazed, unseeing eyes, hoping for some sort of love and understanding.

But the old man sat like a mummy in his wheelchair, unaware that his son was even there. Images of Treblinka monopolized his haunted thoughts.

19 ❧

THE DETAILS OF TRAVEL ALWAYS BORED AND IRRITATED
Bryan, but now it was infinitely worse. He was on pins
and needles. He even started smoking again, buying his
first pack of cigarettes in two years out of a machine in
the motel lobby while he waited in line to check out.
All he could think about was getting home to do
whatever he could to help Julia—although under the
circumstances, what could he do? It might boil down to
comforting her grandparents. Maybe by the time he got
there, she'd already have been released.

Burlington, Vermont, was only six hundred miles
from Pittsburgh, probably an hour and a half on a
direct flight. But the Burlington airport was very small,
out of the mainstream flight patterns, so Bryan had a
two-hour layover in Newark, New Jersey, while his

baggage was being transferred and he waited to get on another plane. Of all stupid things, he suddenly realized that he had left his shaving bag in his motel room. He had to put a long-distance call in to Paul Smith, on the job at the air-science research center, to ask him to get the shaving bag from the motel management. It was an expensive leather bag and had been a Christmas present from Julia.

"Where are you—home?" Paul asked, obviously harried by the pressure of completing the filming with a short-handed crew.

"No, Newark, waiting for the transfer," Bryan said. "How are things going?"

"Okay. Don't worry. I can handle it. I'll get it done."

Bryan didn't push the point any further, not wanting to step on Paul's exaggerated sense of professional pride.

"Are you feeling any better?" Paul asked.

"Not really. The cramps are pretty bad. I'm going to see a doctor as soon as I get home."

"I hope it isn't appendicitis. Oh-oh, gotta run, Bryan. Riley Morgan is calling me to discuss the next camera angle."

Although he had checked out of the motel in Burlington at seven in the morning, Bryan didn't arrive at Greater Pittsburgh International Airport until nearly noon. The sky was blue and crystal clear on a bright spring-like day, the panorama of the city spread out so shiningly and innocently in the sunlight as the plane made its approach that it seemed impossibly unkind that Julia should be a prisoner somewhere down there, possibly in danger of losing her life.

Again Bryan had to wait for his luggage. Keyed up as he was, he smoked several more cigarettes while waiting. He kept thinking about Julia. He didn't want to be left out of any decisions affecting her; in his mind, she was already his wife. He was responsible for her; he was her protector. It saddened him to imagine what her grandfather must be going through, trying to deal with such a frightening, complex situation. He wasn't sure the old man could handle it. Not that he had total faith in himself, either; tinkering with circumstances involving a human life, especially Julia's, was very scary.

Checking his station wagon out of valet parking, he drove as quickly as he dared to the Valenti house. The old man and his wife both looked as though they had aged ten years, and they hugged and kissed him and started crying as soon as he came through the door.

Theresa fixed him a plate of bacon and eggs, despite his protests, and to his surprise he nearly ate it all. It hadn't dawned on him that he could be hungry with all that was on his mind, even though he hadn't eaten since yesterday evening. With the eggs he downed a couple cups of strong black coffee, then chain-smoked cigarettes till the pack was gone while he pumped Julia's grandparents for as much information as possible.

Sitting at the kitchen table, Dominic recounted as best he could the exact words of the kidnapper. Then he repeated the dialogue with Jim Mallory, both conversations in their entirety. Bryan listened intently. "I t'ink it musta happen when they was onna their way to see Tiffany," Dominic concluded, smacking the tabletop with the palm of his hand.

"How do you know they even made it to ballet practice?" Bryan asked. "They might have skipped it."

"I donna t'ink so," Dominic said.

Neither did Bryan, but it still should be checked out. "If the police were working on this," he explained, "they'd talk to Nicolai Artov and Andrew Blake in order to pin down the probable time of the abduction. The last time you saw Julia was when she left here at six o'clock, an hour after dinner. Then the call from the kidnapper didn't come till nine. A three-hour time span. For that matter, if they got to Blake's but didn't stay long for some reason, they could have been abducted after they left there. That would explain why you haven't heard from him. After all, you'd think either he or Tiffany would want to know why Adrienne and Julia never showed up."

That's what had been bothering Dominic that he hadn't been able to put his finger on. Why hadn't Blake phoned? Dominic had been almost ready to call and find out when he had thought better of it. He now told Bryan, "If we start inna askin' questions, people gonna know somet'ing is wrong. Maybe we shoulda listen to Mista Mallory. He t'inks it's best notta to go to the police. He donna want to scare the crooks. He just wanta pay da money and hope ever't'ing goes smooth."

"Well, how about if I ask a few questions on my own?" suggested Bryan. "Since I'm not a professional lawman, the kidnappers might not get too scared if it's only me nosing around. And we won't be taking this thing sitting on our hands. If something worse happens to Julia while we sit around waiting, the trail will be cold, and we'll have ourselves to blame if Mallory's do-nothing strategy doesn't pan out."

Dominic thought over this proposal, frightened of it. It could be like stirring up a hornets' nest if it went wrong. Julia would pay the price.

"I'll be careful," Bryan said. "I don't think we should just sit still. That would be a compromise."

"Will I need to tell Mallory whatta you're doin'?" asked Dominic, beginning to lean Bryan's way.

"I wouldn't tell him right away," said Bryan. "Reassure him that you're not going to the police. If I find out anything important, or get to a point where a decision has to be made that might jeopardize Adrienne *or* Julia, we won't make a further move without leveling with Mallory."

"All right," said Dominic with a desperate sigh. "Whatta you say makes sense. God bless." He looked over at Theresa, who gave her silent assent.

Now that he had them on his side, Bryan felt the pressure of his decision even more. He could get himself or Julia killed, and Adrienne, too, if he didn't handle himself properly. "First thing to do is phone Nicolai," he told Dominic. "Tell him that Julia has come down with influenza and won't be able to rehearse for a week to ten days. Ask him if she looked ill at practice last evening—that way you'll find out if she was there at all."

Bryan wrote down the number of the Artov Ballet Studio on a slip of paper for Dominic, and the old man picked up the kitchen phone and dialed. He found out from Nicolai that Julia had done well in rehearsal yesterday, had looked and sounded healthy, and had left with Adrienne to go and visit Tiffany Blake.

"She didda not getta tired?" asked Dominic, playing the solicitous grandparent. "She stay for entire practice?"

"She worked hard all the way till eight o'clock, or even a little later," said Nicolai. "Maybe it's my fault she's ill. I could have been pressing her too hard. Maybe she's run down and depleted. If so, though, she gave absolutely no indication. She wanted very badly to dance the lead role in *Giselle*. I hope she recovers in time to do it. If not, I suppose Adrienne will have to fill in."

So Bryan found out that Julia did have the part in the bag, but somehow knowing it only made him feel worse. He pushed it out of his mind and tried to analyze what he had just been told. "If they didn't leave till after eight," he said, "then that means they must have been grabbed on their way *to* Blake's. They wouldn't have had time to get there, visit, and leave, for you to have gotten the threatening phone call by nine. That makes me very curious about something. Did Andrew Blake know that Adrienne and Julia were coming to see his daughter?"

"You bet," Dominic said, chewing on what was left of his cigar. "Julia talka to him to set uppa the time. He ask if they will eat somet'ing with him and Tiffany after da ballet practice, but Julia says no, she watcha da weight."

Bryan stood up, brimming with nervous energy, and nearly bumped into Theresa, who was coming to wipe off the kitchen table. "Excuse me," he told her. Then, to Dominic: "Why didn't Blake phone you to find out why they never arrived?"

"I donna know. Maybe he t'inks Adrienne and Julia change their minds, go home instead of to his-a house."

"I'll have to talk with him," said Bryan, beginning to pace. "There's no way to avoid it. I'll have to trust him to be discreet."

Nodding his head to nobody in particular, Dominic looked up at Theresa for her approval, hoping he was doing the right thing. She nodded grimly, affirmatively, but did not quit her silent prayers as she wiped the table.

Bryan asked Dominic, "Did you phone the hardware store and tell them Julia wouldn't be coming to work?"

The old man shook his head yes.

"What excuse did you use?" Bryan asked.

"Sick," said Dominic, feeling old and tired and futile. A tear rolled from his eye as he looked away toward the kitchen wall, wondering if his granddaughter would ever be going to work again.

20 ❦❦❦

WEARING A DARK BLUE SUIT THAT HE USED TO LOOK GOOD in, Andrew Blake tapped lightly on his daughter's bedroom door. Without waiting for her response, he entered, coming a few feet into the room. She looked up, surprised once again at how bad he looked. He had lost so much weight that the suit was too big for him, and the clean-shaven skin stretched over the bones of his face seemed almost transparent, with a sickly hue. "Someone is here to see you," he said, "someone I'd very much like you to meet."

Tiffany had been reading a book. She was annoyed at her father's intrusion and by her own inability to prevent it. He could have waited for her to call out her permission to enter, instead of acting as if a cripple had less right to privacy than a whole person. "Who is here,

Father?" Tiffany asked accusingly. "You know I don't want to see anyone."

"This is a special person," Blake said, forcing a smile of confidence which looked grotesque to her as he beamed it down upon her bed. "I've found a doctor who knows how to help you."

Tiffany scoffed bitterly. "By sewing on a new leg?"

"Approximately that, yes," said Andrew in cold seriousness.

Tiffany's eyes widened, meeting his unflinching stare. "You're serious, aren't you?" she said disbelievingly.

"Will you talk with Dr. Augenstein?"

She wondered if her father was losing his mind. She didn't dare let him get her hopes up. Yet, he seemed so serious it was frightening. "I suppose I've got nothing to lose by humoring your doctor friend," she told him, snapping her book shut and plopping it down beside her on the bedsheet.

Relieved that she had given her permission, Andrew Blake went downstairs to his study, where Louis Augenstein was waiting. Louis looked well. There was more color in his cheeks than there had been, and he was dressed impeccably in a brand-new three-piece black suit that helped project the image of the sober, successful physician. Andrew escorted Louis back up to Tiffany's room, then shut the door, leaving his daughter and the doctor alone.

Back in his study, Andrew Blake poured fresh gin over the melting ice cubes in his tumbler and took a long sip. This was his second refill. It was nearly noon and he had not eaten anything, but he needed the drinks to ease his nerves while he waited out the results of Tiffany's first meeting with Dr. Augenstein. The doctor was going to try to convince her to go ahead with an operation. The operating room was ready in the basement, the remodeling done, and the equipment moved in while Tiffany was still in the hospital. If she didn't give her consent to go ahead, it could be done, anyway, by slipping her an anesthetic when the time came; but it would be better to have her wholehearted cooperation.

Her chance to be whole again was Andrew's opportunity to redeem himself. As he stared at Tiffany in an action still from *The Nutcracker* in a gold frame on his desk, his mind went back over her childhood, the death of her mother, and his attempts to raise her well and make her love him by giving her everything money could buy. She had taken all that came from him for granted, because it came so easily. The only thing she had really valued was her dancing, because the success came from her own effort, her own sacrifice. Andrew realized that now, and he berated himself for being the one to shatter her dream of becoming a great ballerina. Now he must try to put the pieces of the dream back together.

Carrying his glass of gin with him, he paced out to the foyer, his gaze fastened anxiously to the top of the stairs, waiting for Dr. Augenstein to come out. When at last the doctor descended the staircase, his eyes met Blake's with not a hint of the outcome of the conversation with Tiffany. He was playing his role to the hilt for drama and suspense.

"Well?" Blake inquired, urgency and desperation in his voice.

The doctor remained inscrutable, all the way to the bottom of the stairs, till he stood on the landing. Then he allowed himself to smile slightly. "She'll do it," he announced. "I explained what we can do for her, described the procedure, emphasizing that the operation is surgically no different from the reimplantation that was already done—except that this time the new limb will be a genuine transplant, from a terminally ill donor. She said she'd rather have that than a leg from a cadaver, which, in her words, would give her 'the creeps.' She had far fewer qualms to overcome than I expected. She wants very badly to dance again, Mr. Blake."

"And do you think she will, Dr. Augenstein?"

"The dancing will be up to her. I will make her whole again, Mr. Blake, but she will need to furnish the energy and the will to attain her former status. Of course, I had to be honest with her concerning why Bernard and I were sent to prison, how we came to make our discoveries, and so on, so she would understand and believe in our capabilities. I had to convince her, much as I had to convince you. I suggest that you go up and talk with her now, to cement her resolve to go through with it."

"When will the operation take place?"

"Tomorrow. The sooner the better, so she won't change her mind. I told Tiffany that the girl who is donating the limb is not expected to live long. That was my way of making her see the urgency of an immediate decision on her part."

"That is satisfactory," said Blake. He sipped his gin, pleased that the more he got to know Dr. Augenstein, the more the man impressed him. Now that Louis had quit his job at the morgue and had some money in his pocket, he had recaptured the confident demeanor and obvious self-esteem of the true professional.

"Don't worry, Mr. Blake," Louis said with assurance. "My brother and I know what we are doing. Your daughter is in excellent hands."

"Thank you, Doctor, for all you've done so far," Blake told him. "Will you be leaving for the day now?"

"No," said Louis. "I'll want to spend some time downstairs first, making sure everything is in proper order. Up to this point all has gone well because of our thorough preparations. Bernard, Doris, and I believe in paying minute attention to every detail. It's the only way to minimize risks."

Andrew nodded approvingly, and Louis went down the hall to the basement door, opened it, and began descending the staircase as the door slowly shut.

After finishing his gin and rinsing out the glass in the kitchen sink, Andrew went upstairs to talk to Tiffany. As he climbed the steps, he tried to think what to say. They had not communicated on any meaningful level since the accident. Why, he wondered, should things be any different now?

She looked up at him as he entered her room. Her book was still closed, beside her on the bed, so she must have been thinking over what lay in store. His heart went out to her; her shorter left leg was poignantly obvious, with legs and feet outlined under the covers. To him, she was still very pretty, in frilly blue pajamas that complemented her blue eyes and blonde hair, although her long confinement had made her complexion pale. To his surprise, she gave him a slight, trembly smile, the first one she had favored him with in months.

"Promise me one thing," she said in a hushed voice. Her attitude toward her father had softened; she needed his strength, what remained of it, to see her through another operation.

"Anything. Just ask," he whispered, gazing fondly upon his daughter.

"Never tell me the name of the dying girl who is giving me a new leg. I want to think of it as my own. I don't want to know anything about her. What she died of. Anything."

He stared at her, not answering.

"Promise me, Father. *Please*. Or I won't go through with it." She tightened her lips determinedly.

"Yes. Certainly. What you ask is reasonable," he

told her finally in a hoarse, husky voice, knowing he was making a false promise. He didn't have the slightest idea how he was ultimately going to keep the results of what he was doing out of the newspapers, off the radio and TV, and away from Tiffany.

In the end, would he lose her respect forever? Or would she be grateful and forgiving? Would she realize that he did it out of love? And would she love him in return, as much as she did when she was a little girl?

On his way downstairs to get ready to go to the office for part of the day, Andrew crossed paths with Doris Augenstein, who had been the live-in nurse ever since Tiffany came home from the hospital. "So, Tiffany gave her consent," Doris said. "I knew Louis would talk her into it."

"Yes," said Andrew. "We're going ahead with it tomorrow."

"That's certainly good news, isn't it?" Doris said, smiling. "Bernard and I have been checking over all the equipment and now Louis is down there, too. We shouldn't have any unforeseen difficulties, Mr. Blake. We're set up better than any hospital I've ever worked in."

"I hope so. It cost plenty."

"I'm going up to see Tiffany now and give her a sedative. She's still in plenty of pain, you know, and I'm doing my best to control it without making her dependent on morphine."

"How much more of this can she take?" Blake said anxiously. "She'll have to go through it all again after the operation tomorrow."

Doris answered brightly, enthusiastically. "But this time she'll be whole again, Mr. Blake! That alone will give her the spirit to endure pain and recover beautifully."

Provided God doesn't curse us for what we're doing,

Blake said to himself as he went into his study for another tumbler full of gin. One more before going to work wouldn't hurt, he told himself. He poured from the bottle in the liquor cabinet, and as he was plunking in ice cubes from the bucket on his desk, his eyes fell upon a newspaper article that had come from Louis Augenstein's files. Louis had purposely brought the article in this morning, to show Andrew what might be accomplished for Tiffany with a successful transplant operation. It told of a woman who had severed the bottom half of her right leg in an automobile accident three years ago. The limb had been reattached, and in the week the article was written she had been able to compete and run the distance in a six-mile marathon. She had spent six months in a cast after the operation, then more months on braces and crutches, but with constant exercise and therapy, plus gritty determination, she finally was able to use her leg again.

The disappointing part was the three years. That was a long time for Tiffany to be away from ballet. Even with a successful operation, it would be difficult, if not impossible, for her to regain the level of proficiency required by the stage. But if she really wanted to do it, she would. And her father was bound and determined to give her the chance. Together they would share the dream and possibly the reality of a miraculous comeback.

In the basement, Louis and Bernard Augenstein made final preparations for the transplant, which would take place the very next morning. The equipment they had installed was the best money could buy, and it gave both brothers a pleasureful feeling to think that ultimately they would own it, according to their arrangement with Andrew Blake. Their operating microscope alone cost better than a hundred thousand dollars. It had twin binocular viewing heads; a hookup for color television which might be used sometime in the future; foot controls for zooming, changing focus, or adjusting magnification; and a through-the-lens lighting system so the surgeon's hands would not cast any shadows on the operating site. Specialized accessories included needles, clamps, scissors, irrigation cannulas, and forceps scaled down to Lilliputian dimensions; and sutures fine as spiders' silk, yet strong enough to withstand surgical tension. There was also a special microsurgical chair that was designed to brace and support a surgeon's entire body, making it easier for him to accomplish infinitesimally precise tasks with only his fingers manipulating the tiny instruments during the long hours of painstakingly complex operating procedures.

Louis and Bernard had rehearsed with this equipment over the past several weeks, honing their skills to an optimum level of teamwork, efficiency, and accuracy. Three days ago, for practice, they had performed a successful arterial bypass on a laboratory rat. Their instruments were capable of rejoining blood vessels as small as four-hundredths of an inch in diameter—about the size of a pinhead. When joining vessels so gossamer in texture, they had found that the most demanding aspect was maintaining the patency, or opening, of the connection. It was like connecting two pieces of tubing, each as tiny and fragile as a strand of spider web. Yet, the ends had to be lined up so the openings met perfectly, under the microscope. Then a dozen or more precise stitches had to be applied neatly around a minuscule circumference, and the tension had to be sufficient to prevent leakage, but not so tight that the tubes would pinch, tear, or bunch up.

The professional skills involved, especially when they brought off a success, gave the two brothers a deep sense of satisfaction and pride. Just being able to do such work took an extra measure of physical stamina and mental alertness over and above what was normally required in the operating room. Louis and Bernard knew that many experienced surgeons who swore that they had rock-steady hands couldn't begin to hold a microscalpel or microscissors steady enough under a forty-power microscope which transformed the finesse of the real world into spastic clumsiness under the scrutiny of tremendous magnification. When putting the stitches in the artery of the laboratory rat they had experimented on, for example, Bernard's and Louis' hands never moved through more than a one-eighth-inch arc. They did all the blood vessel work with their arms and hands braced solidly on a table, using only minute finger movements to open, close, and reposition their instruments.

Tonight they would get a good night's sleep and refrain from consuming alcohol, caffeine, and nicotine. Come morning their nerves had to be perfectly steady, for all their skills would be called into play in order to give Tiffany Blake a new leg.

Waiting for his late-afternoon class to arrive, Nicolai Artov stood at one of the front windows of his ballet studio, looking down into the street. The class was for youngsters aged six to twelve, and although Nicolai normally enjoyed teaching them, today he wasn't at all looking forward to it. His mind was on the company rehearsal of *Giselle* scheduled for this evening. It was bound to be a disaster. In fact, there was almost no sense going through with it.

Drained of his usual resiliency, Nicolai Artov was just about ready to give in to despair. Ever since arriving in America, he had worked terribly hard to build his ballet company, but in a span of a few short months it was on the verge of being ruined—by bad luck.

First he had lost Tiffany, after spotting her innate ability and cultivating it since she was in grammar school. And now his two principal female dancers were not showing up for rehearsal. By coincidence, both Adrienne Mallory and Julia Valenti were suffering from influenza.

Nicolai knew that Adrienne and Julia probably caught the germs from each other, by competing too strenuously, and being run down. He blamed himself for putting too much pressure on them.

He couldn't begin to guess how long they would be confined to bed—maybe a week or more. How could *Giselle* open in Heinz Hall as slated? If it didn't, the advance ticket sales and the refunds would be a mess.

It was too late to teach the lead role to another dancer from the Artov Company, and besides, nobody else was capable of doing something so demanding. The only other choice would be to bring somebody in, maybe from Atlanta or New York. But Nicolai didn't want to do that; bringing in stars from elsewhere would result in a good performance, but it wouldn't enhance the prestige of his own company. If either Adrienne or Julia couldn't be back to rehearsals within the week, he would have to take out a costly series of newspaper ads, canceling the show.

He was just about to turn away from the window when he saw Bryan Sinclair's station wagon pull in by the curb across the street. This was a surprise, since Julia had said that Bryan would be out of town for a week, doing some filming in Vermont. Nicolai's first reaction was a rush of fear that Julia's condition had worsened, causing Bryan to come back. He expected Bryan to get out of the station wagon and come into the studio—but Bryan merely pulled into a stream of light traffic and kept going. Nicolai tried to open the window in time to call out, but the seldom-used lock was hard to turn, and by the time it broke loose, Bryan was gone. Nicolai turned around angrily and yelled at the little girls running around the studio in their street shoes, streaking the hardwood floor that he had laid with his own hands.

Bryan was retracing the probable route taken by Adrienne and Julia on their way from Nicolai's ballet studio to the Blake home. Smoking a cigarette from a fresh pack he had just bought, he drove slowly, looking all around, not knowing exactly what he was looking for. He felt a bit silly and more than a bit helpless, although the cops would undoubtedly have done exactly this if they were working on the case. He couldn't imagine how they would know what to look for any more than he did. If a clue were spotted, it would have to be by sheer luck.

The ballet studio was in a high-crime neighborhood to begin with. If Adrienne had parked her car on any of the lonely and quiet side streets, she and Julia could've gotten jumped right there, even in broad daylight. Rapes and muggings were common around here. Bryan couldn't help thinking of how he had often warned Julia to always stay on the main street. Another thing about the studio, which occupied the floor above a bakery, was that the front windows had no curtains, so that from the street you could look straight in at the dancers. It was a perfect setup for a potential rapist to get his sights set on a particular girl, while working out a strategy for attacking her. Bryan had even told Nicolai that he ought to get curtains for those windows, but Nicolai always had something more important to buy for the company.

When he had stopped in front of the ballet studio, Bryan had considered going up and talking to Nicolai Artov and telling him the truth about what had happened to Adrienne and Julia. The ballet instructor might have noticed any suspicious characters hanging around—he kept valuable costumes and props upstairs and was always afraid of being burglarized. Bryan trusted Nicolai personally but decided not to open up to him without thinking it over a little more and discussing it with Julia's grandfather.

Making snap decisions could be dangerous. Bryan hadn't had much sleep over the past thirty-six hours; he was physically and emotionally depleted. His thoughts were disorganized. He had no real plan of action. Now that he had set out to do something on his own, what could he hope to accomplish at best? His only answer, unrealistic as it might be, was that if he could somehow find out who the kidnappers were, he could let them know that he knew, so they wouldn't kill Adrienne and Julia to protect their identities.

One irony that he couldn't forget was his screenplay, *Beautiful Victims*, in which young ballerinas were terrorized and assaulted. The parallel was creepy. In his script there was a detective who questioned people to try to find out if they had seen anybody strange hanging around the ballet studio, or had noticed anything suspicious at the times the crimes were committed. The police would assuredly ask such questions in real life, but Bryan couldn't think of any way to ask them on his own without making the situation more risky. The only people he would dare talk to would be Nicolai Artov and Andrew Blake. This didn't give him much to go on, but despite his feelings of frustration and uselessness he still knew that he had to be out doing something; he couldn't just stick around waiting for the worst to happen or not happen.

He lit another cigarette as he left the area of rundown houses and shops and boarded-up storefronts and got on Bigelow Boulevard, heading for the Liberty Tunnels. This was the fast crosstown route that avoided the business section. Adrienne and Julia would probably have taken it. Bryan drove at the speed limit here since it was an unlikely place for an abduction. Coming out of the Liberty Tunnels, he headed south and took the turnoff toward the Marlboro Park neighborhood, where the Blakes lived.

Now he was on a two-lane blacktop that wound through a wooded section with few houses. He drove more slowly and resumed his close scrutiny of his surroundings. Even though he spotted nothing significant, he felt keyed up just traveling over the same ground that Julia and Adrienne must have been on. It was the same feeling that he had when he'd gone to the street where he had lost a wallet some time ago, hoping it would be there but knowing it wouldn't.

Bryan thought over the route from the ballet studio to where he was now, trying to imagine how the kidnapping may have been pulled off. It still seemed to him that the easiest way would've been to hit the two women before they had a chance to get in Adrienne's car, but if it had been parked on the main street, this tactic would've taken a lot of nerve. The cops, of course, could easily solve the question of where the car had been parked, merely by interrogating people from the ballet company, but Bryan didn't have that luxury; instead, he had to try to reason things out.

Once Adrienne and Julia were on the road, some ruse would have had to have been used to make them stop—force or trick them out of the car and take them prisoner. The likeliest place for this scenario had to be somewhere along the back road Bryan was presently on. Would the railroad tracks have caused Adrienne to slow down enough for somebody to try something? Perhaps. But it seemed so preposterous, like a highwayman stopping a stagecoach. Some more clever plan would have been needed—unless the kidnappers had been tailing Adrienne for some time, possibly weeks, waiting for exactly the right circumstances.

What had they done with her car? The police would have been able to put on an all-out search for the red Fiat. The kidnappers would have had to either ditch it or take it with them. Considering this, Bryan again mentally went over the route he had traveled, trying to recall any spot where the car might have been dumped.

Coming down the hill to the railroad crossing, he remembered the biking and jogging trail that led through the woods. A car could be driven back in there and hidden. On impulse, Bryan pulled his station wagon off the road onto the beginning of the trail, turned the engine off, and got out. He realized what a pretty day it was. The sun was shining and there were buds on the trees, but the peace and beauty of his surroundings mocked rather than comforted him. He started walking, looking for the red Fiat. Dead leaves from the retreating winter crunched under his feet.

He passed four or five joggers, several of whom gave him long, careful glances because he was obviously not a runner. He ignored them and kept peering right and left into the budding branches. When he came to a cul-de-sac, he walked into it and back out, finding nothing. It took about half an hour for the trail to circle around to where he started, and all he had to show for it was the exercise.

He got into the station wagon and sat behind the wheel, thinking. The Blakes lived across the tracks and up the next hill, and it didn't seem that the kidnapping could have taken place that close to their house. Blake Enterprises, Inc., was up the hill a couple of miles past the house and near the intersection of another main highway. Bryan looked at his watch. Four o'clock. Andrew Blake would probably be at his office, and he would be able to answer the question of whether or not Adrienne and Julia ever arrived for their visit with Tiffany. If they had, then the kidnapping could have happened when Adrienne was driving Julia home, and Bryan would have that route to check over. He was beginning to feel his limitations. He could nose around as long as he didn't stir up a fuss. That was the disadvantage of listening to Jim Mallory about not going to the police.

Blake Enterprises, Inc., was a low stucco building set back off the road in a fenced-in area with a gravel parking lot. The gate to the cyclone fence was open, and Bryan drove in and parked in one of the few remaining spaces. The lot was big enough to hold about twenty cars, most of them belonging to Blake's employees who managed the operation of the Hot Dog Heaven chain and related businesses.

In the reception area, Bryan discovered from Mrs. Simms that Andrew Blake was in, although she didn't seem too willing to divulge the information. "Please tell Mr. Blake that I'd like to speak with him," Bryan said.

Annoyed, the plump secretary pursed her lips as she looked up from a stack of papers on her desk. "Do you have an appointment?" she asked petulantly. "Because he got a late start on some things he had to do today, and he told me he doesn't want to be disturbed."

Bryan had never liked the way Blake's secretary treated him. She knew him well enough to act friendlier, since he had been in and out of the place many times during the production of the Hot Dog Heaven commercials. But he supposed that she never took him seriously because of the casual way he dressed, and also because, to her way of thinking, making films couldn't possibly be as serious an operation as making wieners.

Bryan glanced quickly around the reception area to make sure he and Mrs. Simms were alone. Then he said, "He'll want to be disturbed for this. Tell him I have reason to believe his daughter may be in danger."

It was an indiscretion, but Bryan didn't care. Mrs. Simms raised her eyebrows and her mouth opened. Flustered, as he intended her to be, she buzzed her boss on the intercom and in a low, quavery voice relayed the message. Then, looking at Bryan disapprovingly, as if she now realized he must be pulling some kind of stupid stunt, she made her eyes go in the direction of Blake's office.

"I know where it is," said Bryan, heading down the corridor.

Blake opened the door and poked his head out, and Bryan was shocked. The man was a grotesque parody of his former self. His skin was almost yellow and he had lost so much weight that he looked like a grinning skull. His shirt collar was way too big for him, and the corners of his eyes were startlingly red. "Hello, Bryan," he said. "Come in. Have a cigar." He followed Bryan in and shut the door.

The filmmaker saw the box of good, expensive cigars on Blake's large mahogany desk and took one.

"How could Tiffany be in worse trouble than she already is?" Blake asked, getting right to the point and not bothering to disguise his skepticism.

"She *could* be in danger," Bryan said, stalling. He sat in a leather chair facing the desk and took his time getting his cigar lit. "First I'd like to ask that anything we discuss not be repeated outside this office. Tiffany may not be in any immediate danger, but two of her friends definitely are."

"What friends?" Blake asked, sitting down. "And how could it affect Tiffany?"

"Do I have your word," said Bryan, "that what I tell you won't go any further?"

"Yes. Certainly."

Bryan waited a long moment before taking the plunge. His instinct was that a man of Blake's status in the community could certainly be trusted to keep a confidence pertaining to a life-and-death matter. "Adrienne Mallory and Julia Valenti have been kidnapped and are being held for a large ransom. It seems that they must have been abducted on their way to your house to visit Tiffany. I don't have to tell you my feelings about Julia. I want to find her, Mr. Blake, before it's too late to save her. Kidnappers seldom return their victims alive."

After thinking a moment, Blake said, "Bryan, you have my sympathy and best wishes, I assure you. But I still fail to see what any of this has got to do with my daughter."

Of course, Bryan's hint of possible danger to Tiffany was only a ruse to get him in to see Blake. He didn't want to admit this, so he said hesitantly, "If someone's making a career out of snatching young women affiliated with the Artov Ballet Company, don't you think Tiffany could eventually become a prime target—especially considering the amount of ransom you could afford to pay?"

Blake grimaced. "Maybe. But she's no longer affiliated. And Jim Mallory has money, too. I'm afraid you're shook up and getting carried away, Bryan. Have you told the police what's happened?"

"No. We've decided not to. We don't want to give

the kidnappers an excuse to do something drastic. That's why I'm asking you not to tell anyone, either—not even Tiffany."

"But I'd have to tell her if she was truly in danger," said Blake. He used the fingertips of both hands to massage the bridge of his nose, as if he had a headache; even his hands were bony and yellow. "In any case," he added, "I'll keep a close eye out for my daughter's safety, although I see no reason to expect a chain of kidnappings based on what's happened to Adrienne and Julia. I won't alarm her by telling her what you've told me. And I won't tell anyone else, either."

"Mr. Blake, when Adrienne and Julia failed to show up at your place—I gather that they did fail to show—why didn't you check on them?"

Bryan had tried to ask the question innocuously, but it still hit Blake the wrong way, and he replied sarcastically, "I figured they had changed their minds. I've noticed that many of my daughter's so-called friends don't come around so often anymore, including Nicolai Artov and the girls in the company. Apparently they don't enjoy being around a cripple."

Snuffing his cigar out in an ashtray, Bryan got up to leave. "I'm sorry that you feel that way, Mr. Blake. I happen to know that Julia cares very much about Tiffany and feels sorry for her. So do most of the other girls. Allowing yourself to become needlessly bitter can't do your daughter any good."

Blake did not reply, merely stared from behind his desk. Bryan left hurriedly, shutting the office door. He knew that so far he had gotten nowhere; he had, in fact, even lost ground by letting Andrew Blake know about the kidnapping. How much was it really worth to find out for sure that Julia and Adrienne had never arrived at Blake's house? Now that he knew, what could he do with the information?

In the parking lot he glanced at his wristwatch before getting into his station wagon. Almost five o'clock of Julia's second day of captivity, and he didn't even know if she was alive or dead. He hoped that his urge to snoop around was somehow a correct instinct.

What to do next?

Earlier in the afternoon Bryan had remembered that there was a .38 revolver down at the film studio. A couple of years ago he had used it as a prop in a film about crime prevention produced for the police academy. It was registered in his name. The more he thought about it, the more it seemed that he ought to carry it with him if he was going to continue sneaking around. While at the studio, he could check the telephone-answering machine in case there was word from Paul, or any messages from clients. He doubted that the kidnappers would try to get in touch with him, although it had crossed his mind.

When he finally found the gun buried at the bottom of his file cabinet, it looked bigger and uglier than he had remembered. He loaded it and put it in a film can to carry it out of the building. Then he played back the tape on the answering machine.

There was a message from Paul, saying that the filming today had gone fine and they had even finished a bit early. Client is happy. Hope you're feeling better. Click.

Then there was a message from the manager of the film lab in Cleveland, requesting a return call on a problem with the Roth Auto print, but Bryan decided to let this go till tomorrow since it was past business hours.

Then there was a message from Dominic Valenti that sent Bryan's adrenaline racing: "Please calla me as-a soon as-a you can."

Bryan dialed the Valentis' number and the old man

answered and immediately blurted that there had been word from the kidnappers. "Mista Mallory is inna my livin' room now. He's mad like-a a hornet and I try to getta him calm down. I made mistake to tella him you are gonna talk with Andrew Blake. He screams at me we no canna trust Blake to keepa his mouth shut. He smash down the phone and drive over here. Theresa gives him coffee now with anisette to make-a him relax. Someone has to do whatta the kidnappers say, deliver the payoff money, and I t'ink it shoulda be you. Mista Mallory has too hotta head. He tella me that when you talka to Blake, or anyone else, it's same as takin' his daughter's life inna our own hands. Come over here, Bryan, please. Right away."

Bryan let out a deep breath. "I'll be there in ten minutes," he said. On the way down in the elevator with the revolver in a film can under his arm, he tried with little success to formulate what he would say to Jim Mallory.

21 ❦

RUSH-HOUR TRAFFIC HAD DISSIPATED BY NOW, SO IT WAS A fast, easy drive for Bryan to Dominic Valenti's modest two-story home. He parked in front, behind Jim Mallory's silver Mark V, which he recognized. A group of surly-looking teen-aged boys was standing around gawking at the car and arguing over "how much bread it would take to own such a righteous piece of machinery." If it was still parked there after dark, Bryan thought, they would probably try to steal the hubcaps. A couple of the boys gave him some insolent stares as he threaded his way past them and went up onto the porch.

He knocked and then entered and Jim Mallory immediately jumped to his feet. He had been sitting in Dominic's leather chair. "What's the big idea, Bryan?"

Mallory challenged. "Letting this thing out of the bag to every Tom, Dick, and Harry! You want to get Adrienne and Julia *killed?*"

"I spoke to Andrew Blake and no one else," Bryan defended. "I think he's intelligent enough to be discreet. If he wasn't, he wouldn't be such a successful businessman."

"What makes you think *he* cares about Adrienne and Julia?" Mallory shot back. "Maybe he likes seeing somebody else get hurt, besides his *own* daughter. He never cared for Adrienne, anyway, because she was too much competition for Tiffany."

"And Julia, too," said Bryan, meaning that Julia was also competition. But Mallory took it the other way.

"See?" he pounced. "He never liked Julia, either. So why did you tell him what's going on?" He glowered at Bryan, but Bryan didn't answer him. Instead, he said, "Theresa, may I please have some coffee?"

The old lady, who had been standing in the kitchen doorway, turned around and Bryan followed her past Mallory and over to the stove, where she poured him a cup of black coffee. It was steaming-hot and he blew on it, giving Mallory time to calm down. When Bryan went back into the living room, Dominic was standing by the television, his hands behind his back, and Mallory was once more sitting in the leather chair. He was still angry. He had on a white shirt which matched his shoes, and red trousers which clashed with the red in his face. "You people don't have any sense of responsibility," he said. "I'm making the money drop on my own."

"You may need help," Bryan pointed out matter-of-factly.

"Why?"

"They may jump you and then kill you once the delivery is made."

This was something Mallory hadn't considered. Mulling it over, his attitude toned down a little. Finally, he asked, still maintaining a touch of defiance, "What do you suggest?"

Bryan sipped his coffee before answering. He wanted to sound reasonable and practical, rather than adventuresome and foolhardy. "I'll go along with you, hiding in the back of the car. I'll bring along a pistol. I have a .38 revolver that we used once in a film. It's in a film can in my car. Somebody should back you up in a thing like this. You ought to have some protection that the kidnappers don't know about."

"You'll get trigger-happy."

"No, I won't. Listen, Mallory, I want Julia and Adrienne alive as much as you do. But it's foolish not to take steps to protect ourselves, and to have an ace in the hole in case we have to rescue the girls."

For a time, Mallory sat there shaking his head, drumming his fingertips, and grimacing. "Okay," he agreed reluctantly. "I suppose it makes sense, as long as you control yourself and don't do anything rash."

"All right," said Bryan. "We understand each other. Now, how is the money drop supposed to work?"

"I don't know yet," said Mallory. "They told me to stay home tomorrow. I'm to expect a phone call at ten in the morning. They'll give me the instructions then about making the payoff. I already have the money for them—two hundred thousand dollars in unmarked fives, tens, and twenties. I'm not about to pull any funny business. It's going to them exactly the way they want it."

"Hmm," Bryan said, exhaling cigarette smoke. "There's another good reason for me to be with you. Suppose one of the kidnappers decides to go against his partners? He could waylay you and take all the money

202

for himself. You wouldn't be able to make the payoff, and Adrienne and Julia would be in deep trouble."

"What do you think they're in now?" snapped Mallory.

Bryan let the remark pass. He tapped cigarette ash into the ashtray he was holding on his knee. "Do you think I ought to sleep at your house tonight?" he asked Mallory.

"I don't follow you," Mallory responded. He shot Bryan a look that said: *Okay, let's hear some more of your flea-brained reasoning.*

"They might have somebody watching you tomorrow all the way," Bryan said. "Your house might even be staked out right now. If so, they'll see me arrive. But if you pull into the garage, tomorrow morning I can hide in the back seat of the car. They'll think you're leaving alone."

"I'm not sure all this cloak-and-dagger stuff is necessary," Mallory complained. He ran his thick, stubby fingers through his hair, disheveling it. "Okay, okay," he agreed reluctantly, not wanting to have himself to blame if he turned an option down and it resulted in harm to his daughter.

"Betta be careful, Bryan," Dominic said, his voice husky.

"I don't see how you can hide in the car," Mallory grumbled. "They'll spot you. You can't get down low enough between the seats." He pinched the bridge of his nose as if the unworkability of the idea gave him a headache.

"Cover uppa with blanket?" Dominic volunteered, but nobody responded. Bryan was trying to think of something before Mallory backed out. The blanket idea sounded pretty lame.

"How about the trunk?" Mallory said, perking up suddenly and shooting Bryan a probing look. "I have the lid release inside the car. If I get in trouble, I pull the release and you pop out with the gun."

"And if you don't pull it, I stay safely squared away," Bryan said. "I won't be able to 'meddle'—as you put it—unless you want me to."

"I hadn't thought of it that way," Mallory said, lying. Actually, he liked the advantage of having Bryan under his control. He pushed for it, saying, "The trunk may be a little hot, but you'll have plenty of room if I remove my golf bags. It can't be that hard to hide in a car trunk. Kids do it to sneak into drive-ins."

"But they don't get into the trunk till they're pretty close to the theater," Bryan pointed out.

"What's that got to do with it?"

"I don't know for how many miles I'll be locked up," Bryan said. He was going to say more, but he decided to let it drop. He would let Mallory have his way, for the sake of the opportunity to help Julia. But if Mallory were killed or incapacitated before he could pull the trunk-lid release, then what? It could be weeks before Bryan was found starved, suffocated, or dehydrated to death inside the car trunk. Just as he was considering this, to his surprise Mallory came up with an alternative.

"Okay, how's this? I've got a camper. You can hide in the back and nobody'll see you."

"Perfect," said Bryan, "so long as they don't specify which vehicle you're to drive."

Mallory clearly hadn't thought of this. He scratched his head. "For Christ's sake," he muttered, "if they were that smart, they'd be out making a decent living."

It might have been a funny comment, under different circumstances.

Julia was lying on a hospital bed in a locked and windowless room. Her wrists and ankles were shackled to the bed rungs; she couldn't move or turn over, but had to keep lying on her back. Her eyes were still taped tightly shut. She could feel and hear the air circulating through a vent in the ceiling. Her gag had been removed, so she knew that the kidnappers did not mind if she yelled; nobody must be around to help. Still she felt like losing her head and screaming her lungs out, but something told her it would only get her a beating and a reapplication of the gag.

She had been transported to this place in the van that left the warehouse. Since being put here, she had had no further contact with Sammy or Big Tony. This made her feel a little safer. She wished she knew what had happened to Adrienne. Trying to keep up hope and not expect the worst, she presumed that her friend was being kept prisoner in some other room. Probably a room similar to this one, deathly quiet except for the drone of air through a vent and the sounds of a door locking or unlocking whenever somebody came in or out.

One reason for hope was that her captors were making a sustained effort to keep her alive. Twice today she heard a key turning in the locked door, and a woman entered, said "Good afternoon" in a low, shockingly pleasant voice, then sat down on the edge of her bed and spoon-fed her: cereal the first time, stew the next. It was difficult swallowing, lying flat on her back. The woman who was feeding her became impatient with it midway through the first meal and unshackled Julia's legs after making her promise not to kick. It was a blessing to stretch and get some proper circulation back. She could even slide the wrist shackles up the verticle bed rungs high enough to enable her to sit up and eat.

When the feeding was done, the woman asked her if she had to go to the bathroom. She said that she did. "I will unshackle one wrist," the woman said, "and bring you a bedpan. If you give me any trouble at all, I will never again loosen any of the shackles and you will lie there in your own excrement."

After the embarrassment of the procedure with the bedpan, Julia tried talking to the woman, but she would not answer her.

Sometime after the stew was fed to her, she again heard the key turning in the lock, but this time a man joined her female captor. They both said good evening. Julia did not answer. The woman spoke soothingly to her about what she was going to do, as she stuck a thermometer in her mouth and took her blood pressure. The man said very little. He handled Julia carefully, with a practiced kind of tenderness, although when he pushed her skirt up, she was badly scared. But all he did was feel and massage her legs, particularly the left one. If she had to guess, she'd say he could have been testing the muscle tone, possibly taking some kind of measurements. Something ice cold touched her bare skin, an instrument of some sort, probably made of metal, and then she heard scratching sounds, like a pencil writing on a pad of paper.

"She'll do just fine," the man said at one point. "But so will the other one." And then he and the woman went out, turning the key in the door.

But at least the man had brought good news. Adrienne must still be alive; she had to be the "other one" he referred to.

When the man first examined her leg, Julia had been surprised, but perhaps he had just been intrigued by the muscle tone and development produced by years of ballet dancing. A dancer's legs with their unusual musculature and definition might be a curiosity to someone not used to seeing them. Some people even thought they were over-developed instead of nice looking—something Julia had often worried about.

Somehow that explanation did not suffice.

What reason could there be for the measurements, and the taking of temperature and blood pressure?

The man and woman seemed like a doctor and a nurse. They had that aura, that sort of rapport. They had never once mentioned ransom money, although Sammy and Big Tony had done so numerous times.

Julia had tried to believe that she was safer in this new place. Now she began to feel a deep fear. What could the man and woman be planning to do? What was it that she and Adrienne would do "just fine" for?

Although she could conceive of no logical answer, the mere speculation sent chills up her spine. Adrenaline shot through her, filling her with unbearable high-strung tension; yet, she couldn't move—she was shackled to the bed. She tried to calm herself down. At an atavistic level, the memory of the man's probing and measuring made her feel like a human guinea pig. He had handled her with a scientific detachment and skill, and whether she wanted to be handled had not mattered to him.

Afraid of being beaten, she had not protested, except to gasp at his very first touch. Then she had been so relieved to find that she was not going to be raped. Shackled and blindfolded, with no way to escape, Julia now began to experience a terror of something nameless and formless—something worse than rape. The dread of the unknown consumed her, sapping her energy and numbing her brain. Finally, it sucked her down into a tortured sleep.

She came awake, perspiring, with a jolt that hurt her wrists as she yanked against her shackles. Parts of her body were cramped and she gingerly tried to change position to relieve the physical discomfort while she fought off the effects of intertwining nightmares. Sleep had left her more tired and tormented than before.

She tried to picture the steps she had been rehearsing for *Giselle,* but they wouldn't come to mind. She couldn't focus on them, couldn't conjure them up, even though she wanted desperately to think about something pleasant, to chase away the terror. Shackled to a sweat-dampened mattress in the darkness, her former life, her hopes and desires, seemed intangible, illusory, unreal.

The plans and preparations she and Bryan had made for their wedding, their future life together, seemed remote and unattainable. She couldn't imagine being married to him and living as man and wife, doing the everyday things that married people do. This scared her badly; maybe she wasn't going to be set free.

It gave her little solace to recall that she hadn't been able to imagine marriage before, either. At the time she had thought it was because she was too used to being single; she couldn't intuitively feel what married life would be like. Now she worried that maybe all along some deep part of her had known it was never to be.

22 ❧

IT WAS DARK OUT AND THE STREETLAMPS WERE ON BY THE time Bryan Sinclair and Jim Mallory left Dominic Valenti's house. Coming down off the porch, Bryan noticed that the teen-aged boys weren't loafing on the sidewalk and the hubcaps were still on the Mark V. He jumped into his station wagon and followed Mallory out to his home in an expensive suburban area north of the city.

On the way, Bryan anxiously checked his rearview mirror for a tail, but every time he thought he had a suspect, the car eventually dropped off. By the time the silver Mark V led the way into Mallory's neighborhood, it and the station wagon were the only two vehicles on the access road.

But that didn't mean that the house wasn't being watched. As Bryan pulled into the driveway, he realized that the wooded hillside across the way was a good place for someone to be hiding. The idea of a spy skulking around up there in the woods at night seemed preposterous, but then every aspect of this whole business seemed that way, even though the danger to Julia and Adrienne was real.

Mallory used his automatic garage-door opener and pulled the silver Mark V into the four-car garage. Carrying his film can with the loaded revolver in it, Bryan entered the garage, forcing himself not to look around suspiciously at the hillside. He saw the camper that he would possibly hide in tomorrow. It was a red and black Chevy Blazer. The garage door shut and Bryan followed Mallory into the main part of the house.

He had been here once before for a party that Adrienne threw, so he wasn't surprised by the elaborate layout. The family room alone probably cost more than the entire three-bedroom home he had shared with his parents and younger brother in Philadelphia.

"Let's go up to the kitchen," Mallory said. "Smells like the wife's up there making coffee." Here in his own abode, he seemed more relaxed and under control, and he led the way up the shag-carpeted stairs, taking the steps in a stride that was almost jaunty.

Sarah Mallory was not in the kitchen. But there was fresh coffee being made on the Mr. Coffee machine. Mallory got out cups and saucers while Bryan stood around wondering where to put the big shiny film can containing the loaded revolver. Finally, he just put it on a stool and sat down next to it at the breakfast counter.

Sarah Mallory made her appearance, wearing a frilly pale blue housecoat. She was a nice-looking woman, Bryan thought, and, though she must be awfully worried, she didn't look haggard and wasn't showing her age. The truth was, she had just taken a hot bath which had made her feel more alert, although it had done nothing to relieve her anxiety. "Sit down, Jim," she told her husband, and then poured coffee for him and Bryan and set out a small tray of cookies.

"Bryan wants to come along with me tomorrow," Jim Mallory said, then explained the plan they had arrived at. He didn't leave any details out and didn't prejudice the explanation by a skeptical tone of voice, but still Bryan had the feeling that he was looking for his wife to poke holes in it.

She listened intently, occasionally sipping coffee or taking a tiny bite of chocolate-chip cookie. "This is very brave of you, Bryan," she commented succinctly, making it clear that she approved, after she heard it all.

"You don't think it's too risky?" her husband prodded. Her objections, if she had any, could be his way out.

"I think it's a good idea for you to have someone backing you up," said Sarah. "That way you're not totally at the kidnappers' mercy—as long as they don't figure out what you're up to."

"How could they do that?" asked Bryan.

"Well, I don't know," Sarah replied. "They may be two steps ahead of us. They may already have figured out some way to guard against exactly what you're proposing."

"I don't see how," Bryan said after thinking it over.

"Humph!" Jim Mallory snorted. "You're too naïve, Bryan. You think you've got all the angles covered, but you don't think the way a criminal thinks. You're going up against people with God-knows-what on their consciences. They could probably commit murder without batting an eyelid. Sure, you'll have a gun—but so will they. Have you ever even fired a weapon?"

"At targets," Bryan said, aware of the inadequacy of his response.

"Hah!" Jim Mallory pounced. "These will be *human* targets. And they'll be shooting back at you!"

"Don't scare him more than he is already," Sarah interjected.

"I'm hoping it doesn't come to that," Bryan said, trying to sound calm and resigned and not foolish. "But if it does, I'll do whatever I can to protect you and me and help save Adrienne and Julia. I'm well aware of the fact that I may fail."

After a long moment of silence, Sarah Mallory said, "I still think we're doing the best we can, even though we're all frightened. And we deserve each other's sympathy and help. When you're ready, I'll show you to your room, Bryan. We probably all ought to make some attempt at getting a decent night's rest."

The room Bryan stayed in obviously once belonged to one of Mallory's sons. The room was maintained as if the son was still there, surrounded by mementos of his interests and activities through his growing-up years. A wornout baseball glove hung on a post of the bunk bed, with its bedspread of "masculine" plaid earth colors matching the window curtains. Photos on the walls portrayed the boy at various age levels from infancy on up. A composite of his college fraternity hung next to a large fraternity paddle on a leather thong. The bookcase was a personal history, filled with everything from Dr. Seuss to college physics. On top of a maple dresser was a glass case displaying a collection of expensive-looking toy automobiles. And hanging above the boy's desk in a corner, where Bryan deposited his film can containing the loaded revolver, was a precisely crafted model of a Piper Cub.

Crawling under the covers, Bryan felt like an interloper, out of place and out of time. Being surrounded with treasures of childhood wasn't a conducive environment for contending with the reality of why he was here. He probably wouldn't have been able to sleep well in this room, even if he had had nothing momentous on his mind. As it was, he kept worrying about Julia and what might happen on the following day. If all went well, the nightmare could be over. On the other hand. . . .

He tossed and turned, and managed to sleep for only a couple of fitful hours. In the first light of dawn, he lay awake staring at the dangling Piper Cub and the film can underneath. He waited till eight-thirty, which seemed to take an eternity; then he went to the bathroom and washed up, got dressed, and went downstairs to the phone. He called the lab in Cleveland to check on the trouble with the Roth Auto print. It seemed ironic that he had to concern himself, at a time like this, with a thirty-second strip of film about a man in a rabbit suit. The lab manager got on the line and said that the print had to be remade because the processing equipment had broken down in the middle of a run and all the shots were streaked. This presented a deadline problem which could be solved if the new print could be pulled right away and shipped directly to the client by air express. The lab manager promised to do his best, "provided we don't have another breakdown."

Jim Mallory came into the room during Bryan's telephone conversation and glowered at him till he hung up. "What are you doing?" Mallory demanded hotly. "Don't you realize the kidnappers might call?"

Bryan glanced at his watch. "Not till ten, you said. It's only nine now." Actually, it was ten minutes after.

"They could call early!" Mallory snapped. But he went to the phone himself and dialed his office and talked business for several minutes.

Bryan went into the kitchen, where Sarah was preparing breakfast. In a little while, they all sat down to scrambled eggs, toast, and coffee. They didn't talk much, but stayed on edge, waiting for the ringing of the phone. It was only nine-thirty when breakfast was finished.

Bryan would have liked to sip another cup of coffee to make the time pass, but to get away from Jim Mallory he went back upstairs to the room he had slept in. He made the bed; then finally wandered down to the family room, bringing along the gun in the metal can. He sat in a plush leather chair, the can in his lap, and leaned his head back. He kept his eyes closed for what he thought were long stretches, but every time he looked at his watch he would find that only three or four minutes had passed. Across from him was a telephone on the family room wall.

He jumped when it rang. Jim Mallory took the call upstairs in the middle of the second ring. For a while Bryan stayed put, listening to Mallory's voice in short sporadic bursts. Then he paced over to the phone on the wall and very carefully eased it off the hook, holding the hook down with his hand and letting it up slowly when he had the receiver to his ear.

Mallory was receiving instructions from somebody with a hoarse, muffled voice. "Drive to the abandoned Amoco station one mile past the intersection of Route 8 and Murray Road. Go straight there. Don't try anything fancy. Someone will be watching you at all times. When you get to the station, look on the floor of the phone booth. Under a small stone there will be a scrap of paper with further instructions. If you do everything right, and we get the money, we'll return to you *one girl only*. In about a week, when we've had time to make sure the currency is unmarked and we've gotten away clean, the second girl will be set free somewhere in the city."

"*Which* girl?" Mallory shouted, panicked.

The phone went dead.

Bryan replaced the receiver on its hook and went upstairs to the kitchen, where Jim Mallory, very upset, was explaining the situation to his wife. "They say they'll release only one girl today. When they check out the money and feel safe, then the other girl will be let go."

Sarah bit her lip, digesting these new facts.

"Don't you see what this means?" Mallory ranted. "Our daughter might not be released!" He glowered at Sarah as if it was somehow her fault.

"There's another possibility," Bryan interjected.

"Huh?" said Mallory, whirling around.

"Julia might be the one who doesn't get released."

The pointed suggestion that he had been thinking only of his daughter stopped Mallory short. He ran his fingers through his hair. His face was sweaty.

Sarah broke down crying and said, "We'll be lucky if we ever see *either* of the girls again." Her reaction startled Bryan, because it was the first time he had seen her lose her composure. She left the room, still sobbing.

"We've got no time to waste," Mallory barked gruffly. "We have got to do what we're told. The kidnappers gave explicit instructions. I'm to take the Mark Five, not the Blazer."

"I didn't hear them say that," said Bryan.

"Jesus Christ!" Mallory's eyes widened as he smacked the top of his forehead with the palm of his hand. "You mean to tell me you listened *in*? If they would've heard you, they would've thought it was the police tapping the line!"

"I was careful," Bryan defended, wondering if Mallory was lying about having to take the Mark V. Locked in the trunk, he would be totally under Mallory's control. And in a toss-up situation, Mallory's decisions would favor Adrienne. Of course, he might not be lying; he could have been told to take the Mark V before Bryan got on the line.

Sarah, who had dried her tears, came back into the kitchen carrying a leather satchel which she handed over to her husband. Bryan presumed that it contained money. Two hundred thousand dollars.

Jim Mallory kissed his wife, then started down the stairs, lugging the satchel in a way that made it look heavy. Bryan followed, taking the revolver out of the film can as they passed through the family room. He breathed in deeply, trying to calm himself.

"Keep low going past the garage windows," Mallory cautioned gruffly. "I don't doubt that they've got somebody out there watching."

"What about the golf clubs?"

"I took them out last night." Mallory saw the look Bryan flashed him. "Just in case," he added defensively.

But Bryan's suspicion that Mallory had intended all along to lock him in the trunk of the Mark Five was now confirmed.

The trunk had a new-car smell mixed with the odor of the tar-like substance used for rustproofing. It was hot and stuffy. Bryan tried to curl up in such a way as to prevent his muscles from cramping, but he was not successful. He told himself that the first leg of the journey wouldn't be too hard to take—the defunct Amoco station with the message in the phone booth was only about twenty minutes from Mallory's house. Still, it seemed to take forever to get there, and Bryan felt every jolt and turn in the road—especially the potholes. Now that he was doing this, he felt silly. Maybe he should've stayed home and let Mallory handle it alone. But if there was even a slight chance of helping Julia in any way, he wanted to try, even at the risk of coming off like an ass. He didn't necessarily believe that either Adrienne or Julia would be released, even after the money drop was made. The paying of the ransom was no guarantee that they wouldn't be killed.

At last Bryan felt and heard the tires on gravel, and the car stopped. The door opened and Mallory got out. Presumably he was going into the phone booth. In a little while, he got back in the car and slammed the door. He pulled out of the gas station lot onto the smoother surface of the road.

Bryan soon lost all track of where the car might be. Two more times it came to a stop and Mallory got out, did something or other, then got back in and kept driving. Obviously, he was following a series of instructions—and the kidnappers must be watching him closely from secret places, making sure he complied perfectly at each stage and was not being tailed by the police. Mallory couldn't tell Bryan what was happening, either; he was afraid the kidnappers could see his lips move—in which case they might assume he was talking into a hidden microphone.

Each time the car stopped, Bryan listened for the sounds of the satchel full of money being hoisted out. But he didn't hear it until the third stop. Bryan heard the back of the driver's seat being pushed forward and Mallory's grunt when he picked up the satchel. Then came the sound of footsteps going away from the car—soft footsteps on unpaved ground. Probably someplace in the woods. Bryan waited, perspiring and nerve-wracked, listening for the chance to pick out the voice of Adrienne or Julia, whichever one had been released. But only Mallory came back to the car. Again he slammed the door and pulled out.

Losing his patience, Bryan called out, "For God's sake, what's happening?" He didn't expect any replay, and he got none. He should have known better than to sound off like that. Mallory wouldn't risk giving away the fact that someone was concealed in his car.

Mallory stepped on the gas and the Mark V picked up speed. Bryan could feel it bouncing over the road and swerving around curves. The money drop had obviously been made. Mallory must have received final instructions about where to find one of the girls. In his anxiousness, he was driving like a maniac, liable to get both himself and Bryan killed.

Bryan felt the jerk and pull of the brakes being forcefully applied and the car careening into a hard right turn, then bouncing over a stretch of rough, unpaved—possibly gravel—road. The bounces and jolts got worse, hurting Bryan's elbow, shoulder, and hip. Finally, the car squealed to a stop. The door opened and Mallory got out. He didn't bother closing the door behind him.

In the trunk, Bryan wondered what was happening. His fears for Julia and Adrienne mingled with relief that the wild ride was at an end.

Following the kidnappers' instructions, Mallory had driven to the site of an abandoned strip mine. In the middle of a totally denuded area, fifty feet in front of him on a mound of yellow clay, he could see Andrienne's car. At first this spurred him to walk faster, hoping his daughter was inside instead of the Valenti girl. But then some deep, inner, gut-wrenching fear took hold of him; he slowed down and almost timidly pulled open the door of the red Fiat.

When he saw what was inside, he emitted a loud,

ugly moan of animal despair and collapsed against the side of the car, his eyes bulged wide in horror and disbelief.

Adrienne was lying tied up and unconscious on the front seat. Her left leg had been amputated at the thigh.

23 ⋘

FROM A MEAT-PACKING PLANT OWNED BY BLAKE ENTERprises, Inc., Sammy Triglia phoned Andrew Blake and said, "Everything worked like a charm and we got the goods."

"No problems?" Blake asked.

"None. It went off like a charm." Sammy winked at Big Tony Fallon, who had just laid a package wrapped in brown plastic on a meat-cutting table.

"Is the cash in the safe?" Blake asked.

"Yeah, and the safe is locked," said Sammy Triglia. He had been tempted to split with the money, but now that temptation was removed; once the safe door was shut, only Andrew Blake could open it.

"I'll be out to pick it up," said Blake. "In the

meantime, follow through. There may be a bonus for you."

When he got off the line, Sammy Triglia went over to the meat-cutting table and watched Big Tony unwrapping the package they had brought with them. It was a girl's leg, in a plastic garbage bag. The blood drained from it, it was white and shriveled. "It looks like a chicken leg," said Big Tony, grinning.

Sammy didn't reply. He stared down at the leg, trying to pretend he wasn't queasy.

"Boss said to bury it with quicklime," said Big Tony. "But what we're gonna do is better."

"Yeah," Sammy managed to agree. His voice came out dry and husky, and Tony looked up at him and giggled. It pleased Big Tony to know that he wasn't as squeamish as his partner.

Alone in the processing plant, they disposed of the leg by stripping the meat from the bones, grinding the bones to powdered fertilizer, and feeding the meat into the machine which made wieners for Hot Dog Heaven.

In his study, over a full glass of gin on ice, Andrew Blake went over everything in his mind. Sammy Triglia and Tony Fallon had done a good job. He felt he could trust them to follow through, but at this point it hardly mattered. No matter what happened now, the most important part of their contribution had already been accomplished. Even if they were caught and ratted to the police, Tiffany already had her new leg. They might try blackmail at some future point, but Blake didn't think so—they were incriminated themselves. They were both ex-convicts who for the past year or so had worked at Blake's meat-packing plant. Nobody else would give them a job. He had hired them because he knew they wouldn't balk if he ever had need of men who would do something not exactly legal, although at the time he had nothing definite in mind. Now they had come in quite handy.

They had argued that the Mallory girl should be killed instead of released. But Blake didn't want to kill anyone unless he had to. And the police might be kept out of this for a while longer, on the dangling hope that Julia might be returned alive and in one piece. Adrienne, kept drugged or blindfolded from the time of her capture to the time of her release, would be able to tell nothing about her kidnappers or where they had kept her. She wouldn't even know why she had lost her leg. But the catty bitch would now know how Tiffany had felt lying in the hospital crippled.

Julia Valenti, still being held prisoner, was insurance; if something went wrong with the first transplant attempt, it would be tried again.

Disguising the purpose of the kidnapping by going through the rigmarole of ransom demands, threatening phone calls and so forth had served two purposes: to buy time for the transplant operation to be performed without fear of interruption by the police; and to produce a sizable chunk of extra cash to cover expenses, including the large payment to the Augensteins and to Paul Smith.

Kidnapping the two girls on their way to visit Tiffany was a clever part of the plan. If the police had been called in, Blake would have known it immediately, for they would have questioned him right away as to whether or not Adrienne and Julia ever arrived at his house. Since he wasn't questioned, except rather ineptly by Bryan Sinclair, Blake knew that his threats had worked to keep the Valenti and Mallory families quiet.

Blake assumed that Bryan Sinclair would probably try snooping around some more. He'd be more upset than ever once he saw what had happened to Adrienne. But Blake didn't really consider Bryan much of a threat. Sipping his gin, he told himself that it didn't really matter how much the young man poked around or what he found out.

The cops didn't even scare him. In the final analysis, he didn't care if he got caught. As long as the operation was successful, whatever happened to him was of secondary importance. He would cheerfully go to prison or give up his own life as long as it benefited Tiffany. She would be made whole again, because of him. At last she would know how much he loved her, and that he had done the most for her that a father could ever do.

24 ⚜

PUMPED FULL OF ADRENALINE AND SATURATED WITH
perspiration inside the car trunk, Bryan listened for a
long, heart-stopping moment, having heard Mallory's
moan. For all he knew, Mallory or one of the girls
might be dead. He might be abandoned and left to die.
"Mallory! Mallory!" he began shouting. "For God's
sake, let me out!" He kicked and thrashed inside the
trunk.

Walking in a daze, Jim Mallory finally came over and
got the keys out of the ignition and unlocked the trunk.
Bryan got out, woozy from breathing hot, oxygen-
depleted air, and looked around. A sick, blood-drained
expression on his face, Mallory's eyes flickered toward
Adrienne's car. Bryan lunged toward it as fast as he
could with his cramped, aching leg muscles.

When he saw what had happened to Adrienne, he was stunned. A feeling of horrified helplessness overwhelmed him as he realized the true depths of the danger Julia was in.

Jim Mallory was so shattered by what had been done to his daughter that Bryan had to bark orders at the man to get him to help transfer Adrienne to his car. Bryan drove to the hospital, while Mallory sat numb and gray-faced opposite him in the front seat. Now and then he glanced back at Adrienne, who was still unconscious, breathing deeply, the lower part of her covered by a raincoat of Mallory's which allowed her right foot and calf to stick out.

At the hospital, Bryan pulled into the emergency-room area and ran in to get help. A couple of white-suited attendants hustled into action, wheeling Adrienne through a door and down a corridor, with people gawking and the whole place in turmoil.

While waiting for a report on whatever emergency treatment was possible, Jim Mallory went to a pay phone and put in a call to his wife. Bryan overheard the conversation and was amazed at how poorly Mallory handled it. Instead of waiting to give out the details gently when he could talk to Sarah face to face, he told her everything, and he ended up panicking her. When he hung up the phone, he had a new worry: that his wife was now so frantic that she might wreck her car on the way to the hospital. "My God!" he said to Bryan. "I said all the wrong things, didn't I?"

Bryan abstained from a direct answer. He had other things on his mind. He asked Mallory to step outside so they could talk. In the parking lot outside the emergency room he lit a cigarette, his ninth or tenth one since loading Adrienne into the Mark V at the site of the abandoned strip mine. He offered a smoke to Mallory, who refused with a tired, jerky nod of his head.

"I need to know what you're going to do," Bryan said bluntly.

"What do you mean?" Mallory responded, too dazed to think clearly.

Bryan looked him in the eyes. "Well, Julia is still in danger. I'm hoping you won't go to the police. I can understand that you'd be anxious to catch whoever did this now and see that they get punished. But I'd like a chance to rescue Julia before they do something to her—if they haven't already."

"You're talking crazy, Bryan. The cops are going to find out about this. I can't simply keep my mouth shut. I'll have to tell them something."

"I don't want them jumping in on this," said Bryan. "It's pretty clear we're dealing with maniacs, and putting the cops on their tail will only make them crazier. At least Adrienne was returned alive. Julia may not be."

"The cops might stand a better chance of rescuing her than you do," Mallory countered.

"Maybe so," Bryan admitted. "But I'm asking you to give me the benefit of the doubt. Yesterday you were against calling in the police. Please, for a few more days, put Julia's well-being ahead of your urge for revenge."

Mallory turned away, his hands behind his back, his gaze going out to the edge of the lot or beyond, as if the rows of parked cars made fascinating scenery. It was a balmy spring day, the kind that mocks personal tragedy. After a long silence, Mallory said, "It's a lot to ask, Bryan."

"Just as a suggestion, you could tell the cops that Adrienne was the only one kidnapped—if it comes down to it, and you have to tell them anything."

"What kind of story can I give the hospital? Won't they report this?"

"Look, Mr. Mallory, the bottom line is, Julia's life is in danger. Surely that gives you the right to withhold information from anybody, including the police. In fact, it morally obligates you to do so."

"That's only your opinion," snapped Mallory. "But I'll think about it and talk it over with my wife. I won't make any decision until tomorrow."

"I'll phone you," said Bryan. "If Adrienne's up to it, I'd like to talk to her. She might know something that could help me find Julia."

"You're not going to be able to find her," Mallory said. "You're clutching at straws. You'd be better off preparing yourself for the worst. But I hope I'm wrong."

Leaving Mallory waiting alone for his wife, Bryan took a taxi to Dominic Valenti's house. Beside him on the seat of the cab, he had his revolver in a brown paper bag. He hated the thought of telling Dominic and Theresa that Julia had not been released. What had happened to Adrienne would fan their wildest fears. Bryan would try to convince them that it was better not to have Julia returned as yet, than to have her in the condition Adrienne was in.

Or were the kidnappers going to do worse to her?

Dominic and Theresa wept quietly when they heard the bad news. The old lady eventually went up to her bedroom to pray. Dominic sat in his leather recliner, looking more than ever like a broken old man, ten years of his life wrung out of him, along with his remaining hopes and expectations. The pathetic thing was that he had shaved and put on a fresh shirt and tie in the event of welcoming Julia back. He consented with the faintest nod of his head when Bryan said that he still didn't want to call in the police.

It was now late afternoon. Bryan phoned Andrew

Blake at his home, and Blake immediately asked how the kidnapping case was going.

"This morning we paid the ransom," Bryan said. "That's what I was calling about. We followed the kidnappers' instructions precisely. But things have taken a bad turn."

"How do you mean, Bryan?" Blake asked

"This thing has something to do with your daughter, Mr. Blake. Adrienne wasn't returned to us in one piece. Her left leg has been amputated at the thigh."

Through a long silence at the other end of the line, Bryan waited for Blake's reaction.

"I feel sorry for Adrienne," Andrew said, doing a credible job of feigning shock.

"What it tells me," Bryan went on, voicing his conjectures, "is that at least one of the kidnappers might be a fan of Tiffany's—a psychopath. If *she* can't dance again, he's going to make damned sure none of the other girls can, either. The money is probably less important to him than his perversion. Julia and Adrienne were Tiffany's top rivals. That doesn't strike me as a coincidence."

A chill shot through Blake as he held onto the phone. Too much of what Bryan was saying had hit home. Was it true, Andrew wondered, that deep inside himself he was out to harm the other girls as much as he wanted to help Tiffany? Would he be pleased to see them maimed even if she wasn't cured? Had his love for his daughter caused his mind to become unhinged?

No! He only wanted to help Tiffany, to preserve a great talent, no matter what the cost to himself. And the others, less talented, would have been maimed instead of Tiffany, if the world were more fair. On still another level, the morality of what he was doing didn't really concern Andrew Blake. He was blinded by the goal, the desire, to see his daughter whole again.

"Then you think the same thing might happen to Julia?" he heard himself asking Bryan Sinclair.

"Yes. If it hasn't already."

"I have a feeling she won't be harmed," Andrew said. And he really believed at this point that what Dr. Augenstein had done would work; the operation probably wouldn't have to be performed again.

"I wish I had your confidence," Bryan said. "But it's all I can do to keep my spirits up, Mr. Blake. Can't you give me any help? If you can just think of anyone who paid the wrong kind of attention to Tiffany . . ."

"If it's the work of a psychopath, he's certainly succeeded in remaining anonymous," Blake said. "I don't know anyone, even peripherally, whom I would suspect of such a hideous deed."

"A butcher!" Bryan said angrily. "An insane butcher!"

"Yes," Blake agreed, commiserating, before getting off the line.

25 ❀❀❀

ARTHUR SILVERA WAS ON THE COVER OF THE *Newsweek* Tiffany Blake was reading as she lay propped up in bed. This was the week of the ballet master's sixty-first birthday, and inside the magazine was a feature article about him, reciting his accomplishments of the past, and highlighting several promising young ballerinas whom he had recently given a chance at stardom with his New York National Ballet Company.

If things had gone differently, Tiffany might have been featured in the article, too. But her chance would come again, thanks to Dr. Augenstein! Reading and thinking about ballet was now an inspiration to her. It helped her build the necessary willpower to recover and get to the top once again.

A ballerina must learn to live with pain, and this training had been of much use to Tiffany in the ordeals she had faced over the past five months, since her accident. The pain-killing drugs could only do so much, and then it was up to the individual to refuse the pain its dominion and live through it. Live *with* it, more appropriately. You had to treat it as if it didn't exist.

As Tiffany studied the magazine article about dancers and dancing, she concentrated her psychic energy on the hopes for the future which had been restored to her by that most wonderful of persons, Dr. Louis Augenstein.

She was going to dance again! She truly believed it. And if she could make herself believe it, then it would come to pass.

This operation was different from the last one, the one that had left her with no hope. This time the pain and anguish she was going through would result in a whole and healthy body instead of a crippled one, unable to perform.

When Dr. Augenstein first told her he could transplant a limb from a young girl who was dying, it gave Tiffany chills and made her half-sick to even contemplate such a thing. But she fought down her qualms and agreed to the operation, because when all was said and done, she would rather die than not dance. She didn't really want to be a choreographer's assistant or a costume designer. She needed this new chance.

Dancing was Tiffany's life, the only thing that could ever give her a sense of accomplishment, importance, and worthiness. She had realized that incontrovertible fact over the long days and weeks of suffering when the train accident had apparently killed her dreams and she wanted to die along with them.

Now, through the pain, she nurtured the bright

knowledge that, thanks to this miraculous operation, she had been truly reborn. A glorious future stretched ahead of her.

In the basement operating room, Dr. Louis Augenstein told his brother, Bernard, the bad news. "The tissue cultures have confirmed our worst fears. Thymocites are present in the bloodstream. Rejection has begun, in spite of the serum. In a day or so we can expect gangrene, if we don't amputate."

Hearing it made Bernard sick. He stared in amazement at Louis, who could state such devastating information with such an outward calm.

"How can we tell Blake?" Bernard whispered. "He'll go crazy." Of course, he knew his brother would have some kind of answer. Louis had answers for everything. If you could go on believing in Louis, your world would never be shattered.

Louis answered confidently, as usual. 'We warned Blake to expect possible complications wit. .he first try. This shouldn't come as such a great shock to him. He may react badly at first, but we can get him calmed down. We can use the antibodies the patient s producing to refine our serum. The transplant should be successful with the second girl as donor."

"What if it isn't?"

"It *will be*, Bernard! Please try to remain objective and analytical. Otherwise, your effectiveness in the operating room will be impaired."

Perspiring, Bernard pushed his glasses up farther on his nose. He cleared his throat and swallowed dry saliva. "Louis," he said, his voice quavering, "Blake will probably tell those goons of his to kill us if the second attempt fails."

Louis remained unperturbed. "It won't fail, I tell

you. A slight adjustment of some sort is all that's necessary. Now, let's get started on an analysis of those new antibodies, and the antigens that produced them, as well."

"Another girl to be operated on," Bernard whined. "It's getting to me, Louis!"

"I regret these necessities as much as you do," Louis told his brother. "But millions have died already to put us on the verge of this breakthrough. If the girls knew what they were part of, they might willfully go ahead with it, as a noble sacrifice."

Then why don't you give them the opportunity to say yes or no? Bernard thought. But he stopped arguing. He began preparations for analyzing the antibodies and immersed himself in the task, feeling intimidated and quite sorry for himself. He also felt guilty about allowing Louis to talk him into doing their first operation, not with a cadaver or a terminally ill donor, but with a kidnapped girl. Evil had spawned evil, just as his father had predicted. The curse of the concentration camp was running its course, down through the decades.

Bernard was weak. He always ended up doing whatever his brother wanted. But underneath it all, he knew that Louis was as demented as any Nazi. He was just as ruthless in his quest for what he defined as scientific progress, the so-called "revolutionizing of modern medicine." The concept had infected Louis' mind, his very being. He was not his father's son any longer, but the spiritual son of Adolf Barkema, the madman of Treblinka.

In the small windowless room in the basement of the Blake mansion, Julia Valenti was still blindfolded and shackled to a bed. Since it was mid-evening now, the air conditioning was more efficient, and the room was too cold. Julia had goosebumps all over her flesh, but she was so heavily sedated that she continued to sleep.

Using a key that she took from the pocket of her nurse's uniform, Doris Augenstein unlocked the steel door to Julia's cell and stepped in to check on her. Doris shivered when the frigid air struck her in the face, and she moved quickly to the thermostat on the wall and lowered the setting.

Afraid that Julia might have caught a chill, the nurse took the sleeping girl's pulse and felt her forehead to make sure she wasn't running a fever. Then Doris administered a hypodermic injection to keep her patient unconscious so she wouldn't fight back when it was time to operate.

Before leaving the room and locking the door, the nurse pulled a woolen blanket over the oblivious young woman, who was shackled flat on her back on the white sheets of the hospital bed. The nurse knew that it was important for the patient to be kept healthy and in a passive condition for the second transplant attempt.

On his way back from Vermont, during the plane ride, Paul Smith wondered how everything was going. Either Adrienne or Julia must have been operated on by now. He hoped it was Adrienne. It would serve her right for thinking she could dump him. Now he wouldn't need her or her money ever again.

He didn't need Bryan Sinclair, either. Hadn't he just handled a major production all by himself, doing the camera work *and* the directing, and hadn't it come off beautifully?

Paul Smith Productions. It had a nice alliterative ring to it. Backed up by fifty thousand dollars to capitalize it, fifty-one percent of the stock to be held by Andrew Blake, and forty-nine percent by Paul Smith.

Hey, wait a minute! Why should Blake be the major shareholder?

Suddenly Paul realized that, knowing what he knew, he could have squeezed a lot harder for more money and a bigger piece of the company. It wasn't too late to do so, the papers weren't drawn up and signed yet.

Paul figured that he was contributing all the talent and the expertise. His efforts would make the enterprise fly. He was the one who knew how to make movies. So he should have a bigger slice of the pie.

He would make Andrew Blake see it his way, as soon as he got back to Pittsburgh.

26 ❦

ON THE MORNING FOLLOWING THE PAYMENT OF THE
ransom money, Bryan phoned the Mallorys to ask how
Adrienne was. Her brother James, the one who helped
run the construction business, answered the phone.
"My mother is at the hospital," he told Bryan. "She's
been there all night, and my father and I are about to
drive over there. Adrienne has been moved out of
intensive care into a private room. But she's not
allowed any visitors."

This last statement was obviously meant to discourage Bryan from going to see her. "How is she doing?"
he asked.

There was a long pause, as if the brother thought the
question foolish. Then: "If you mean mentally, we
don't really know. It took most of the night for the

drugs to wear off. But the toxicologist said she wasn't given anything that would do permanent harm. Whoever amputated her leg did it as skillfully as a surgeon, and whoever administered the drugs must've had training in anesthesiology. Of course, Adrienne is now aware that she has lost her leg, but she seems numb, in shock. An orthopedic surgeon is in charge of her case. We're going to talk with him some more this morning. He's already recommended a complete physical checkup for Adrienne, by an internist, and a psychiatric consultation."

"Well, I don't know what to say," said Bryan, "except to wish for the best, under the circumstances. May I speak with your father for a minute?"

Reluctantly, Mallory's son called him to the phone. He snatched up the receiver and barked angrily, "You can't talk to Adrienne, Bryan. She's in no condition for it. You'd only upset her worse."

"I wasn't even going to ask," Bryan said soothingly. "I only wanted to know if you're going to keep your word about not calling in the police."

For a few seconds there was no reply, only the sound of Mallory's breathing. Then: "I couldn't keep the police out of it, Bryan. I had to tell the people at the hospital *something,* so I told them Adrienne had been abducted and returned to us in the condition she's in. But I didn't fill in most of the details—I didn't even mention Julia."

Stunned, Bryan didn't respond; he merely held the phone, his fingers clenched white around it.

"I had to come up with a story that made sense," Mallory went on, defending himself. "I couldn't say she had had an accident—that was too obviously not the case. But I think I can keep the police from talking to her for a day or so, while she's under psychiatric care."

"Thanks," Bryan murmured. "I'd appreciate anything you could do."

"I'm going to ask the police not to leak the story to the newspapers," Mallory said. "I think they want it hush-hush, anyway. There's no reason to publicize it, and, in fact, it may put the kidnappers on their guard—make them harder to catch."

"You're right. It's best to keep it quiet," Bryan encouraged, with no real hope that the news wouldn't leak out. "I'd still like to talk to Adrienne as soon as you feel you can give your permission. She might know something that can help me."

"We'll see," said Mallory, making it clear that his daughter's interests came first.

When Bryan got off the line, he felt a greater urgency than ever about getting to Julia before something terrible happened to her. He could see Jim Mallory's point: How could he have kept his mouth shut without coming off like a crazy man, without seeming not to care sufficiently about what happened to his daughter? But still, there was no guarantee now that with the cops fumbling around, even with partial facts to work on, that the kidnappers wouldn't be alerted—and moved to do something drastic, out of sheer panic. Although, what could be more drastic than what they had already done?

At least, Bryan now felt a certain freedom about making his moves. He no longer had to take Jim Mallory's opinions into consideration. Any decisions he made from now on would affect only Julia, but they had better be right ones, for Julia's sake. If he had to get concurrence from her grandparents, or even if an emergency precluded it, he could pretty much assume that he and Dominic were on the same wavelength.

Last night had been another sleepless one for Bryan, as he lay awake agonizing over what had gone before, trying to think up some logical way to proceed. His ideas and choices were few. As far as he could see, he had to take it one step at a time, trusting to luck and gut reactions until, he hoped, something would click into place and the puzzle would begin to make more sense.

One thing he could do now was talk with Nicolai Artov. He trusted Nicolai. The only reason he hadn't talked to the ballet director before was because of Jim Mallory. Bryan knew that Dominic Valenti liked and respected Nicolai as much as he did. Nicolai was a person they both could confide in and know that he would keep silent. Also, it would only be fair to let Nicolai know what was happening because of the way it was threatening his company.

It was ten o'clock, according to Bryan's wristwatch. Paul Smith would probably be down at the film studio. He and his crew of freelancers should have returned from Vermont the night before. Dialing the office number, Bryan considered whether Paul could now be leveled with, too. He decided no, and felt guilty for deciding so. If he couldn't trust his business partner, what was he doing in partnership with him in the first place? On the other hand, business was different from personal relationships. You didn't need to trust someone down to the most minute personality detail in order to find some advantage to working with him. After all, hadn't Paul cheerfully taken over the handling of the air force film without a complaint?

The ringing of the office phone was stopped by the answering machine. So, Paul wasn't in. Perhaps he had canned the Vermont footage and was taking it to the Greyhound station. Or, he could be running some other errand. Bryan waited for the beep and left a message for his partner, saying that he had called to check in, and he'd be on the run but would call back later. Then he phoned Mr. Roth of the Roth Auto TV commercial and found that the finished print of the spot had arrived satisfactorily. Mr. Roth was very happy with the way it had turned out, and Bryan went along with his enthusiasm, although he would never understand how anything but embarrassment could come out of seeing oneself on screen in a giant rabbit suit.

Bryan knew that Nicolai taught morning classes on Fridays, so he drove to the ballet studio. Climbing the stairs from the street, he heard strains of music for the second act of *Giselle*. When he reached the landing, he was surprised to see Nicolai dancing the part of Albrecht, while Markian Teslovic stood by watching. Bryan nodded a hello, but Markian was so absorbed he didn't notice. Nicolai was dancing the scene in which Albrecht is in mourning beside Giselle's grave in the forest when he is caught by the wilis—the ghosts of maidens who have died after being betrayed by their lovers—who surround Albrecht and try to dance him to death.

Although he was wearing rubber-soled sneakers, Bryan kept to the edge of the hardwood dance floor so he wouldn't risk putting marks on it. The irony struck him that ordinarily he would have welcomed the opportunity to see Nicolai in action, but now he had to wish it wouldn't go on too long.

Nicolai seldom danced anymore, except to illustrate something for one of his students. He preferred to concentrate on his directing and his choreography, but clearly this time he had started out to show a step or two to Markian and then had gotten carried away. He was enjoying himself. It would have been a splendid sight to watch, if Bryan hadn't had such a weight on his mind.

When Nicolai caught sight of Bryan, he brought what he was doing to an abrupt halt. Out of breath, he strode to the tape recorder and let the tape screech as he rewound it and started it over. "Now, you do it, Markian!" he cried. "I must go and talk to Bryan." Like clockwork figures with their gears out of mesh, Markian and the corps de ballet worked themselves into step in the middle of the number.

Nicolai watched till they got started. In gray sweatshirt and black warm-up trousers, he looked small, but this was deceptive because he was all muscle, and muscle is denser than fat. He was five-eight and weighed one-sixty-five, and when he had been onstage, he impressed audiences with the effortless grace and power of his "lifts." After the action on the studio floor was synchronized, he came over to Bryan, smiling, brushing back his sweat-matted black hair. He extended his hand and shook Bryan's heartily. "Come! We will have a drink!" As always, he left no room for doubt. Bryan followed him into his plush air-conditioned office.

From the liquor cabinet, Nicolai produced a bottle of expensive Russian vodka and poured two tumblers half-full. He handed one to Bryan, saying, "Sorry. I have no ice. You must drink it like a Russian." He chuckled, going around and sitting in his tan leather desk chair and facing Bryan, who had sat in a chrome-and-leather director's chair on the opposite side of the palette-shaped glass top of Nicolai's paper-strewn desk. "*Giselle* is such a beautiful ballet!" Nicolai said enthusiastically. "It was choreographed in the nineteenth century by Jules Perrot, an ugly little Frenchman with a funny-shaped body. But he was a great dancer and an even better choreographer, with a magical and true sense of beauty—he knew how to create what he himself did not outwardly possess."

Nicolai stopped suddenly, as if all at once aware that he had been rambling on, not allowing Bryan to state the purpose of his visit. Most ballet terms were in

French, and the ballet director invariably mispronounced them all, although he understood perfectly what they stood for—and Bryan usually found this quirk amusing. This time Nicolai had pronounced Perrot's name as if it were "per rot." But Bryan was too preoccupied to be amused. "I've come because of Julia," he said, allowing the inflection of his voice to turn the discussion to seriousness.

"What is the matter?" asked Nicolai, alarmed. "Is she not getting well?"

"She never was ill," Bryan confessed. Then he went on to explain why the influenza story was a lie and what had really taken place in the past several days.

Nicolai listened with an intense, puzzled look that soon evolved into intense anger. The more he heard, the more agitated he got, rocking back and forth in his chair and finishing off his glass of vodka in short, spastic gulps. "Oh, my! Oh, my!" he said, outraged. "What can we do, Bryan? What can *I* do to help?"

"I'd like you to answer some questions," Bryan said. He took too large a mouthful of his warm vodka, which he had been sipping. It made his eyes water and his throat burn. "Also," he added, in a voice constricted by the smarting liquor, "I don't want you to say a word about this conversation to anyone—not even to Natalia."

"Of course, of course," Nicolai agreed adamantly, hunching forward with his lips pursed.

"Trying to figure out who the kidnappers could be is the hard part," said Bryan. "Did you ever notice anyone hanging around the studio—as if they could be casing the place?"

"What does it mean—'casing'?" asked Nicolai.

"You know—looking the place over, as if they were intending to rob it. Only in this instance they were planning to capture Adrienne and Julia."

"Poor Adrienne!" Nicolai sighed, a sigh of sadness and exasperation. Then he laid his head back with his eyes half-closed, thinking. "I did not notice anything," he said finally. "Nothing unusual. Nobody doing some casing."

"Are you sure about the time they left the studio?" Bryan queried.

"Yes. As I told Julia's grandfather, she and Adrienne left here at approximately eight-thirty, and they were going to Andrew Blake's house. In fact, Adrienne asked me if I would like to come with them, to visit Tiffany, but I told her maybe some other time, because Natalia was waiting with supper for me."

"Where was Adrienne's car parked?"

"In front. Not far from the streetlamp. I watched from the studio window till they got in safely."

"When they drove away," Bryan asked, suddenly excited, "did anyone pull out behind them? In other words, did it look like they were being followed?"

"I'm sorry, Bryan," Nicolai said dejectedly. "I wish I had stayed at the window longer. But I only watched until they were safely in the car. Some of the other girls were going to their cars, too. I always watch them, if I can. But Adrienne and Julia were just about the last to leave."

Bryan didn't know what else he should ask Nicolai. For a while he had imagined that he might be accomplishing something, but now he felt a sense of futility. If this were a wide-open investigation, all the members of the Artov Ballet Company could be questioned to see if *they* had seen anything unusual. They may not have thought anything of it at the time, but if a car had pulled out behind Adrienne and Julia, it could be helpful to know the make of car. The license plate number would be too much to ask for. But the make might be enough, if any of the kidnappers were connected to the girls in any way. If the police were in on this, they would probably try to ferret out and check up on every single car that had been parked up and down the block.

Bryan thanked Nicolai and risked insulting him by reminding him to keep quiet about it all. Leaving the ballet studio, he noticed Markian still rehearsing and thought about the shock Markian was due for when he found out that his girl friend was not merely out with the flu.

A couple of storefronts away from Nicolai's place, Bryan stopped in a neighborhood drugstore to buy a pack of cigarettes and make a phone call. Paul still wasn't at the office. Bryan slammed the receiver onto the hook without waiting for the beep from the answering machine. Where could Paul be? Usually there were too many follow-up details to take care of after a job was done filming; it wasn't wise to stay out of the office the next day.

It dawned on Bryan that Paul was the one who called up on the night before the Vermont trip, to suggest that Adrienne and Julia go to visit Tiffany Blake. In fact—Bryan's mind went leaping—Paul had said on the phone that Andrew Blake had hinted that he would like Adrienne and Julia to visit his daughter.

If Bryan didn't know better, he would have viewed all this as a possible setup—but the idea was so farfetched it seemed silly. He rejected it, and told himself he was tired, clutching at a straw, and in danger of making a fool of himself.

He stood outside the drugstore, puffing away on a cigarette. He didn't know what to do or where to go next. Andrew Blake and Paul Smith had never gotten along. It was far too absurd to entertain even a hint of a possibility that they could be mixed up in this together.

Paul might do something crazy to further his own ambitions. Even something illegal. Something shady. But not something barbaric? Would he?

As for Blake, what reason could he have? Not the money. He didn't need it.

Could Blake be twisted enough to punish the other ballerinas for what had happened to Tiffany?

Hadn't Jim Mallory said something that had struck close to such an idea?

Bryan felt ridiculous and then almost ashamed of himself for even harboring such notions. But *someone* was mad—that much seemed clear. And if nothing else, he ought to try eliminating Paul Smith and Andrew Blake as possible suspects, oughtn't he? That's what the police would do, wouldn't they?

Paul's apartment wasn't too far away. Rather than phoning there, Bryan was still so reluctant to talk to his partner about his wild conjectures that he decided to drive to Paul's place and let whether or not Paul was home determine whether the subject would be broached. Anyway, he didn't need an excuse, there was business to be talked about now that Paul was back in town—unless the shooting in Vermont had gone over schedule and Bryan had never gotten the word. It startled him that he had not thought of this logical possibility before. He continued through the motions of driving to Paul's apartment, sure now that Paul wouldn't even be there.

When Bryan rang the front bell, he was admitted by Mrs. Engle, a well-preserved lady in her mid-forties who would have been considered attractive if she didn't always wear an incredible excess of makeup. She and her husband received half their rent free, according to Paul, for acting as overseers.

"Looking for Paul?" Mrs. Engle chimed, doing her best to look and sound charming. She had often thrown hints that she'd like to be in a TV commercial. Also, Bryan had the feeling she'd probably like to seduce him. As usual, she had on the sort of dress that ought to be worn to a cocktail party, or at least to a day of shopping in elegant surroundings; yet, she never seemed to leave the building. She had had a fling at show business at one time, in a very minor way, and was still convinced she could have been a star performer. Once she had pointed out to Bryan that Farah Fawcett wasn't really discovered till she landed a series of Noxema spots.

"Yes. Is Paul in?" Bryan responded carefully, not wanting to take the slightest risk of encouraging her advances, either sexual or career-oriented.

Again, the charming, dulcet voice: "You can go up and knock. But I haven't seen him come or go in about a week."

Bryan said, "He's been out of town on one of our filming jobs. But he should be back now. I've been trying to reach him for something important."

"What's he filming?" Mrs. Engle asked, always ready to talk show business.

"A documentary about a part for an airplane," Bryan squelched. "Nothing glamorous, Joan."

"Oh," Joan Engle said, disappointed, then perked up. "Well, keep me in mind if you ever have a part that's right for me, Bryan. Go up and knock, like I said. Paul might have come in late last night, after George and I went to bed. If so, I didn't hear him." She added, with a wink, "It isn't as if George keeps me awake for any reason."

Bryan didn't wait for her to finish, but was already mounting the red-carpeted stairs with the curving mahogany banister. He knocked several times on Paul's door without any result. Then he came back down the steps and Mrs. Engle was still standing outside the door. "Can you let me into Paul's apartment?" he asked her. "I won't steal anything. You can come in with me. But there's a roll of film in there I've got to have. It has to go to the lab. Paul said he would send it, but he forgot. We'll lose a lot of business if the client doesn't get it on time."

"Who's the client?" Mrs. Engle asked, titillated. "Is it a TV commercial?"

"Yes, for Sears," Bryan said, lying some more.

"Why didn't you put me in it?" Joan Engle said petulantly.

"It was all kids," Bryan replied. "Can you let me into Paul's place?"

"I'll go get my master key."

Waiting for Joan Engle at the top of the stairs, Bryan had the feeling that she was probably delighted at the excuse to go into Paul's apartment uninvited and nose around. She put the key in the lock, opened the door, and they went in. "He keeps it neat," she commented, obviously surprised and disappointed that there wasn't a pile of personal belongings left out for her to inspect.

Bryan moved from living room to kitchen to bedroom, not knowing what he was looking for. Joan Engle followed closely behind, as if really watching to make sure he wouldn't steal anything. He hoped she wouldn't choose this moment to cozy up to him. Moving away from the bed, he went into the bathroom, wondering if she'd think his behavior strange—it was hardly a likely place for a can of film. "Sometimes he uses it as a darkroom," he started to say.

But then he saw Paul, in the tub.

Mrs. Engle peeked in behind Bryan and let out a horrible scream. Bryan was rooted in shock, his heart pounding, his eyes riveted wide, stretching the skin of his face taut. At the same time he was dimly aware that Mrs. Engle had backed into the bedroom behind him and was retching, vomiting on the carpet.

There was no question about Paul's being dead. He was nude, his slashed wrists submerged in water that was bright red. The bloody straight-razor was pasted to the linoleum floor in a blackish-red clump of dried blood. Bryan recognized the razor as a prop he and Paul had once used in a cheapy thirty-second spot for a chain of hair-styling emporiums. Paul's knees were up, his head down, the back of his hair soaked. His eyeballs were wide open and rolled so far upward that the pupils were nearly gone. Strings of mucus connected his nose and mouth to the reddish water like thick strands of a spider's web.

When Bryan staggered out of the bathroom, Mrs. Engle had finished vomiting and was groping her way out of the apartment. "Phone the police!" Bryan called after her, wondering if it would sink in. He tried to gather his senses about him, so he could do whatever needed to be done.

While Joan Engle was gone, he forced himself to take a quick inventory of the apartment, going from room to room. He opened closets and drawers but saw nothing that struck him as a clue—but in the state of mind he was in, he doubted that he could recognize one. Paul's clothes, the ones he must have been wearing, weren't folded neatly, but were strewn on the bed. Quickly, furtively, feeling guilty, Bryan went through the pockets and flipped through the wallet, finding nothing of note. He dropped the trousers in the approximate ball he had found them in, thankful Mrs. Engle or someone else hadn't popped in to catch him in the act.

He looked around the kitchen once more. In the toaster on a counter there were two pieces of toast popped up, cold and dried out. It flickered through

Bryan's mind that Paul Smith had decided to commit suicide while making himself a couple of pieces of toast.

He sank down onto a couch in the living room, and for a time went numb. He couldn't think or feel. Behind his inertia, like the ticking of an alarm, was the fog-filtered awareness that somehow he had to keep going to help Julia; he had to find out if Paul Smith's death tied in.

But, how did it tie in? Bryan didn't know. It just didn't seem like a coincidence. Paul wasn't the type to commit suicide. The cliché mocked Bryan as soon as he had thought it—after all, who did seem like the type? But Paul always had such driving ambition, one would think he would hurt others before he would hurt himself, in his drive to get what he wanted.

A Lieutenant Manko and a Sergeant Pavlack arrived, glanced at Bryan as they strode past him, and went to have a look at Paul's corpse. After a few minutes, during which Bryan could hear them moving around and talking, they came back into the living room. They introduced themselves. Bryan gave his name and showed his driver's license. Manko was tall and thin, and Pavlack was tall and stout. They both wore three-piece suits—Manko's was brown, and Pavlack's was a light shade of gray, grayer than his hair. "Have to wait for the coroner," Manko said. "In the meantime we'll take your statement."

They sat down and wrote on their pads while Bryan told them what he had done and how he had come to be in the apartment, using once again the excuse of the can of film, and then explaining his relationship to Paul.

The detectives didn't bring Joan Engle back into the apartment. Apparently to spare her any further upset, they were going to question her downstairs. They took down Bryan's addresses and phone numbers, business and personal, and told him he was all through. It surprised him that it was over so soon, but he couldn't think what else the cops could have asked or done. The coroner still hadn't arrived. Bryan was relieved that he hadn't had to see Paul's body carried out in a shroud.

"Are you too shook up to drive?" Manko asked. "Want us to give you a lift wherever you're going?"

"No, thanks, I'm okay," Bryan said, wondering if it was true. He forced himself to ask the question that had been nipping at the edge of his mind. "Will you be able to tell if he was conscious when his wrists were slashed?" It sounded nutty as soon as it was out of his mouth.

Pavlack raised an eyebrow, giving his flat, swarthy face a bemused look. "Why? You have reason to think it wasn't suicide?"

Bryan backed off. "No, not really. Except he never seemed the type. But I guess you've heard that before. What made me wonder was the toast in the toaster—it seemed odd."

"Not significant," Manko pronounced. "People who kill themselves leave all kinds of things unfinished. My bet is that the autopsy will turn up nothing suspicious. We'll talk to his family and friends to get an idea of his psychological frame of mind at the time of his death. Probably turn out to be something simple—trouble with a girl friend or something."

"How about business pressures?" Pavlack interjected. "We neglected to ask you that."

"There always pressure in the film business," Bryan said. "But lately, if anything, there's been less than usual."

"Well, obviously he had a problem," Manko said. "Health or business or personal. It'll come out in the wash."

Getting into the car, Bryan kept thinking about what Lieutenant Manko had said about trouble with a girl friend. Adrienne. Could it be that Paul had committed suicide because he found out, somehow, about what had happened to Adrienne? And, could he have had something to do with it? Spurned by her, had Paul set her up for a kidnapping? Would he have done such a thing believing she wouldn't be harmed?

Bryan sat in his car, the key in the ignition, realizing finally that Paul's death at this particular time was just too much of a coincidence. He didn't start the engine because he didn't know where to go. Yet he knew he had to do *something*.

Could Paul Smith and Andrew Blake both have been involved in the kidnapping? Could Paul have been killed to keep his mouth shut? Could Andrew Blake be the demented mastermind behind it all?

These outlandish thoughts churning in his mind, tormenting him with the overriding feeling that they were only wild speculations, all but groundless, Bryan decided to drive out to Blake's home to have another talk with him, or possibly with his daughter. Blake would either be home or at his office, which was close by. It might even be better to talk to Tiffany. She might be the one to shed some light on the puzzle. Perhaps she would know just which one of her fans might have turned into a maniac.

Bryan couldn't shake the feeling that money was not the motive behind the double kidnapping and the maiming of Adrienne. Tiffany lost a leg; then Adrienne lost one. This could not be a coincidence. Time was obviously running out for Julia.

27 ❦

WAITING TO BE TAKEN TO THE OPERATING ROOM, TIFFANY mentally prepared herself. As she always did before going onstage, she summoned psychic energy, storing it to see her through the situation, even though she would be unconscious. The will to survive, to heal, would not be dulled by the anesthetic.

She believed that her transplant operation had been successful; she did not know that tissue rejection had occurred. She had been told by Dr. Augenstein, whom she trusted, that the operation today was for the purpose of doing nerve grafts to help the sciatic nerve in its regrowth. She accepted this—even, in a way, looked forward to it as a necessary step toward getting well.

Since the train accident, she had undergone much

physical pain and emotional trauma. But the hope of dancing again, which had been absent before, was the ingredient which now helped her to face each new ordeal. In her room, lying in bed, she concentrated on visions of what she would accomplish as a ballerina once she became whole again.

In her cell in the basement, Julia was being prepared to be wheeled out into the operating room by the nurse, Doris Augenstein. Julia was unconscious. Her shackles were unlocked, her wrists and ankles no longer bound. She was wearing a white hospital gown, which Doris tugged on, pulling the hem up as far as her patient's hips. Julia's shapely, muscular legs were exposed, the left one already shaved and ready for surgery.

In the operating room itself, Louis and Bernard, in surgical gowns, masks, and gloves, were getting ready for a second attempt at a limb transplant, with Julia as donor. Their preparations were being observed by Andrew Blake, who was full of anxiety.

Andrew looked terrible, emaciated by drink and guilt, as if he had a secret death wish. He, too, was wearing a surgical gown and mask, so he could watch the operation. The green gown hung upon his bony form, way too large for him.

More and more lately, Andrew had been tormented by the gnawing fear that the Augensteins might be quacks or maniacs who were deluding him into believing there might be hope for his daughter. But he so desperately wanted to make Tiffany well again that he *had* to believe in Louis and Bernard. If their effort today failed, Tiffany would be left with only a stump of a leg. And, Andrew knew, she would never be able to forgive him—again.

If that happened, the Augensteins would pay.

Sammy Triglia and Big Tony would take care of them.

Andrew looked up as Julia Valenti was wheeled in, flat on her back. The first step of the operation was to amputate her leg. Blake told himself that he felt nothing for her, only the hope that the saw of the surgeon would do a nice, clean job, so that Tiffany would not have an ugly scar. Measurements had been made during the past few days to ensure a nearly perfect match of Julia's lower left leg to Tiffany's upper one, limb to limb.

Bryan pulled his car into the driveway of the Blake home and got out, instinctively easing the car door shut gently so it wouldn't make much noise. Was Andrew Blake home or not? Bryan went up to the garage doors and peered inside. He saw three cars, one of which was Blake's Cadillac, which he usually took to the office. Bryan backed away from the garage and mounted the steps to the porch, glancing left then right, overcome by an inexplicable wariness, as if something might leap out at him. The weight of the .38 revolver tucked in his belt, under his jacket, did not give him any comfort. In fact, he felt silly carrying it and could not have said exactly why he had taken it out of the glove compartment.

From inside the house, Sammy Triglia covertly had his eyes on Bryan, peeping from behind the corner of a heavy drape. Sammy welcomed the possibility of action. In his pocket he had a blackjack; it grieved him that he probably wouldn't get to use it—instead, he'd have to try to scare this young guy off because the boss had said he didn't want to stir up any unnecessary trouble.

When Bryan rang the doorbell, Sammy pulled the door open. Bryan stared at the wiry, tough-looking hood, whom he had never seen before. His presence here somehow convinced Bryan that something was wrong, but he tried not to show it. Sammy could read the fear in Bryan's face.

"What can I do for you, young man?" Sammy asked, giving the words an edge of blatant unfriendliness.

"I'd like to speak with Mr. Blake."

"He ain't here."

"Tiffany, then."

"She ain't available. Mr. Blake don't want her bothered—by you or anybody else. What are you, a reporter? Ain't you got no sympathy for what she been through?"

All of a sudden it dawned on Bryan that the man he was talking with could be a bodyguard, hired to protect Tiffany because of the story Bryan himself had spun. Maybe Blake really did believe his daughter could be kidnapped. If so, Blake couldn't be part of the kidnapping plot. Still, Bryan needed to talk to Tiffany, to see if she could shed any light on anything.

"I have plenty of sympathy," Bryan said in all sincerity. "But I'm trying to protect someone else from going through something similar."

"Bully for you," sneered Sammy. "Now get movin', snooper, and don't come back." He refrained from reaching for his blackjack, though he was itching to use it.

Bryan got stubborn. "I'm camping out right here till I see either Blake or his daughter. I know he's home. I saw his car in the garage."

"You ain't campin' nowhere, punk!" Sammy shouted, and he swung the storm door at Bryan, knocking him back. To avoid falling, Bryan jumped off the porch and scurried around the side of the house, with Sammy walking after him, a confident, amused smirk on his dark-complexioned face. Sammy slowed up and sneaked around the corner, peeking from behind some

255

shrubbery. Bryan suddenly leaped out and clobbered him on the top of the head with the butt of the .38 revolver. Sammy groaned and sagged, crumpling to the grass.

With a weird feeling, Bryan saw the blood trickling from the top of Sammy's now bald head, his prized toupee having flopped forward, the front edge still being held on by glue. Bryan was relieved to see that the man he had hit was still breathing. He didn't want to kill anybody. But the strong-arm tactics had convinced him that Blake might have something to hide.

He bent over Sammy, making sure he was out cold to stay, then looked and listened in case anyone had heard the scuffle. Everything seemed still and quiet, so Bryan creeped toward the house, mounted the porch steps, and tiptoed softly in by way of the front door. He found himself in the living room. The house seemed eerily silent, a portentous silence, as if something strange was about to come to fruition.

"Sammy, is that you?" a voice called out, startling him.

The voice had come from upstairs. With a shock, he recognized it as Tiffany's. Bryan found his footsteps taking him toward her, and in midstride he remembered to put his revolver away. Halfway up the stairs, he tucked it in his belt, under his denim jacket. Tiffany looked up at him when he walked into her bedroom. She looked pretty, excited, full of hope somehow—he might even say "vibrant." He remembered how despondent she had been the last time he saw her, and he could not reconcile the two images.

"Bryan!" she exclaimed, puzzled at his presence.

"Sammy said I could come up and talk with you. He just stepped out for a cigarette."

Bryan felt funny lying to Tiffany.

"But . . . I'm having an operation today," she said, uncertainly. "How have you been, Bryan? What do you need to see *me* about?"

For an electrifying moment, Bryan couldn't answer, for he was stunned; he saw Tiffany's legs, straightened under the covers. Both legs appeared to be the exact same length. But the train accident had left one leg shorter than the other—Bryan knew this for a fact. His mind boggled, trying to assimilate the contradiction.

Tiffany realized what he had taken note of, and acted flustered. Hesitantly, not sure she should be telling it to him, she said, "I've had a transplant, from a donor, a girl who was terminally ill. At first I could barely accept the fact. . . . Now, though, I can talk about it. You see, I'm going to be able to dance again. The whole world will know, when they see me onstage. It's not anything to be ashamed of, is it? After all, I think going around with someone's . . . a dead person's heart . . . inside you would be worse. . . . I mean . . ."

"This operation you're having today—what's it for?" Bryan interrupted, half-shouting.

"Nerve grafts," she said meekly, in the face of his excitement.

He leaned over, blurting a shower of words at her. "Do you know that Adrienne Mallory was kidnapped? And that she was returned to her parents minus a leg?"

"Oh, my God!" Tiffany wailed. Her face became distorted and went pale as the meaning of what Bryan had said struck her full force. She began crying and moaning piteously, and then started striking her left leg, pounding on it with a ferocious will to destroy it, so that it flopped up and down on the bed.

Bryan seized both her shoulders and shook her, shouting in her face. *"Where* will the operation be performed?" He knew she was innocent, a part of him knew it, but he found himself so repulsed by what was done on her behalf that for the moment he hardly cared how much he hurt her.

She babbled, "In . . . the . . . basement . . . I . . . didn't know . . . I . . . poor Adrienne . . . my father . . . aaagh!" She began gagging and retching dry heaves. Because of the upcoming operation, nothing was in her stomach, so nothing could be vomited out.

Bryan was already out of the room, running down the stairs. His pistol was in his hand. Crossing through the kitchen, he spotted a door that looked like it might lead to the basement. He yanked it open savagely and in the semi-darkness plunged headlong into Doris Augenstein, knocking her backward down the cellar stairs. He kept moving, descending after her, shocked by the sound of her head hitting against the concrete block wall with a loud crack and a simultaneous snap. Atavistically, Bryan knew what these sounds meant. Her neck was broken; she was dead.

He leaped to the bottom of the stairs, stepped over Doris' limp form, and saw the operating room. At a glance, he took in the sight of Julia, helpless on an operating table, two masked surgeons with sharp instruments in their hands, and another man in gown and mask who didn't seem to have a function there. This third man pulled his mask away, and Bryan saw that it was Andrew Blake.

Louis and Bernard Augenstein looked at Bryan, appalled, then at Doris, with her twisted, broken neck. Then—with malice—they looked back at Bryan.

"Don't move!" Bryan yelled, pointing his gun.

"Sammy! Sammy!" Blake called, shouting up the stairs.

"He won't help you; he's out cold," Bryan squelched.

"Get him!" Louis Augenstein shouted. "He's going to ruin everything!" And he came at Bryan, raising his sharp surgical scissors, threatening to stab. Bernard advanced, too, slashing the air with a scalpel, as at first Bryan tried backing away.

"Stop!" he shouted, not wanting to shoot. But the two brothers kept coming, slashing and stabbing at him as they got close.

Bryan fired his revolver at point-blank range, and fired again, and again. Blown back by the force of the slugs, Louis and Bernard sank to the floor, dying in pools of their own blood.

"Don't shoot!" Andrew Blake said, his hands up. The skin of his face was yellowish. He looked evil, demented, like a skeleton in a green shroud.

"*Damn* you, Blake!" Bryan yelled, agony in his voice as he struggled with himself not to pull the trigger.

Suddenly Blake's emaciated jaw began twitching and he trembled, looking past Bryan at something behind. Bryan pivoted, then backed away.

It was Tiffany, who had made it down the cellar stairs and was limping toward her father, dragging her "new" leg along like something dead.

"Daddy!" she cried out, wailing the word in the echoes of the basement, her face a mask of anguish and tears.

"Baby . . . baby . . ." Blake muttered, moving forward to embrace the object of his fanatical love.

Bryan permitted the embrace to happen as— numbed—he saw too late the flash of the sharp scalpel in Tiffany's hand and she plunged the surgical instrument into her father's back. His dying weight toppled the two of them to the floor, locked in each other's arms. But Tiffany extricated herself, using all of her strength, and continued to stab her father's corpse again and again—even when Bryan tried to restrain her and pull her off, until out of desperation he had to slug her with the barrel of the revolver, knocking her out.

With a mild whimper, she sank to the floor, half-sprawled over her father and covered with his blood.

Bryan turned away. He shuddered and felt weak all over, sick to his stomach. For a long moment he didn't move, just stood still, the gun hanging limply at his side. His fingers uncurled and the gun dropped, clattering on the concrete. He didn't notice.

Moving slowly, afraid of what he might find, he approached the operating table where Julia lay.

He pulled a sheet away from her and saw that she was all right. She was merely unconscious. Bryan knelt and kissed her on the forehead, and his tears wet her face. Her heart was still beating, but she was oblivious to Bryan and the carnage that lay all around. He rose to his feet and bent to lift her into his arms. He didn't want her to wake up till he could get her out of there.

He began climbing the cellar stairs.